THE
MEMORY
BONES

BOOKS BY B.R. SPANGLER

THE MEMORY BONES

B.R. SPANGLER

bookouture

Published by Bookouture in 2021

An imprint of Storyfire Ltd.
Carmelite House
50 Victoria Embankment
London EC4Y 0DZ

www.bookouture.com

ISBN: 978-1-80019-829-6
eBook ISBN: 978-1-80019-666-7

PROLOGUE

THREE YEARS EARLIER

Birds were singing as they flitted about the branches, their early morning chorus filling Janice Stephen's ears while she walked to her death. She brushed away a misty web from her arm and cried out when she felt the gun barrel slam hard against her head. A soundless gasp followed, her eyelids clapping shut. Janice waited for the bullet to come next.

It didn't.

He was tall and had to kneel to lower himself close to her face, his excited panting hot and stinking sour. The gun rattled in his grasp. Was it a reconsideration? Was he having second thoughts?

There was frustration in his eyes for a brief moment before he shoved the gun hard enough to rock her head sideways, the tip of it cutting her scalp. She dared to look into his masked face, tattered holes in the black knitted material for his eyes and mouth. She shuddered at the sight, the mask making him look like a scarecrow. A scarecrow who had a gun, who'd abducted her and dragged her to his truck.

The other one was shorter and wearing a mask too. Unlike the tall one, there was fear blazing from his hazel eyes, and his hands were shaking. She dared a look at him too as he stood quiet and tried to remain still.

Like Janice, he was doing as he was told, taking orders from the taller one.

She thought she knew the shorter one. His voice had seemed familiar. She decided to try pleading again.

"What do you want with me?" she begged.

The taller one motioned to her clothes as he stood over her. "Strip!"

Hesitant, Janice did as was demanded, shoes and socks first, spreading her toes, pushing them into the cool soil. The other one held his hands out to collect each article. Gooseflesh rose on her arms and chest as cold air brushed over her bare skin, her shirt being the first to be surrendered. Her pants were next. She lowered each pant leg with hands that she couldn't stop from shaking. Unfurling the new pair of pink scrubs from her feet, she clung to a sinking hope that she might wear them again.

The taste of bile rose from the back of her throat, stinging her tongue. The men saw her nausea coming and stepped back, twigs crunching. They had brought her to a place thick with trees bordering marshy wetlands. After she'd vomited, she gazed beyond the tree line, searching for a glimpse of life, the motions of an early morning jogger perhaps. But the disappointment was fierce. She lowered her head, seeing they were completely alone.

The taller of the two stomped his shoes, his demeanor becoming more anxious. He waved his gun at her bra and underpants. She stared down at her pale skin with bashful fright. He wanted the last of her clothing. He wanted her naked.

"Okay," she said, trembling, slipping her panties down, the silky touch of them falling onto her toes. Her bra was next, one of the clasps sticking. When he tensed again, she jerked it free. "It was stuck."

Pointing to a place off the trail, he growled. "Now walk!"

"Please!" she said, tears welling as she begged. When she didn't move, he shoved the tip of the gun against her forehead. "Please let me go. You don't have to do this."

"Do what he said!" she heard the other one plead. Her arms

and legs trembled violently, the tears cold on her face. Terror was driving her heart through her chest hard enough to hurt.

"That way." The gunman pushed the gun into her back, moving her off the trail, taking her into the swamp. Tall sawgrass blades parted as she walked through, the cattails snapping, her feet sinking into the marshy ground. When they reached an opening, the first of the day's light became bright for a moment, until a harsh strike came from behind. Janice tumbled over, her bare chest and elbows scraping against the coarse grass, a white streak blowing up behind her eyelids.

"This will do."

Dazed, the pain inside her head peeled away her fears and turned her body cold as primal instincts took over. *Breathe*, she told herself. Footsteps circled around her as she sensed them staring. She looked up, seeing the shorter of them scared while the other was wild-eyed. "Please," she begged. Without word or warning, the gunman yanked the knitted mask from the other, jerking it hard enough to pull it off his head and reveal his face. Janice went wide-eyed.

She did know him. She had known him for some time.

A strange sense of relief came at the sight of his face, but with it, so many questions.

"You?"

His voice belted shrilly. "Why did you do that!? Now she's seen my face!"

Slowly, the taller one removed his mask too, his grim smirk telling Janice the truth of what was to come. He saw her resignation and told her, "Don't lose your hope just yet. How about we play a game?"

"Come on! Let's get this over with," the other pleaded, beginning to pace, his face shiny with sweat.

"Tell me why?" Janice asked him directly, her head clearing.

"I'm so sorry, Janice," he answered, blubbering.

"Tell me why!" she yelled, smacking her hand against the ground, making him jump. "Now!"

"Because you saw too much," he answered, sniveling. "Janice, you saw too much."

"Saw what? What did I see?"

The taller one let out a laugh and clapped his hand onto her shoulder. He turned serious then, kneeling close enough she could smell his breath again. "Do you want to live?"

"Fuck you!" Janice answered, knowing it was too late.

"I'm being serious with you," he added, his brow raised. From behind him, he revealed a bundle of rope, a white nylon like a clothesline. "I'll let you pick. You can have a bullet to the head. It'd be quick and simple. Or, I tie you up and we walk away."

"Walk away?" Janice asked, wondering what the catch was. She didn't wait for his answer, speaking quickly, "The rope. I'll take the rope."

"Awesome," he said with a loud clap. He went to work immediately, her front pinned against the sodden ground, the plants scraping and pinching her belly and chest. She cried out when he wrenched her legs up and tied the ropes around her ankles. He took hold of her arms, twisting them behind her, the sharp touch of nylon cinched around her wrists. "Hanging in there, Janice?"

"This isn't right," the other one complained. "You said this would be quick and simple."

"It will," he answered, grunting while he worked the ropes, forming a noose that he placed around her neck.

"This is the game?" Janice asked, breathless, unsure of what to think.

"It is," he answered, his hands large, fingers fanned across her hands and feet, keeping hold of them, the rope slack. "And when I let go, we'll walk away."

"She'll get away!" The other one shouted, trudging back and forth, flattening the plants in his path. "This is too risky."

"You're next if you don't shut the fuck up!"

Still holding her hands and feet, the nylon around her neck warming with the heat of her skin, he asked in a soft voice, "Janice, are you ready?"

"And you're just going to walk away?" she asked, heart skipping wildly with hope. But another glance at him, she saw evil. He wasn't going to stay true to his word. Tears stinging again, her voice a rasp, "You'll let me live?"

He lowered himself, his expression emptying when his gaze met hers. "Cross my heart and all that nonsense." He checked the rope once more, saying, "Now take a deep breath."

She breathed in the dirt she faced, gagging at it while he held her arms and legs firmly behind her. Roots and stones jutted into her gut. She braced for him to let her go, to begin his game. But before she could fill her lungs again, his hand went free. The muscles in her legs relaxed, and her arms fell, the weight of both jerking the rope around her neck.

He let out a giddy laugh when the rope snapped tight as though she'd just been hung from a tree limb. Janice braced against the strangling force, blood and air cut off from her brain. Her nose against the ground, her gaze went to the killer's feet as they moved into position to watch her die.

"Oh this is cruel," she heard. There was regret in the other one's voice, but it wouldn't help her. "Just kill her already."

Janice strained to look up, trying to ease the rope's tension. "Wait!" the taller one said. "A promise is a promise."

She found a short breath. And then another. But her strength was disappearing, the noose tightening as she moved to fight the restraints. Her heartbeat pulsed like a bomb in her head. Janice shifted her arms and legs, fires forming in the shadows of her mind that turned bright and shot into a sky until she could no longer see. Desperate and nearing a blackout, Janice stretched until her fingers brushed an ankle, close enough to snag hold of the nylon wrapped around it. In this game, she only needed to add slack, to grab hold of the rope and not let go. She held on to it by a fingertip, the immense pressures around her neck lifting enough to steal another breath. This *was* the way to get out of the trap. She only needed to hold the weight of her legs and arms like he'd done. Otherwise, the noose on her neck would tighten.

It'd strangle her. Muscles quaking, could she do it? Was she too late?

"Is she going to get it?!" the other asked, stammering nervously.

The killer raised his hand, rearing up as though he was going to strike. "Shut up and wait for it!"

When the muscles in her arms shook uncontrollably, her grip began to slip. Janice tried with everything she had to hold the rope, to slide another finger into the loops cinched around her ankles.

But she couldn't keep hold. Her strength waning, the noose collapsed a final time. The men turned their backs then. Their game was over.

Janice Stephen died in the quiet noise of the marshland. The fireflies shone as though the stars in the sky had magically descended.

And she died never knowing why. Never knowing what she had seen too much of.

ONE

We left the safety of a Buxton Woods hiking trail and entered into an open grove of oak and pine with long purple flowers someone on my team called pickerelweed. It was a summer day, cloudless and warm. Cobwebs were strung across the bushes and sparkled with dew as the sun burned off a morning haze. My team was responding to a call to travel south on Hatteras Island, a caller describing what they believed was a body, naked and exposed to the elements.

As the designated lead, I was the one who'd rallied the team for this morning's drive to the southern part of the Outer Banks. We'd piled into a few cars, coffee sloshing in our cups, and headed to the jut of wetland that shouldered the Atlantic Ocean. It was a short distance from the tranquil beaches most come to the Outer Banks to see. But we weren't here for a walk on the white sands. We were here to find a body.

The team was quiet as we passed a row of trees that glistened with sap; a steady and soft snap of branches was our background noise, along with leaves rustling, frogs croaking, and birds singing to the rising sun. The coordinates on my phone were only an estimate and had been based on the caller's location. *Perpendicular to the trail*, was what he'd said. I checked over my shoulder, making sure we stayed straight, seeing hikers on the trail stop to watch with curious gazes, their voices a distant chatter.

We made it fifty yards and then the ground changed, becoming wet and mushy, a marshland. I looked at my team's faces, gauging their remaining confidence for us to continue. I questioned it too. We'd traveled well beyond the established terrain which had been touched by civilization. This was raw nature.

The air was humid and salty, and the cattails and sawgrass grew more crowded. The sting of sweat teemed on the back of my neck and on my upper lip. We passed pools of bubbling waters the shade of black tea. I spread my arms for balance, the others doing the same, our boots getting stuck in the murky soft loam. There were gnats darting in and out of our faces, and dragonflies hovering above flowering plants. The sight of the insects had me thinking of the flies that might have found the body, if that's what it was. Depending on their species, they could be used to establish a timeline.

When the breeze shifted, it came with an odor I knew. I could smell it in my mouth and nostrils and feel it on my skin. It was death.

"We're close," our medical examiner, Dr. Swales, said. She stopped dead and tilted her head, her frizzy gray hair leaning with it. She wrinkled her nose and sniffed the air as her thick glasses fogged. She found the direction like a well-trained dog, and pointed, giving me a hard look. "You smell that?"

"I do," I answered, continuing forward, leading us to the body. I noted the location, pinning the coordinates on my phone. "Not exactly a hundred yards, but close enough."

"Let's see what we have." Dr. Swales came to my side and squeezed my hand with her tiny fingers. I gripped her fingers in mine when the earth swallowed one of her boots whole, the ground covered with bright green moss and too soft to trust.

"Lift," I told her as Detective Emanuel Wilson, all six foot six of him, took hold of her other hand. I froze then, a gust parting tall grass aside like a curtain blowing through an open window. Beyond it, I caught the first glimpse of pale gray skin, the body naked and face down. It was possibly a man, his body without bloat which meant death had occurred within the last three days. "Guys, over there."

"I got you," Emanuel said, the doctor's size like a twelve-year-old compared to him. She held out her arms as he hoisted her effortlessly, the muck releasing her boot with a muddy burp.

"My handsome knight coming to my rescue," Swales kidded, but her face turned grim when she saw the body over the swaying grass.

I turned toward the team, wrinkling my nose at the growing stench. "We've arrived."

We circled around the body, carefully noting the ground and any disruptions. Nichelle Wilkinson, our team's IT lead, held a camera in hand and started taking picture after picture. She'd caught the crime-scene bug on a recent case and was training for her certification. I pointed out what might have been a path from the hiking trail, its coming from the northern side of the open grove. The path before the marshes was evidence of someone having been here. From the looks of the body, we knew immediately there had to have been at least one other person involved.

I glanced toward the divot made by the doctor's small foot. "Nichelle let's get pictures of footprints. And anything that resembles one." With a careful step, she went around the body, continuing to photograph the scene. "And any pictures where there's broken plants and bent cattails. Also search for clothing, blood, anything that shouldn't be here."

"Got it," she said, looking confident. She'd confided in me to being nervous, this being her first time working a crime scene without working on the technology side. But we were here, a team, and we wouldn't let her fail.

Tracy Fields caught up to us after taking a statement from the man who'd reported seeing the body. He'd been out with his son, the two hiking and watching a pair of nesting owls. She was breathing heavy and her hair was matted flat against her sweaty forehead.

"You guys found it then," she stated, her expression emptying as she stopped to stare at the body. Tracy was the youngest on my team, a crime-scene technician I've known since her first day on the job. She was also the smartest of us, having acquired every certification while working toward a second master's degree, her latest in criminology.

I nodded as I went to the body, squatting, staying still a moment as I took in the sight, assessing the biggest and most obvious piece of evidence. This was not a case of a summer picnic turning into a drunken foray, and the man ditching every stitch of clothing. This was a victim of foul play. His ankles and wrists were tied hog-style, a thin nylon cord strung around his neck. Almost certainly murder.

Then something caught my eye. *That shouldn't be there,* I thought to myself, catching a breath, my lungs rattling with the humid air. The victim had a birthmark on the inside of his right thigh. It was a dark blemish, about the size of a small fruit, a jagged blotch that was shaped like a lightning bolt. I'd seen one like it before and the sight of it now gave me pause.

"There's no bloat," Swales began, plucking the taut line like a guitar string. "The body has been here less than three days."

With the nylon rope, the victim's hands and feet were hoisted, and had drained of blood, turning them ghostly white, veins and arterial paths clear like branches on a tree bared by winter. On the victim's torso and thighs, at the lowest point where his skin touched the ground, there looked to be one massive bruise. "Livor mortis is evident, the victim's blood settling. From the size of the patches, I'd say death was well past twelve hours?"

"We have more than twelve hours and less than three days. Let's add the flies to the lividity," Dr. Swales said, her newest assistant, Samantha Watson, by her side and taking notes. With a deeper than normal southern twang, Swales added, "By the way, Samantha, meet Detective Casey White."

"Welcome to the team," I said and put on my best welcoming smile. Samantha gave me a shy wave and returned to her note-taking. She was in her early twenties with a short crop of black hair and ivory-colored skin. Her pale blue eyes were big and round as she wrote everything. When she lowered herself close to Dr. Swales, I saw the resemblance—same eyes and nose and mouth and brow. A niece perhaps, a second cousin? Dr. Swales pegged the air with her finger, estimating the count of bugs on the victim. "The blowflies appear to be arriving. I'd expect their numbers to increase."

"Increase?" Samantha asked. "What are they doing?"

Swales looked over her shoulder, nodding. "They're going to lay their eggs."

"Oh," Samantha said, writing a note, her lips puckering as she held in a gagging reflex.

"Blowflies arriving," I said, watching them buzz around the corpse, a frog interrupting with a croak. "That puts us at less than three days?"

"Possibly. I'd say seventy-two hours is on the far side. Time of death could be as early as thirty-six hours, based on lividity and the weather having trended on the warmer side."

As I moved toward the neck, the nylon disappearing into a fold of torn skin, I found my study of the victim returning to the sight of the birthmark again. "Hard to tell the height and weight and age in this position."

"We can get those details at the morgue," Swales commented as she picked up one of the flies. "Is that knot peculiar?"

"Is it a kind of slip knot?" Tracy asked, moving closer. "I think it is. I used them sailing."

"You're right. It's a slip knot," I said as Emanuel joined from the other side. With my gloves on, I tugged on the stretch of rope leading to the victim's neck, the fold of skin moving slightly. "Look at how the line is threaded through this single loop on the ankles and wrists."

Emanuel pushed on the victim's feet, the legs cracking with rigor mortis. The nylon line leading to the neck went slack, the noose loosening. "It's like the weight of the arms and legs was used to strangle the victim."

"Oh my God!" Samantha said, letting out a gasp. A dead body can make excruciating sounds when moved. And to the inexperienced, the first time hearing it can be like something from a horror show. "What was that!?"

"It's normal," Swales said. She turned back, adding, "The knot here at the center, what do you make of that?"

I stared at the line with an idea. "It looks as though it is acting as a fulcrum."

"A fulcrum?" Tracy asked, moving the victim's feet with Emanuel, the line around the neck loosening.

"That's exactly what it's doing," I said, seeing what had happened. "The killer made the victim lie down on their belly. He then held their legs and hands in position and used them as a counterweight to the noose around the victim's neck. Tracy, what do you think happened next?"

Tracy frowned, thinking through the physics of the victim participating in his own death. "Well, I'd think the weight of his legs and arms tightened the noose."

"Why couldn't they hold their legs and arms behind them so the rope didn't get tight?" Samantha asked as she put her arms behind her back to try and understand.

"Time," I answered. "Like doing planks or holding your arms out at your sides."

"Eventually your muscles will give and you won't be able to keep the line slack," Emanuel added. "But how long could he have held them?"

"A couple of minutes?" I answered, guessing, but having no

idea. I went back to where the path led back to the trail. "The killer stood here and watched the struggle. When the victim couldn't hold their arms and legs any longer, the slack in the rope tightened."

Tracy ran her finger along the part of the rope that ran the length of the victim's back. "And when the slack was gone, the rope tightened the noose around the victim's neck."

"That must have been horrible," Samantha said, her complexion as gray as the dead. It might have been the combination of heat, humidity and the ever-present smell. Or simply that it was her first time seeing the cruelty of a killer. "Does that mean the guy killed himself?"

"Technically, that would be a true statement. It was the weight of his legs and arms causing him to asphyxiate," Swales answered, handing her assistant a bottle of water. "Drink, dear, this heat requires it."

"Regardless of the technical details, this man was murdered," I said, assuring the team as a pair of birds sang in unison. Tracy raised her hand, but I shook my head before it reached her shoulder. "It's an open discussion."

"Would it be possible to do this to yourself?" Tracy asked, moving to the other side of the body.

I knew where she was going, the idea already floating in my mind. We'd have to prove or disprove it as standard procedure. "Explain," I said so the others could think it through.

"Okay. He's alone with a rope, and he gets everything tied together, including the main part, the arbor knots. He then lies down on his stomach, slipping the noose around his neck. Then he reaches behind him and ties his hands and ankles."

"A suicide?" Swales questioned, voice drifting as she considered it.

The birthmark stole my attention a moment, the sight of it unnerving me again. "Tracy, your task. Figure out if that's possible."

Swiping errantly at a fly, she asked, "You want me to try and tie myself up like that?"

"Correct. Have a go. Using Nichelle's pictures, answer the question for us. Is it possible to put yourself into this exact arrangement? Make sure someone else is with you so you don't end up..."

"Uh-uh," Emanuel said, shaking his head. "Won't work. Someone else had to have done it."

"I'm thinking the same," I said, agreeing. "But we have to rule out the possibility of this being a suicide."

Swales cradled her chin, her fingers knobby. "When the will is strong enough, it's amazing what a person can do."

Nichelle snapped a picture of the victim's head, the brow flat against the ground, a crimp in the neck, hoisted by the rope. "There's a lot more flies over here."

Swales leaned forward, looking at the victim's ear, saying, "Yep. They're doing their thing."

"The egg thing?" Samantha asked, a look of disgust returning to her face.

"Correct," Swales said in an as-a-matter-of-fact tone. "It's nature, and we can use the maggots, if there are any."

Samantha swallowed. "I'm going to go over there a moment."

"Oh, Dr. Swales," Nichelle commented, shaking her head, her bronze skin turning pale too. "Please, no more about maggots."

"What?"

"The feet," I said, changing the subject. "The clothes for that matter. There was a case when I'd first arrived to the Outer Banks where the victim's feet were clean of mud and dirt and injury. That's the same here."

"Yeah, look at our shoes," Tracy said. "There's no way he could have walked out here without getting dirty."

"He was wearing shoes and clothes," Swales said with a grunt as she inspected the victim's head, pushing aside the graying hair to search his ear.

"That puts a pin in the idea of this being a suicide," I said. "Clean feet. No clothes discovered here or on the trail."

"You think the victim was forced to disrobe?" Emanuel asked, the ground making a squishing sound as he joined Nichelle at the other end. I gave him a nod. "The killer also took the victim's phone and anything else too."

"If the phone is on, we'll be able to track it down," Nichelle told him.

"You want me to study the knot?" Tracy asked as she studied the nylon, taking notes, measuring the noose and loops around the ankles and wrists. "Make a mock-up back at the station of the ropes and its arrangement?"

"I do," I said, my focus shifting back to the birthmark, the sun's light getting bright, showing it in greater detail. Dread touched my heart, but I shook it off, the idea being impossible. "I want to know exactly how the killer arranged this and if it was at all possible for the victim to get out of this."

"As in escape?" Tracy asked, a brow raised. She held her thumbs, motioning while considering the idea.

"Could be that the killer may have designed this arrangement on purpose, to make it a game."

Tracy stopped, hands hung in the air, saying, "That's brutal."

"Murder often is," I said, my voice glib, my need to see the victim's face growing like a fever. I put my hand over my eyes, looking at the sun's light and feeling the heat on my face. "If it was a game, it didn't last long."

"How do you know that?" Emanuel asked.

"Sunburn," Swales answered, and then motioned for me to continue.

"You can't burn or tan if you're dead. The skin cells aren't alive to react to the sunlight," I said as I searched every inch of exposed flesh, all of it white and gray. "Since he was naked and we haven't had any rain this last week, his death may have occurred before sunrise."

Nichelle worked the camera, centering on the birthmark to take a picture. "We have got a distinguishable mark on the inside thigh," she commented.

"I saw that. It could help to identify the victim," Swales commented, touching the rope, a knife in hand. "Shall we?"

"Let's do it," I answered, my eyes fixing on the birthmark, apprehension building the way it does when imagining the worst of a loved one. I stood abruptly, waving a flash of heat away from my face. Swales's eyes followed me with concern.

"Are you okay?"

"I need to get some water in me," I said, assuring her I was okay. "A touch of dehydration."

"Everyone, take a minute and drink your water," Swales demanded. "We don't want to be carrying two bodies out of here."

After a moment of swigging, I just had to know for sure. Abruptly, I took the knife and cut the rope. "We'll leave the rope on the victim but release the arbor knot."

"Understood," Swales said. I could feel the worry coming from her, my hand trembling slightly as I handed the knife back to her. "Casey?"

I ignored her concerns as I lowered the victim's legs, the rigor keeping them stuck in place. "Can I get some help turning the body over?" I asked, my words on a hot breath.

"Yeah, we got it for you," Derek said, the doctor's lead assistant, his hands joining mine, "And one, two—"

Together, we put muscle into the move, grass crunching as the victim's face showed, his eyes filmy and bulging. Blood had settled into his face, turning the skin into a large purple blob. With death, I saw the impossible, terrible truth.

"It can't be," I nearly screamed, pedaling away onto my backside, the fright stealing my composure.

"What!?" Derek asked, alarmed, searching around the corpse, arms straining.

"Casey?" Swales asked with alarm. "What's going on?"

"The victim, he's—" I began. I tried to look away from his face, my throat closing around his name.

Tracy and Nichelle knelt next to me, my arms and legs like

rubber as they held me. Nichelle had met him before and recognized the victim. "Oh, Casey!" She squeezed my shoulders and put her head against mine. "I'm so sorry."

They held me as I got back to my knees. "His name is Ronald Haskin. He's my ex-husband."

TWO

Gasps came at a fevered pace, forcing me to take a dizzying walk away from the body. I fell hard onto one knee and gripped a handful of cattails, needing the leverage to hold me up. But the plants were flimsy, and their chutes broke against my strain. Somewhere deep inside my chest, I think a part of me was breaking too.

Ronald had been my husband of eight years. The two of us were together since early high school. Outside of my immediate family, I'd known him longer than anyone. There was a time when Ronald was the love of my life. He was also the father of my only child, Hannah, who'd been stolen from us fifteen years ago. While I'd gone on to pursue Hannah's kidnapper, to find our daughter and bring her home, Ronald couldn't join me. We tried to make it work, but our marriage had ended.

My eyes stung with tears for him, tears for his family who would hurt with the horrible news about their son and brother. Feeling grief for him was unexpectedly confusing, and yet, I felt an immense loss. I'd seen Ronald last when he'd been to the Outer Banks during the latter part of the summer almost a year ago. It was a brief window of time when a kidnapped girl was thought to be our daughter. But then the unfortunate news came that the girl was the daughter of another couple, another family, the victim of a kidnap. Ronald moved away after that, his life resuming in the city where we both grew up, the city of brotherly love, Philadelphia. I hadn't spoken to him since, and like before, we'd lost touch, his name becoming a character in my story whenever I'd share about Hannah.

Tears on my face turned cold with a breeze, sawgrass brushing my arms as Tracy knelt beside me. I looked at my hands and tore off the gloves as though they'd been touched by Black Death. A thousand questions whirled around my mind. In a shaky breath, I asked, "What was he doing in the Outer Banks?"

She shook her head, the touch of her hand warm on my shoulder. "I'll get you a fresh pair," she offered, not answering my question for now—how could she?—but taking the gloves I'd discarded.

"Thank you," I answered with a rasp as I wiped my fingers across my cheeks to dry them. But the idea of what happened, the torture he must have suffered... a pain welled deep and threatened to make me burst with a fresh cry. A man I'd loved, a man I'd had a child with was now brutally murdered.

"Casey?" Tracy said, approaching again, her figure a blur. I turned away to shield myself, waving to be alone.

I didn't want to give anyone a reason to suggest recusing me from the case. I know it was a fine line, but since I hadn't been married to Ronald in a long time, and since our daughter had never been found, we had no relationship at all. I could work this. I could find his killer. I could do that for him. He deserved more.

When I was ready, I stood and pegged my fists to my hips. A summer wind carried the sea air from the nearby ocean. I filled my lungs with the taste of brine and shook off my grieving moment, telling myself that'd be all of it, that I was done. It was time to get to work.

I faced the team and Ronald's body, the sun gaining ground above him which put a buttery-colored spotlight on the morbid scene. By now, Swales had covered Ronald's middle, including the birthmark on the inside of his thigh. She'd perform a thorough autopsy, but for now, neither necessitated viewing more than was needed as part of the crime scene.

"We can call in Cheryl?" Emanuel suggested, taking to his feet and stretching out his back. "She's still on desk duty, but the physical therapy is almost done."

"Already ahead of you," I said, showing my phone as though I'd texted her. It was a lie, but I would follow up and contact her, and rest any uncertainties he might be having. Detective Cheryl Smithson was another of the station's lead detectives, the two of us making up the complete roster of leads available to work homicide. We'd worked together on a recent case where a suspect's bullet shattered her hip. The injury had become a complicated recovery with Cheryl requiring a new hip and months of rehabilitation. She'd ride her desk at the station for the immediate future, but I could use her help when the time came.

"That's good," Emanuel said. What Emanuel didn't know was that he was up for a promotion. A basketball player in a previous life, I'd been filing the paperwork to get him promoted. It was time for him to take the lead, to manage his own team. The sad part was, it might mean his leaving our cozy part of the Outer Banks, the station having a limited budget for my team. But change can be good, and it'd be great for him to get the promotion. "We can take it from here."

"I'll be okay," I assured him as Dr. Swales lowered her face with a stare over her thick glasses. It was Jericho Flynn I was texting, a former sheriff and a major in the Marine Patrols. Jericho was also my partner. He'd worked with me on a case when I'd first arrived to the Outer Banks—and we fell in love. We've been together nearly every day since and it was Jericho I told all my stories to, including the ones about Ronald.

Now, I texted, *Buxton Woods. Ronald's body was found. He's been murdered.*

What!?

Jericho replied. Three bouncing dots showing he was typing.

Are you okay?

I'm fine, but I feel horrible for him and his family.

Want me to meet you there? he texted, the thought of my driving back with him appealing.

Yeah. I'd like that.

I sent him the coordinates, adding,

Give me another hour.

An hour he replied, knowing that probably meant three.

"Tracy?" I asked, holding my car keys. I'd have her take my car to the station. She peered up. "I'll take that fresh pair of gloves now."

"I got it," she answered, jumping to her feet. She grabbed the gloves and made her way around Ronald's body. As she approached, her foot caught onto the ground, snagging her step, causing her to tumble forward. Tracy fell to her knees, slamming the ground hard enough to hear. "Shit!"

"Whoa!" I hollered, running to her, searching for old tree roots or rocks, taking care to not join her. There were none though, only the soft earth, thick with green and yellow moss. I knelt next to her, eyes darting to her knees and elbows which had taken the brunt of the fall. "Are you hurt?"

"Just my pride," she answered red-faced, the team ogling. They said nothing as they waited for a sign. She held up a hand, signaling she was okay. "I'm fine, guys—" Tracy stopped mid-sentence and handed me the pair of gloves. She motioned to her shoe, and to what had caused her to fall.

"What is that doing there?" I asked, sleeving the gloves onto my fingers as fast as I could. I held up my hands, telling Tracy not to move, wanting her to remain still while I cleared her foot of what snared her. It was a rope, a foot or more of it with both ends anchored into the ground.

"That's the same type, isn't it?" she asked, removing her foot, and kneeling next to me, her hands joining mine as we wove the thin nylon cord through our fingers, each of us taking hold where the rope emerged. "I mean, like it is exactly the same kind."

"It is, but could be a coincidence," I said, voice muffled as I measured the distance from Ronald's body and judged the age. "But this rope looks older"—The nylon was closer to a brown color, blending into the colors of the moss, and had weathered and frayed —"might have been here a season or more."

"What do you think it's tied to?" Tracy asked, her mind like mine with the same questions.

"There's only one way to find out," I answered. I scooped a handful of the soft ground, a patty of green moss topping it like hair on a Troll doll. I held it up, its earthy smell strong, and told Tracy, "We dig."

Tracy nodded, a look of fierce determination on her face as she shoveled another handful. I joined her while the team continued their work. It wasn't more than a few handfuls of dirt before my finger struck onto a smooth rock.

Too smooth.

Tracy noticed, asking, "What's that end tied to?"

I cleared the ground, digging down an inch, maybe more, the rock appearing, round and a horribly bright yellow-white that was unmistakable. "Dr. Swales?"

Her chin up, glasses edging the tip of her nose, "What is it?"

The need to know came over me, and I shoveled the ground around the rock, the size and shape of it like a small melon. But it was as I'd thought. It was the back of a human skull. "Can you come over here?"

Her hands to her sides, fingers splayed, the doctor carefully made her way to us, watching the ground so she wouldn't trip. Tracy saw and told her, "You'll be okay. What I tripped on was a rope."

"A rope?" Dr. Swales asked. "Coincidence?"

"That's what I said," I answered, her eyes growing round and big behind her thick lenses. Then she saw the bright white bone.

"That's the back of someone's head," she stated calmly.

I scooted to the side, making room for her while she squatted in place and joined in the dig. "Tracy, take a step back." Tracy looked at her feet, realizing where she was and moved around the doctor. "If I'm right, you were standing on this person's left shoulder."

As the doctor removed the soil, Emanuel joined, and a thought occurred to me. Why hadn't the killer buried Ronald? There was wildlife here, and the ground was marshy. I scooped a handful of loose dirt, the dampness of it from brackish water, Buxton Woods being close to the sea. The area must have flooded in the past, the bones sinking rather than being buried.

Samantha and Nichelle joined us, the entire team standing behind Dr. Swales as she completed the recovery.

"Is it what I think it is?" I asked, a hard lump in my throat.

"Definitely a human skull. Take this," she said, handing me the nylon rope, the shape flat, but what had one time been a noose. "The bones to the neck are still buried. I believe we have a complete human skeleton."

The image of her holding a human skull found a place in my brain where it would burn in and stay forever. I followed the rope to the other end of the noose, finding the knot. "Another arbor knot."

"Same one used with Ron... the first victim," Emanuel said.

"Ronald Haskin is fine," I said, hating to hear his name used in connection to a murder investigation. I stood, my legs still wobbly and weak, the toll of this morning feeling like it had been days of an examination we'd barely started. I shielded my eyes from the bright sun, cringing at the stench of death drifting all around. A dreadful hunch stirred in my gut.

"We have two victims," I began addressing my team, showing them the rope and knot. "Killed with what looks to be the same method. I think we've found a killer's dumping ground."

THREE

The Buxton Woods hiking trail had begun to fill with gawkers and onlookers—joggers, hikers, and mothers and fathers with little children in tow—most only passing by. And though we were quite a distance from the trail, I found none of the telltale signs that a killer was in the crowd. I knew what to look for, if this was a serial killer case—a lone individual, spectating amidst a crowd, but cautious of their distance as they sometimes are. Alone, they'd admire their work and watch us tease through the horrors of their creation. And to them, it was a creation, an art.

The excavation from Tracy's find continued. We worked the rope, each of us pulling it slowly with Dr. Swales guiding and instructing. The victim's skull had been set aside, the sunlight shining brightly on the bone. With the clear view, there was no physical trauma showing on the victim's bones, I was convinced that what I had in my hand, the rope with an arbor knot, had been used in a same manner as we'd discovered on Ronald.

"This is going to take some time," Dr. Swales said, drawing her fingers through the loose moss and earth, an outline of a bone forming. "I believe the body decomposed in less than a few years."

"It's a skeleton. I thought that took a really long time?" Samantha asked, her black bangs draping over her eyelids, fake lashes batting them with each blink. "In the movies, when they dig up bodies they're kinda still like real people, only they're all sunken and papery and stuff."

Swales shot me a glance that spoke volumes, her patience with her new intern nearing maximum. "What you saw was a body that's been at rest in a coffin. In suitably dry conditions, the decomposition to skeleton form could take decades." Swales scooped a handful of loose earth, drops of moisture from it running down the side of her hand. She pinched the mud, a clump of it falling, adding, "But with a body outdoors, in conditions such as these with the ground wet and warm and littered with insects and wildlife, skeleton form could be reached in as little as a few weeks."

We continued uncovering the rope, it appearing from beneath the moss as though we were pulling on a loose stitch. But when the rope held firm, I stopped pulling and brushed aside an overgrowth of seagrass to reveal a pair of sticks—or what I thought to be sticks—their color matching the skull. "Doctor, are these a pair of legs?" I said, asking as I assessed the posture and visualized the position with the skull having been facing the ground. "Why would the victim be partially covered?"

"Reasons are many. From seasonal changes to flooding in this part of the reserve," Swales said, kneeling next to me, wiping one of the larger bones clean. She gave me a curt nod. "Yes, these two bones are the femur, the victim's thigh bone."

I chanced a pull, the rope springing through cattail stalks, a loop coming loose, a smaller bone falling out of it. "I think I found a wrist? Or what was part of it?"

"Could be the ankle based on the first victim," Swales answered, sitting up, her hands perched on her hips as she studied what we had. With a heavy breath, she held out her arms, her eyes hidden behind fogged glasses, the humidity thick. "Okay, everyone stop. This is what I'd like to do—"

A zipper from behind us stole my attention, the sound of it making me flinch. I dared a look over my shoulder to see Samantha joining Derek, a body bag being prepared to receive Ronald. Derek raised his voice for Swales to hear, saying, "This one is ready to be transported?"

"I'll deliver him to the morgue," Swales answered, glancing at me a moment before continuing. "For the excavation of this victim, Derek, you and Samantha help with the recovery and anything Casey's team needs."

"Emanuel, you can run this one?" He straightened, towering over us, his lower back popping with a boney grind. He agreed with a wince and a wave. "Nichelle as well, and Tracy." I faced the doctor, saying, "The team here will continue the investigation and I'll join you."

Dr. Swales furrowed her brow, the corner of her mouth curving. "Casey, are you sure you want to do that?" There was trepidation in her voice, but I'd already seen the worst of what could be seen.

"I'm sure," I said, but did have a fleeting uncertainty that gave me pause. In my gut, I believed this to be the best path forward to move this investigation. "I'll need a preliminary report soonest."

With her tall hair swaying with the cattail fronds, she removed her glasses to clean them for a long moment. When Swales was ready, she said, "You can join me." She motioned to the bodies. "I think we know what killed these people, but I'll get you a report with description and cause of death for the investigation."

As they closed the zipper on Ronald's body, I closed my eyelids as if it would help. It didn't though. I was sure to hear it in my sleep tonight. I placed the rope I'd been working carefully atop the exposed bones and got up, offering Swales my hand. Her petite fingers found mine as she got to her feet. "Ready?" I asked, sighting the path we'd made as a second medical examiner's wagon arrived.

"Lead the way."

We were quiet during our walk to the medical examiner's wagon, Derek taking the bulk of Ronald's weight. A strap around my wrist cut into my skin as I bore the weight of my ex-husband's right leg, the thought striking me hard. Another ME assistant named Jonathon held the left side. I'd tried to avoid it, but in the quiet of our trek my mind raced with the torture of Ronald's last hours, the details appearing in my mind like a horror flick on late-night television. I'd instructed Nichelle to get moving on every detail regarding Ronald's car, his driver's license, his credit cards, and his phone. I had no idea what he was doing here in the Outer Bank's reserve of Buxton Woods, but maybe a digital trail would get us an idea of where he'd been and where he was going.

A patrol officer opened a streamer of black and yellow crime-scene tape, allowing us to pass before she hung the first end and lined it along the trail. She'd weave it across the shrubs and red cedars, officially blocking access while our teams investigated the site and excavated the second victim. We entered the walking trail, the day's heat and the heavy walk making me sweat, the packed dirt and stone beneath my feet welcome. Through a ceiling of pine trees, I saw the Cape Hatteras Lighthouse come into view and felt a rush of emotion.

Not yet, I told myself, biting my lip to shut it down, feeling as though there were a thousand eyes on me. Now was not the time to mourn Ronald. I had a killer to catch first.

I'd followed up with more texts to Jericho. He'd shifted plans and was already at the morgue by the time we'd arrived, his blue-green eyes soft with care. He was dressed for a shift on the ocean, wearing a short-sleeved pale gray shirt and dark blue pants, a cap on his head with the Marine Patrol logo, and his sunglasses perched upside down on the visor. The sight of the uniform rattled my already frayed nerves a touch, but I put on a smile, happy to see him. With our line of work, I'd never tell him that I always got nervous when he went out to patrol the waters. The ocean's beauty and tranquility could be deceiving. It could become an unrelenting giant that'd run through his boat with little to no warning.

"Thanks for coming," I said as he descended the granite stairs of the township's municipal building, the lower level being the home to the morgue. I was already shivering and hadn't opened the doors leading to the refrigerated room where the autopsies were performed. As the elevator doors opened, the bell rang, and the tip of Ronald's body bag appeared. I shook, some of it from the cold, the rest from thinking it impossible to feel this way.

"Hey, babe," Jericho whispered in my ear, smelling of sunblock, his broad shoulders blocking the view while they completed the transport of Ronald's body. I wrapped my arms around him and shuddered with a stifled cry. It wasn't until I was with him that I knew how much I needed Jericho. He pinched my chin, our eyes meeting. "I'm sorry about Ronald."

"Thank you," I managed to say, my hand against his bristled cheek. "I need to find out why he was in the Outer Banks."

"You haven't heard from him?" Jericho asked as Dr. Swales came down the steps, her green Crocs kissing stone with an echo bouncing against the high ceiling. I shook my head. "It's been a while since I spoke to Ronald."

"Good to see you, Jericho," Swales said as she stowed her things in a locker and put on a lab coat.

"And you, Terri," he answered. She joined us, her height making her look tiny next to Jericho. When he saw the doctor's lab coat, he asked, "So this is what you call retirement?"

"Maybe someday. Just not today," she answered, gripping his arm to give it an affectionate squeeze. The two had been friends a long time, and like me, I knew Jericho was happy to see Dr. Swales continuing. "I'd stay to chat but would like to get started."

"Yes," I said, agreeing with her. "We should begin."

"Will you be okay?" Jericho asked, concern showing in a weak frown.

"I'm fine," I assured him.

But I wasn't sure at all. I only knew I needed to work this case.

"Then, shall we?" the doctor asked, her hands pressing against the heavy resin doors, the room's refrigerated air spilling around our feet as I sleeved one of the lab coats onto my arms and wrapped it around me.

"Stay safe," I told Jericho, his giving me a wink with the door closing behind me, the edge of it clipping the other, the sharp clap making me flinch.

"I'll walk us through this, dear," Swales said, taking my arm. "And have you out of here soon enough."

"Seriously, Doctor," I said, my breath a cloud, and my voice bordering on tense. "Thank you, but I'm fine. Let's work this like we'd work any other case."

Dr. Swales stepped onto her wood stool, the finish on it gone from the years of service. The attendants moved Ronald's body from the gurney onto her autopsy table, his skin rubbing harshly against the stainless steel. "Very well," she said with a nod. She motioned to the other side of the table, offering a place for me to stand. She flipped a switch, turning on a microphone above the table to record the preliminary report. "Male, approximate age is in early forties—"

"Forty-four," I said, interrupting—a reaction. A muscle memory. The doctor acknowledged the correction. And in the cold, I felt heat rising on my neck, making it worse by continuing, "He... the victim turned forty-four last month."

"—Forty-four years of age with a laceration around the neck, resulting from a nylon rope, the diameter approximately one-quarter of an inch."

"Sorry," I said abruptly, interrupting again. I fidgeted, hating that I suddenly felt uncomfortable. Ronald's face and chest were swollen, and a cloudy purple color where the blood had settled since he'd been discovered face down. I don't know why I thought it'd move back once we'd righted his body, but the dead don't bleed, their hearts don't pump. "I... I'll shut up."

The doctor's eyes narrowed. "Casey, being uncomfortable is completely understandable," she said, continuing to work as she spoke, running her fingers through Ronald's hair and feeling his scalp. Her glasses dipped as she turned her head sideways when reaching behind his head. "For what it's worth, while you are an exceptional detective, it is good to see the human side—"

She stopped, having found something. "What is it?"

"Gloves," she answered, nudging her chin to a counter covered with medical equipment. Swales lowered herself closer to Ronald's face, her study of his head turning intense, her focus concentrated. "You need to be a detective now."

I understood at once. Whatever it was she found, I'd need to record it, detail it, and that meant feel the finding and see it. I put the gloves on, the pace of the motions as fast as my breathing. "Okay, I'm ready."

Swales guided my hand behind Ronald's head, fingers in his hair where I felt his scalp. She took hold of one finger where I felt a lump, the surface raised. "Do you feel that?"

"It's a bump," I said. The center of it was cratered, forming a perfect circle. My emotions drained, the detective in me came to full attention. I knew the shape, understood the injury. It was from a gun muzzle, the last part of a gun the bullet touches before exiting. "Someone held a gun to his head."

"That is my assessment as well," she said as she searched the rest of Ronald's head. "Seems to be just the one. Based on the depth of the bruise, it was held there a while."

"Long enough for him to remove his clothes," I said, suggesting a series of events. "And then long enough to force him to lie face down while being tied up with the ropes."

"Agreed," she said.

"Can we get measurements?" I felt the lump, trying to determine the gun's caliber. Our knowing the weapon would help in the search for the killer. The bruising was larger than a .22, maybe as big as a .9 millimeter, but it could have also been the barrel of a .45. Frustrated, I added, "I can't tell from touch. We'll need the diameter."

"Of course," the doctor answered, a question forming on her face. "Casey, why not just use the gun?"

I shook my head, hating what I thought to be the reason, having already understood the sickening use of the arbor knot, and the weight of Ronald's legs and arms. "The killer wanted to draw it out. And they wanted to watch."

"Awful," Swales said with a grimace, her expression soured by the thought.

"That's not the worst of it though," I said with a heaviness in my words.

Her brow lifted. Her eyes giant behind her glasses. "What do you mean?"

"The killer held the gun, only there's no bullet injury. There's just the threat of one." I shaped my hand like a gun, the tip of my index finger pressing against Ronald's head. "The killer had to be holding the gun long enough, and with enough force, for us to detect a bruise post-mortem. That means someone else had to have tied the ropes around his neck and ankles and wrists. There are two killers."

FOUR

As Dr. Swales proceeded to perform a preliminary findings report for me, I began to investigate the rope. We'd severed a part of it in the field, allowing us to relax Ronald's limbs while the bindings remained tautly in place. With my hands sleeved in purple gloves, their powdery touch on my fingertips, the loops around his wrists came off with relative ease. I shuddered when it came time to recover the rope from around Ronald's neck, Swales nodding an okay for me to proceed. It had done significant damage, disfiguring my ex-husband with his mouth hanging slack, his tongue swollen and his eyes bulging from their sockets. I tried not looking as I worked the nylon cord. Maybe later I'd find our old wedding album and poke through the pages until the horrors of this day were thoroughly diluted.

A moment was all I needed, the brief thought of our wedding album bringing me back to when we'd first met. In the autopsy table's steel surface, I saw Ronald's reflection. Only, it was his face from when he was on the path to becoming the man I'd marry, the man I'd have a child with. The morgue disappeared, the walls gone, death fading. It was just the two of us, our fingers laced, the soft grass of Fairmount Park between my toes as we walked along the Schuylkill River Trail.

My chest and neck warmed as I remembered the day. My shoes held in my hand, we'd stopped at an old stone wall to rest. But really it was a plan he'd put into motion much earlier. A group of his friends appeared from out of nowhere, crashing through the shrubs to surprise me. They held champagne glasses and a bottle, and each of them was dressed in a suit with loud colorful stripes and bow ties to match. Before I knew it, they were all singing as Ronald went to one knee, an engagement ring perched on his fingertips and a marriage proposal on his lips.

I sucked in a breath, a harsh sadness coming with it. I'd forgotten how in love we were. How absolutely head over heels I was about Ronald. About us. The memory seemed like it was only yesterday. We were so young then. Just kids really. But we had one another and were convinced we could face anything together. What if Hannah had never been kidnapped? What if we'd been like everyone else, our family still together? Who would we be now?

I dismissed the memories and the questions. The case of Ronald's murder was between my fingers now. I held the knot, the point where most tension had held, and then had cinched tight when Ronald couldn't keep his legs and arms in position.

I was twelve when I was first introduced to this type of knot, my father spooling a new fishing line onto a reel. He explained that an arbor was the part of a fishing reel's spool where the line wound around. The knot he showed me was a slip knot which grew tighter when pulled, allowing us to reel the new line onto the spool without worry of it coming loose. The killer, or killers, knew this knot and applied the same principle to the rope. I held the clue, taking notes, and then carefully bagged it as evidence.

"Look at this," I told Swales, showing her the pad of Ronald's right thumb. On it, his fingernail had lifted from the nail bed as though it had been pried.

"Here too," Swales said with the rigor mortis cracking as she rolled his wrist for me to see. On his thumb, his fingerprint was peeled raw. We found the same on his other hand. "What do you make of them?"

"Are they rope burns?" I answered. "And his nails... He'd always had strong nails. It would have taken a lot to do that damage."

Swales leaned up, raising her chin for the microphone. "Significant rope burns to the pad of the victim's thumbs, and fingernails pried from their nail beds."

She pinched her lips, her mouth going crooked. I knew she had an idea.

"What is it?"

She replied without a word, showing only a frown.

"What?"

"Well—" she began. She took off her glasses to clean them, continuing, "There was a type of torture I read about while in medical school, the victim hung by their thumbs."

The ideas of what she described slammed into my head. I braced the table, thinking it through, thinking the logistics of it. If Ronald had been tortured, it would have been done elsewhere. We would have more evidence than this. "I don't think that's this." I squeezed one of Ronald's hands, sadly unable to recall the last time I'd held his hand. I wasn't a doctor, but I could tell the bones in his hand felt okay. "With his size, wouldn't that type of torture break the bones in his hands?"

Swales took hold of his other hand, her fingers prodding. "Nothing broken here."

I sucked in a quick breath, an idea coming to mind. "He was working the rope," I said. Swales cocked her head, trying to understand. As much as I hated to do it, I had to visualize and attempt to demonstrate what had happened if we were going to understand the injuries. "Picture this. He is face down, and his wrists and ankles are tied behind him. It's similar to being hog-tied, only there is a rope around the neck too."

I held up one of the four smaller loops. "There was a loop for each wrist and ankle."

She picked up the longer cord, the one leading to the noose that was around his neck. "And this is connected to them?"

"Correct. The killer made it so that the victim had to keep their hands and feet up while they were face down."

Swales's eyelids opened wide, her understanding the difficulty. "And if they relaxed their arms and legs, the bigger noose got tighter."

"Ronald must have figured out how the ropes worked together." I tucked my thumb beneath the loop that had been around his right ankle. "What if Ronald slipped his thumbs into the loops to hold the weight of his legs?"

"So the struggle caused the rope burns," Swales said with firm understanding.

"That's how the arbor knot works... how all of these worked together," I continued and then placed one of the ropes back onto Ronald's wrist, slowly pulling the rope to show its movement. "See how this slides freely back and forth?"

"Through the knot," she answered with a nod.

"If Ronald was able to get his thumbs beneath the ropes around his ankles, even the slightest bit, then he would have been able to add the slack needed to remove them."

Swales cupped her chin, a finger waving, and said, "I think I see what you mean. He'd figured out how to escape by adding slack, which would relieve the weight of his legs long enough—"

"—long enough to remove the rope," I said, finishing for her. "But he couldn't, and if the strain was too great, his legs would give out. And the weight of them surely had to cause the rope burns."

"But he tried," Swales said, her focus returning to Ronald's thumbs. "This is evidence that he fought. Casey, I believe you are right."

"Doctor. This was torture." In my career I'd come to learn when murder was with compassion, the killer not letting their victim suffer. A bullet to the head perhaps. Or a cut from ear to ear, severing blood flow, opening the windpipe, the blood loss and the suffocation coming quick. With a sickening thought I asked,

"What if the killers picked this knot to see if Ronald *could* escape? Maybe this was a game?"

"That's absolutely awful," Swales answered with a grimace. "What sort of person would do that?"

"I aim to find out—" I began, the heavy doors swinging open with a jolt, Derek and Samantha entering, each of them carrying the end of a black body bag, their work at Buxton Woods completed. "Did you bring everything?"

"Everything we could find," Derek replied. "Your team is still there."

Samantha shook when the morgue's frigid air hit her, her teeth chattering instantly, her words slurring, "We found most of the bones at the surface."

"I suspected that'd be the case." Swales joined them, wheeling a gurney into position, one of the wheels squealing. "No burial."

"And the ropes too?" I asked. "Or did my team bag them?"

"Some of it was still attached," Samantha answered, blowing air to clear the bangs in her eyes.

"Good," I muttered, thinking it would help to compare to what was found on Ronald's body.

With a grunt, they placed the body bag atop a gurney and wheeled it next to Ronald's, Samantha's stare fixed on his body. She looked at me, her bangs falling as she spoke again. "But some of the rope kinda like fell off the bone. Know what I mean?"

"We know, dear," Swales said. "Thank you."

I pinched the zipper's tab, the body bag still warm from it sitting in the sunlight. "Doctor? May I?"

"Yes, let's," she answered.

"I want to confirm if the knots are the same."

As Dr. Swales covered Ronald's body, the recovered ropes set aside on a steel tray, I tugged the body bag's zipper, the sound grating, a dark cavity appearing. When the bag opened, I was reminded of the brackish smell and the boggy mud where we'd discovered Ronald. "Lights please."

Swales flipped a switch and dragged her step stool into place, the rough surface worn smooth where she stood. The lamps above the gurney flicked on, the brightness bouncing before turning solid with a low hum to chase the darkness away. "Better?"

"Much," I answered, stretching the bag, making it yawn until we could both see the scatter of bones and rope seated inside. The jumbled pieces were like a sad puzzle, someone's life cut short and stolen. The bones weren't clean like ivory. They were dingy and pale, but some stood out, the shade of them like deadwood. There were a few that had remained connected too, and a few I thought I recognized from my studies.

It wasn't the color or the shape of them that bothered me. It was the sheer number of them. "Doctor? How long would it take to reassemble?"

"How much of your anatomy do you remember?" she asked, her head tipped, her eyes hiding a grin as she stared at me over her glasses.

"Really?" I asked, believing I'd probably connect a leg to a shoulder and have no idea I'd done so.

"No, dear. Not really." She laughed. She got down from her stool and went to a drawer. From it, she pulled out her cassette player and earphones, the orange foamy ear pads aged and dingy like the color of the bones. She held it up for me to see. "I've got company."

"A few hours?" I asked with a guess as she prepared for the work. I slipped my finger through the biggest of the rope's loops, the noose which had come from around the neck.

"There are two hundred and six bones that make up the human skeleton," Swales commented as she unwound the cord to her headphones. With care, I removed the noose, laying it on the body bag. The arbor knot was still functional. "You collect the ropes, and I'll try and have the bones reassembled in a day or two."

From the inside corner, I retrieved the skull and carefully placed it in the light, the victim's teeth straight and complete. "Can we get dental records maybe? This could be a younger person."

Swales opened her cassette player, flipped the tape inside, the label reading *mix-tape '87*, saying, "Go on."

"Well, the teeth are in reasonably good shape." I rotated the remains to look at the rear of the jaw, but the bottom half came off in my hands. My heart seized.

Swales saw my reaction. "Casey, it's perfectly normal for that to happen. Especially when the body is in this state." Swales took the bottom jaw and placed it aside. "Your assessment is correct. There is no wear, no chips, or broken teeth."

"There are no cavities or signs of dental work either. Braces?"

"Perhaps," Swales answered, her study turning more serious as she began to retrieve bones from the body bag. She held up the largest of the bones, adding, "From the length, I'd guess the victim was just over five feet tall."

"You can tell from that?"

One brow rising, she answered, "This is the femur. And with it, I can make a fairly accurate estimate on height."

We had teeth for a possible dental record and a skull to perform a facial reconstruction, digitizing a likeness based on the structure. But could we use DNA?

A recent cold case came to mind, something I'd seen in the news. "What about DNA recovery?"

"It all depends on how old these are." She peered over her glasses again, asking, "What are you thinking?"

I didn't tell her what was seeded deep in the back of my mind. I didn't reveal the question I'd been carrying for the last decade and a half. With every unidentified body we discovered, every victim that was around my daughter's age, I couldn't help but wonder if it was her that I was finally seeing again. To answer the doctor's question... I was wondering if these were Hannah's bones.

But that's not what I told her. Instead, I answered, "DNA, let's do the standard distribution, submitting to national databases like CODIS with the FBI for missing persons."

The doctor cocked her head and squinted. "But you've got

something else in mind too?" Swales asked, reading me like a fortune teller reading tea leaves. "What is it?"

"Well, it's a little out there, but I'd also like to send a sample to some of the ancestry services," I answered as I retrieved another of the nooses, smaller in diameter, the knot still working.

"Like the family-tree types I see advertised on those infomercials?" she asked.

"The same," I answered. Swales frowned, seeming confused with the request. I touched the victim's arm, or what I thought might be an arm, the feel of it smooth. "Doctor, these bones have a memory."

"A memory," she said and blurted a short laugh. When I didn't laugh along, her face turned serious. "Go on, explain."

"I read in a recent case, the DNA was used to find relatives who'd also used the service. When questioned about a missing family member, they mentioned a second cousin who'd disappeared three years earlier."

"Interesting." Swales fetched another of the larger bones, a noose sliding off it. "Those services can make the connections?"

"Apparently, over the years, they've amassed enough data to connect you to distant relatives you didn't know existed."

Her interest piqued. "So for other unsolved cases. Ones dating years back. I can use the DNA with the service to shed a hopeful light on who they were."

"Exactly," I said. "Call it DNA, or simply a memory, our bones carrying them to our graves."

She nodded fervently, lifting the femur. "I'll see what I can do with your memory bones idea." She looked at the work I'd done while we'd talked. The rope now lay next to the bones, showing five nooses, the first four small enough for ankles and wrists, and one large enough to accommodate a neck. "It's the same knot structure?"

"It is," I answered, demonstrating the rope's lead and how the victim's own arms and legs were used as a weight to strangle them.

I held up a noose from Ronald's remains, showing the size difference. "Only these are substantially smaller."

"That supports the size of the femur, the victim smaller in
stature, possibly female."

With her earphones in place, it was my cue to leave. I wanted
DNA and dental records. The rope, the type of knot, and the
pattern used was all the same. But the timing? The first victim,
how long ago had they been murdered? How long had their bones
been in Buxton Woods? And who was looking for them? Who was
posting fliers on old telephone poles or handing them out as people
passed by?

I believed someone was missing them. And it was my duty to
find out who.

As I made my way back to the locker to drop off the lab coats, I
heard a chatter echo across the granite. Thinking I was alone, I
turned around to see the intern, Samantha, in the shadows, an
older woman next to her, a pad in hand and the top of a pen
dancing as she wrote. A reporter.

Knowing Samantha was new, the sight of them together filled
me instantly with worry. We were early in the case and only had
sparse ideas of what kind of killer we were dealing with. There was
also Ronald. If his name leaked, and his relationship to me leaked,
the press would become uncontrollable. It had happened many
times before with our daughter's kidnapping case.

The two hadn't noticed me and I couldn't hear what was being
discussed, but any words to a reporter had to come through the
correct channels with multiple levels of awareness and permissions
first. I decided to make noise by dropping a hanger, the wood clamoring against the floor, the smack echoing loudly enough to startle
the pair. When Samantha caught my eye, shooing her bangs with
the swipe of a hand, I waved her toward me. The reporter saw who
I was and knew the drill, shuttling her pen and paper with one

hand, stuffing them deep into her pocketbook before racing up the stairs.

"Detective?" Samantha asked, her voice subtle and with a southern twang like the kind I would hear from Dr. Swales at times. "How can I help?"

"Was that a reporter you were speaking to?" I asked, sounding firm. Samantha nodded without regard to why I'd ask. "Did you discuss the case?"

With that, a look came over Samantha's face like she'd put on a mask. One that told me she *had* spoken about the case. I began to shake my head, Samantha asking, "We... we don't speak to them?"

I patted my chest, answering, "I speak to them, nobody else does unless they are with me."

She nodded hurriedly, agreeing. "Okay. I understand." She glanced at the thick resin doors, Dr. Swales still in the room. "You won't tell?"

I shook my head, answering, "I can't make that promise." The doctor had helped get Samantha the job. Her face was rigid with concern. I assured her, "Samantha, it'll be fine."

Warm like Dr. Swales, she touched the side of my arm with reserved relief. "Thank you. I... I didn't know not to say anything."

"How much did you tell the reporter?" I asked her, my feet feeling heavy as the concern weighed.

She twisted her mouth, her focus shifting to the ceiling while recounting what was said. "The ropes and that knot you knew. The arbor knot," she answered. My heart sank like a stone. The details about the rope could be treacherously dangerous. She saw my reaction, concern returning to her face, her pale blue eyes growing big. "She asked how they'd died."

"How much detail did you give her?" I asked, snatching my phone to text the team, telling them the use of the ropes was leaked to the press.

"Well, I mentioned the way the ropes were used around the neck and the victims' legs and arms as counterweights."

I didn't think my heart could sink any further, but as she spoke, I sensed the worst was yet to come. "And what else?"

"Well," she began, her gaze falling to the floor. I lifted her chin, seeing a young Dr. Swales, the resemblance in that moment was uncanny. Our eyes met, she answered, "I told her the victim's name. The one we knew. Ronald Haskin."

FIVE

A field of reporters had already begun to gather outside the station. A few stood in a lean against the building, some crowded the white benches to trade stories while working their phones. I took a breath, holding it in while I approached. Ronald's name wouldn't have been published yet. Not on purpose anyway. But reporters had their ways and their networks—a few dollars sprinkled about, the bills landing in the right hands. I considered Samantha's leak to the reporter in the morgue, but didn't see her face anywhere in the reporters waiting. I hoped Derek or Dr. Swales would give Samantha some guidance on how best to interact with reporters. Even if that meant not at all. It might be helpful too to give her some background about me and Ronald and our daughter, the history.

The sun hung behind the municipal building, bringing afternoon sunshine to the Outer Banks. Loose beach sand tumbled along the pavement, pushed by an ocean breeze, the heel of my shoe grinding against it while I climbed the first step toward the doors. One of the reporters gave me a nod. A lanky man with red combed-back hair, I'd known his face since my first days working in the barrier islands. He caught my eye and raised a freckled hand, his phone in the other, the screen flashing with the word, *recording*.

"Detective White!" he exclaimed, and then pulled the phone to his mouth and whispered my name along with a date and time. "Any comments on the Buxton Woods body discovered this morning—"

"There's nothing more than what's already been reported," I answered, easing with the next step as I tried to think of a statement that'd offer enough to keep them busy. And do so without offering too much. Another reporter jumped in, standing close, his holding a spongey microphone that was close enough to record my breathing. Turning to face them, I shielded my eyes from the sunlight, saying, "There was a report of a body found in Buxton Woods. A male, early forties. His... his death is suspicious."

"Suspicious?" the lanky reporter asked, his narrow face inching closer. "A homicide? Can you elaborate?"

My gaze fell to the shrubs lining the station's front, the branches teeming with berries, ripe and bright red, a pair of gray catbirds plucking them. I only noticed because Ronald always fed the birds in our yard and had even planted the same bushes hoping to attract them. "Yes. Death is suspicious. The body has been delivered to the medical examiner."

"What is the manner of suspicion?" he asked, a gust pushing him.

"Have they been identified?" the other reporter asked, speaking over the first.

I shook my head as I jerked on the station doors, opening them, feet shuffling behind to follow me inside. "No additional information or names at this time." But thanks to Samantha's leak, they'd know soon enough.

I let the doors close behind me, hoping they'd remain outside.

"You've had quite the busy morning," I heard from my left, finding Alice, our station's desk officer.

"Alice?" I asked, searching a station monitor, the time showing an hour past noon. "You're not still here from last night's shift?"

She shook her round face as she worked a pin in her graying hair. "I'm getting too old for that eleven-to-seven shift."

"You're on days now?" I asked, making my way to her, the station benches empty, the overnight arrests already processed. While the night was over, it was still early enough in the day that the drunk and the disorderly were still sleeping it off in the tank. It wouldn't be long before the benches were warmed by the pick-pockets and delinquents caught looking for an easy score on the vacationers.

She smiled broadly and answered, "I am!" With a huff, she added, "I am finally back in the land of the living. No more nights for this old gal!"

With my elbow perched on her counter, I wanted to warn about the reporters, and the flood of them that might come when Ronald's name was public knowledge. We'd been a story last year during what was thought to be the return of our kidnapped daughter. At one point the news had gone national, the stories going viral after the news broke that the girl was not our daughter. "Listen, Alice. This morning—"

She took my hand, her fingers pudgy and warm, a deep care in her green eyes. "I know." I returned a puzzled look, believing the count of those in the know being few. I was wrong. "The sheriff stopped in to discuss it with me. Don't you worry none. I'll handle the reporters."

For a moment, I couldn't say anything, the sad look on Alice's face stirring a fresh emotion. "Thank you," I mouthed, leaving her as I made my way through the small gate, the metal latch ringing, toward our cubicles and office desks on the other side of the station.

When I reached my desk, the sight of it felt alien to me, different somehow. Maybe it was Ronald's murder making every-thing feel strange, as though nothing would be the same again.

I dismissed the awkwardness and flicked on my monitor to show my inbox and calendar. Both were empty, which was good. The last thing I needed was a day of station meetings where we talked about the work rather than doing the work. I needed heads-down time to work Ronald's case.

I heard the station gate open and close and saw Tracy and Nichelle arriving. "That was good timing," Tracy said with a wave as they made their way toward their desks next to mine.

Seeing them helped ease some of that strange out-of-place feeling. "You guys finished already?" I asked.

Nichelle said nothing, but surprised me then, her arms wrapping around my middle as she pulled me close to her, the nutty smell of lavender strong. Her breath was warm in my ear as she spoke. "I wanted to tell you how sorry I am about Ronald."

"Thank you," I answered, appreciating the sentiment. Tracy joined in the hug, her face a hot sunburned pink. "Oh, Tracy!"

"It's nothing," she said, her eyes bright and wide, and her dimples deep. "A little color will look good on me."

"Hats for the team," I exclaimed. "I'll push an order through procurement."

"Like the kind the FBI wear?" Nichelle asked excitedly, taking to her desk, chair wheels squealing.

"Sure, like those," I said, feeling more at home, glad to have them sitting near me. The sheriff had offered me a new office recently, one with a window view, but I turned it down. While my position and status warranted it, I believed the closeness of my team's desks was what helped accelerate us. We fed on our energies to solve crimes faster than any other team.

"If you need anything," Nichelle added, brow raised as she nodded until I returned the nod. She'd recently taken to combing her hair flat against her head, losing a few inches in height. With bronze skin tone and golden-brown eyes, she was becoming a beautiful woman. "You promise?"

"I promise," I answered as she disappeared behind her tower of monitors. In my opinion, Nichelle *was* the station's IT Department. She handled everything from printers to phone inquiries. With some of my pushing, calling more meetings than anyone would care to attend, I was able to convince the sheriff and station management to flip the bill and hire more resources. The new team had been assembled to replace Nichelle, taking over her day-to-day which allowed me to utilize her technical skills in a purely investigative manner. Coupling her expertise with homicide investigations was another advantage our team had.

She held up the crime-scene camera. "I'll get the pictures posted."

"There wouldn't be anything on Ronald's phone yet?" I asked, hoping for an early break, but knowing the phone company cooperation could take as short as an hour, and as long as days to a week.

"Let me check," she said, keyboard keys rattling followed by a run of mouse clicks. "No kidding—"

"You've got something?" I asked, wheeling my chair into her cubicle, a map of the Outer Banks on the screen. I wasn't sure what I was looking at. The streets were recognizable, but with red circles. I made a wild guess and asked, "Those are cell towers?"

"Phone company delivered, and we have got his last cell tower pings before his phone went offline," she answered, zooming out to show a string of red circles, a path of them dropped like breadcrumbs.

"Philly," I said, tracing the cell tower pings, their showing Ronald drove from Philadelphia to the Outer Banks. "Nichelle, hover on the pings in Philadelphia. I want to see what day and time he left the city."

She did as I instructed, the first cell tower ping dating three days ago, with his leaving there early in the morning. "We have the date and time he left the city," she said and jumped to the Outer Banks map to hover on a cell tower near the bay. "He then arrived eight hours later."

"He must have stopped for something to eat," I said, commenting about the extra time, the drive taking six to seven hours. "Or maybe traffic was bad. Zoom in on the last cell tower ping. Where is it?"

Nichelle clicked and scrolled to enlarge the map, the street names a blur, the pixels a mirage while the map came into focus. I let out a short gasp when I saw it, Nichelle speaking through her fingers on her lips, "Casey, it looks like—"

"The station," I said, finishing for her. "Ronald's car is parked around the corner from us."

There was only one reason he'd be here. Ronald had come to see me.

SIX

Ronald's arrival location was on one of the streets bordering the station. Nichelle snatched her camera as Emanuel fixed us with an inquisitive eye. He'd returned from Buxton Woods and saw that we were on the move again. Only this time, we were going on foot, and it would be through the station's rear exit, a trick Alice showed me once when I needed to avoid the reporters.

"What is it?" Tracy asked, seeing the commotion.

"I was about to ask the same thing." Emanuel wiped his brow, his head gleaming, the day's heat growing.

"We've got a cell ping on the victim's phone," Nichelle answered, showing a tablet screen, the map transferred from her desktop, a red circle flashing around the tower. "Ronald was here."

As the team headed toward the front, I motioned for them to follow me. I didn't know what we'd find, but if he'd been abducted at his car, there was a possibility of fingerprints or other evidence. "Bring your gear," I instructed.

"Uhm, where are we going?" Tracy asked. I could see the whites of her baby-blue eyes, summer highlights falling in front of her face as she hurried to catch up to us.

"We're avoiding the front exit." I clutched my phone and keys, secured my gun on my belt's holster and straightened my badge.

We fell silent as I navigated the maze of cubicles, passing our team conference room, and entered a narrow hallway with a janitor's closet on one side and a door at the end.

"I can barely fit back here," I heard Emanuel say. A thump and bump followed his words as elbows brushed the walls.

Above the door, the exit sign glowed a bright red. We passed beneath it to leave the station, entering the parking area and a wide stretch of asphalt with white lines marking the parking spaces. There were landscaped grounds around it, along with light posts and young trees. I looked to the lights first, remembering Ronald always parking beneath them, telling me a car was less apt to be broken into at night. "Nichelle, any chance we have motor vehicle records? A car registration with make and model, maybe even the license plate?"

"We should, checking now."

It wasn't until I saw the parking lot full of cars that I realized that I had no idea what Ronald was driving. He'd always favored Fords when we were together, but that was years ago. People change. We were silent as we walked around the lot, shoes grating against the sand, the beach less than a quarter mile away. "After a couple of days, would the car get towed?"

"I don't think so. This is public parking," Emanuel answered. "There's the arboretum behind us, and the township building over there."

"How about we look for a Pennsylvania license plate," I instructed, the team spreading out while I stepped aside as a minivan parked next to me.

"I don't have any DMV records yet," Nichelle announced. "I'll call them direct."

The van's side door slid open, a family of four exiting—husband and wife, two older girls with them—they were dressed for the beach and began to gather their things. I walked around the rear, reading the New Jersey license plate. "You guys from out of town?"

When the husband noticed my badge, he stopped unloading

the van and put a beach chair down, answering, "Visiting for the week, but our rooms aren't ready until later this afternoon."

His wife joined him, a tangle of brown hair sprouting from beneath an oversized sunhat, the shade hiding her face. "We wanted to get an early start." She held out her pale arms, saying, "A little sun, you know?"

"Welcome to the Outer Banks." I hung my thumb over my shoulder. "This is the police station and municipal building. I think what you are looking for is the parking lot closer to the Days Inn and the Best Western," I told them, and realized maybe Ronald had parked there as well. Maybe he was staying at one of those hotels. Cell tower coverage was circular, and we were on one side. What if his cellphone was picked up by the same tower, but across from us by a hundred and eighty degrees?

The van smelled of sunblock, the teen girls slathering their arms and legs while gazing at me. "Is it far?" one of them asked, her face in a pucker.

"Another couple of blocks on Collington and then across 158. The road becomes Ocean Bay—"

"I found Pennsylvania tags!" Emanuel said, his voice distant from the other side of the parking lot.

I hurried with the directions, "—after 158, cross Memorial and you'll see the parking straight ahead with the beach there."

"Thank you," the couple said, murmuring back and forth as I made my way to Emanuel. Nichelle and Tracy joined him, the three staring at the rear of a newer model silver-colored Ford Fusion.

"It's the only car in the lot with a Pennsylvania license plate," Tracy said. She went to the front of the car. "There's no plate on the front bumper?"

"Not in Pennsylvania," Nichelle answered. "Same as here in North Carolina."

"The car is a Ford. That's a sign it's his," I said, sweating and breathing heavy from the run. "Fords are the only cars Ronald ever bought."

"Ford. Found on road dead," Emanuel said, making fun of the name. "I'm more of a Chevy person myself. Always seem to have better headroom."

"I'll run the plate," Nichelle said, rolling her eyes. "We should get something faster to confirm it is his."

I circled the car, finding heavy bug splatter baked onto the windshield and the front bumper—a mishmash of yellow and green and brown. The hood had its mottled share of colors as well, signs the car had traveled the highway for a distance. When I got to the passenger side window, I stopped with a stare, my legs rooting into the asphalt. There was no doubt that this was Ronald's car. There was no need for a DMV license plate lookup to confirm it.

On the passenger front seat was a framed picture of our family. That is, the family we were before Hannah was kidnapped.

From the back of my mind came the memories of visiting a local mall in Philadelphia. I smelled the food court and the doughy soft pretzel Hannah had wanted on the way to the photography studio. I could remember every detail of that day the picture was taken. The photographer had us pose on large eggshell white boxes —Ronald sitting close to me, his arm around my waist with Hannah sitting on our laps. Behind us was a backdrop of what looked like sheets slung from a pole, draped to add shade and contour. I remember the disappointment, remember that it wasn't what I'd expected. Hannah was fidgety and I was happy enough just to get the picture taken. Little did I know at the time, it would become one of my favorites. The last photo with the three of us together.

"Casey?" Emanuel asked, joining me, his towering over the sedan.

"Inside," I answered, my mouth dry like paper as I pointed at the window. Emanuel lowered himself and cupped his eyes to see through the tinted glass, his brow rising with understanding. "It's the picture we had taken to send to family and friends for the holidays. Hannah was cranky, but Ronald got her smiling, even had her laughing while the photographer did her work."

"It's a beautiful portrait," Emanuel said, a familiar sadness in his voice. I cringed at the sound, having come to loathe it in the years following the kidnapping.

"Yeah—" I began, my hands on my hips while I waited for the moment to pass. "We never mailed it though. She was taken a week later." I couldn't break my stare. Although we never sent the portrait to friends and family, I'd used the picture. I'd used the part with Hannah when I started my search for her. And it looked as though Ronald might have been using it too.

With a glove between his fingers, Emanuel rocked the door handle, grunting when it didn't open. In his baritone voice, he asked, "Any idea what he was doing here?"

"No idea," I answered, slipping on a pair of gloves, the team following my lead. Above the Fusion's door handle was a keypad with five pairs of numbers. I swiped my fingers across it, knowing there was only one number Ronald would have coded into the car lock. I plugged in the digits, each pair flashing red in response, the car alarm and locks disarming with an audible ding.

"A birthday?" Nichelle asked, curious about the code used.

I shook my head. "It's the day Hannah was kidnapped," I answered, swinging open the door, the air inside stale with the stench of rotting food. I narrowed quickly on the source, fast-food bags on the floor behind the driver's seat. I'd never known Ronald to be one for drive-thru food, but there was a scatter of bags, and they could tell us when and where he'd stopped. I handed them out, instructing, "Check for receipts, make a note of the time and dates. I want a completed timeline from his departing Philadelphia to his arrival in the Outer Banks."

"Fingerprints?" Emanuel asked, a kit at the ready.

"Let's do it," I told him, finding nothing else in the car except for the picture of our family. I grew frustrated opening and closing every compartment, shuffling the car manual aside along with service station receipts, the dates on them from past months. "His wallet isn't here. Also, there's no cellphone either."

"We'll fingerprint the doors, the keypad and handle too," I

heard Tracy say as I picked up the portrait and placed it on the roof of the car. "Should we fingerprint that too?"

I tilted the frame to let the sunlight flare across the glass, its shine revealing a couple of thumbprints and a smudge to what could be an index finger. While they were likely from Ronald when he carried the framed portrait to the car, we'd want to confirm it. "All of it. Everything is game for fingerprinting." I went around to the driver's side and slipped my shoes into a pair of booties before sitting where Ronald had sat. I shut my eyelids, their feeling sticky with sweat, the car like a hot box. Even with the doors opened, it was already too hot. I could feel my heartbeat thundering inside my head.

"What are you looking for?" Nichelle asked, watching me.

"I'm checking the height," I answered, reaching for the pedals. Ronald was a little over six foot, giving him more than four inches on me. From our years of sharing one car, I knew where the seat position would be if he'd been last driving. Sliding forward, I tapped the brake and accelerator with my toe. "This seat is at the right position, which suggests he was the last driver."

Tracy let out a cough and gag as she rummaged through the bags of junk food, a few receipts in hand. She held them up, saying, "These are all single-orders only."

"That tells us he was alone for the drive." I searched the dashboard and found the release for the trunk. Pressing it, a mechanical click sounded from behind the rear seat. Sweat dripped into my eyes with a sting as I wiped my brow. "Let's see what's in the trunk."

"I got a briefcase," Emanuel called.

Exiting the front seat and walking to the back, I took in the bag. "It's Ronald's."

The trunk was empty, save for a single bag. It was an old brown leather pilot bag that had once belonged to Ronald's grandfather. I knew it immediately. Ronald's family had told stories of travels overseas and the famous hands the bag had passed through. It was known as a Roosevelt Pilot bag and was more than a hundred years old. Made of water buffalo leather, Ronald's grandfather was given it as a gift from a diplomat. There were pockets on both sides, and more in the main compartment, but it was what Ronald packed that I was interested in seeing. "Whatever happened to Ronald, it didn't happen here."

"What do you mean?" Nichelle asked, coming to the rear with Tracy following, their faces bright with interest as they studied the bag. "I've never seen a bag like that."

"I'd think if Ronald was abducted here, his killer would have searched the car." I unbuckled the front pockets, finding lip balm and a roll of antacid. The expiration date on the side of the antacids was more than a year, the pocket's content having been left untouched since a previous trip.

Tracy fanned the fast-food receipts, three in total, her face pinking with heat. "Two of the receipts are from the same day as the cell tower ping."

"And the other?" I asked with interest, hoping for evidence that held a different point in time.

She shook her head knowing what I was looking for. "It was from a few days prior, a bagel cafe with a 19106 zip code."

"City of brotherly love," Nichelle said. "That's from Philadelphia."

"That's in Old City, a part of Philadelphia known for Betsy Ross's house and Independence Hall," I told them. "Ronald might have been living there. He'd always wanted a place in that part of the city."

"I'll get his current address from the DMV records," Nichelle said. "They're a little slow to get back, might take a while."

I stepped back to review, swiping at a bead of sweat before it reached my eyes. "Ronald drives from Philadelphia, stopping for fast food. When he reaches the Outer Banks, he parks his car near our station, and then goes where?"

One at a time, the team shrugged until Emanuel answered, "Wherever it was, he went on foot."

"Or he was picked up," I said, searching the corner of the

station's building for a security camera, hoping it'd give us an eye in the sky we could use. My hopes were doused by the landscaping, the tree behind Ronald's car in the line of sight from the nearest camera.

Nichelle followed my gaze, saying, "Who knows, we might be able to see another car entering the parking lot at the same time?"

"We might see him walking away from his car too," Tracy suggested.

"Let's confirm it," I said and wrapped my fingers around the thick handles of the bag, the leather showing wear from the century of use, the finish worn smooth, the color faded a shade lighter than its original tanning. Feeling the weight, I could tell he'd come for only the one day. Ronald had packed a change of clothes. "I think we might be in luck."

"What have we got?" Emanuel asked, helping me with the buckles. I threw the flap cover over to open the bag. A bundle of clothing was folded tidily and packed tight. As suspected, Ronald had packed with the intention of leaving the next day. But it was what he had packed between the clothes that would open the door to answer why Ronald was in the Outer Banks. I pinched the metal, the feel of it cold between my fingers, and carefully lifted it from the bag, Nichelle's golden-brown eyes beaming wide with a hungry look. "We have his laptop."

SEVEN

On the drive to Philadelphia the sky was black as coal, the stars glimmering bright as a new day began to emerge with purple and orange thick and deep on the horizon. I'd scheduled six hours to make it from the Outer Banks to my hometown. I tried to coax Jericho into joining the drive with me, urging him from his sleep, telling him to take the day off. He had inspections though, the monthly checks and balances of all the Marine Patrol equipment. I couldn't help but notice he'd been shy or maybe a little quiet whenever I spoke about Ronald. I never imagined him being jealous. Not Jericho. Or maybe it was jealousy for the life I'd had with Ronald. There was a marriage and a child with him. Maybe Jericho sensed the feelings I'd always have for Ronald and he didn't know what to say? I dismissed it, telling myself he was only trying to sleep. I said nothing and gave him a peck on the cheek before leaving.

I had Tracy and Nichelle with me—Tracy in the back seat while Nichelle sat in the front passenger seat. While Nichelle worked to access Ronald's laptop, Tracy was wide-eyed and browsing a list of DMV records, reviewing security camera footage, and exchanging texts with Emanuel who was also awake to feed his newborn baby. I kept my eyes on the road, the radio playing soft music and mixing with the monotone whir of the tires against the road.

I had to see Ronald's place, an apartment he rented in Old City, Philadelphia. Home of America's most historic square mile, the birthplace of American independence. It had grown to become a modernized upscale neighborhood. Ronald had moved in last year.

We'd finished with his car. Every fingerprint recoverable had been recorded, and the vehicle secured. Nichelle confirmed the license plates, the DMV records offering the vehicle registration and the apartment's address. A few phone calls from there, and I had the property manager's voice in my ear, gasping as I explained the situation. She'd found Ronald to be an excellent tenant, often helping her with the property, which wasn't a surprise to hear. Ms. Lipton assured us she would have a key available when we arrived. I drove the route Ronald drove, reversing the path, taking the same highways and stopping at the same stops, Nichelle guiding from her laptop.

For the long ride, my nerves had decided to join me, stirring more and more with each mile marker that passed by my window. Ronald was gone. Yet, going to his place in the city made me nervous. I'd been back to Philly before, more than a few times. But this felt different somehow, and by the time we drove past the international airport and the city's skyline came into view, my nerves had become unbearable. I told myself to relax and to breathe. I wasn't going to be much of a lead in the investigation unless I kept things under control.

I don't think either Nichelle or Tracy noticed, even with my leg shaking as traffic came to a stop around construction. Tracy perched her elbows on the backs of our seats, dipping her head to see through the windshield, gawking at the height of the buildings. Coming from the Outer Banks where the tallest buildings are a chain of hotels at four to five floors, Philadelphia's towers were a sight to see. We reached the Ben Franklin Bridge next, the distinct blueish green paint coating the massive structural steel above the masonry base.

Nichelle peered high into the sky now, her gaze following the cabled suspension towers used for the roadway to span the Delaware River.

"Wow," they said in unison as we drove beneath the bridge.

"Yes, wow indeed," I replied. The bridge had always been my landmark for home. "We are just about in the heart of Philadelphia."

We exited I-95 onto 676, the highway dropping below the city with walls towering above us to the left and right, colored with a mix of gang graffiti and historic murals. North Fifteenth was next, and then to Race Street until we reached Eleventh Street, and Ronald's apartment building.

It was upscale with fancy red brick and golden-yellow decorative woodwork, standing four stories tall and occupying a quarter of a city block. I immediately knew we were at the right place. An old woman waited on the steps, eyeing my car's plates as soon as we pulled up in front. A vinyl awning extended onto the sidewalk, protecting the front doors from the weather, the woman staying beneath its shade as though afraid to touch the light of day. She motioned to a man by her side, his bulky size stepping heavily from the curb to move aside a pair of plastic chairs placed to reserve a parking spot in front of the building.

"I hope this will do?" the man asked, his head peering in the passenger side window.

"Yes, perfect," I told him as he backed onto the sidewalk to give me room. I rolled the steering wheel and reversed the car, swinging the front into place to parallel park. I opened the car door, muscles relaxing, and asked Nichelle and Tracy, "Ready?"

"Ready," Nichelle said, stuffing her computer into her backpack as Tracy carried the gear.

I put my badge around my neck and stood on the street, catching the warm smell of the city after a spring rain. There were puddles drying and rainclouds turning the sky gray. Thin, delicate trees lined the sidewalk, the flowering dogwoods dropping their white petals, the city block quiet and with little traffic, but every parking space taken. "Thank you for holding the spot for us," I said to the building's owner, extending my hand with my card between my fingers.

"Not at all," she answered. There were deep creases on her forehead and at the corners of her eyes as she accepted my card, then shifted her focus to my badge. Her white hair was pinned back and she wore thick mascara and lipstick and blush, the colors standing out on her ivory-colored skin. She made a tsk-tsk sound, shaking her head and saying, "I was so very sorry to hear about Mr. Haskin. He was such a wonderful tenant. Always very helpful when my boys couldn't come by."

"You said he's been here this last year?" I asked her.

"Most of it," she answered, but sounded unsure.

"Ronald always wanted to live here," I said while staring up at the brick building, noting the immaculate state, not a single broken window or chip in the paint. "It's a gorgeous building."

"This place has been in our family forever," she commented, her gaze following mine, a cozy city breeze lifting my hair. She counted her fingers then added, "Mr. Haskin has been here at least the last nine months. I can check the lease to confirm."

"That'd be fine, you have my number. Did Ronald... Mr. Haskin, did he have a lot of visitors?"

She considered the question, the corners of her mouth drooping, "None really. Occasionally I'd see a woman with him, but he mostly went for walks alone."

"A woman?" I asked, interested if there was someone else we would want to speak with. "The same woman?"

She nodded and put her hand around her head, "Younger with yellow hair. She was tall too. Looked a little like him."

I nodded, recognizing the description and believing it was Ronald's sister Patti who must have visited with him.

The woman checked her watch. "I'm sorry, but I have a previous engagement. I trust I can give you the extra key," she said, surprising me as she handed over a fuzzy keyring with a pair of dangling keys. She hesitated before letting go, her stare turning hard. "Have you ever been here to visit before?"

"No, ma'am. Not this part of the city," I answered, thinking back to the last time I'd been to Independence Mall or to see the Liberty Bell. "Not in a very long time."

"Huh," she grunted, letting go. "You look so familiar to me."

"I get that a lot."

"Okay then. My office is on the first floor," she said, making her way inside as we followed. "Please do remember to drop off the keys when you're done."

"Thank you, ma'am," I answered, finding the building stairs next to the elevators, a pair of antique doors in front of them. There was a half-moon shaped brass floor indicator above the elevator, an arrow pointing between two and three. "This way, guys." Ronald's apartment was on the second floor, and I didn't waste another minute. I climbed the steps two at a time, walking hurriedly until we were in front of his door.

"Let's hope she gave us the right key," Nichelle said, sounding winded.

Before inserting the first key, I saw the scratches. Two marks in the paint by the door handle. I put on a pair of gloves, handing a latex pair to Tracy and Nichelle. "Take a picture," I said, kneeling and shining my phone's light on the scratches. "These could have been from brushing against it while he was carrying groceries, but they look recent and deep."

"You mean like from metal on jeans?" Tracy asked.

"He did like his Levi's," I answered, the height of the scratches matching a back pocket. "Or these could be from someone trying to shimmy the lock."

When Tracy finished with the photographs, I opened the door, a narrow hall leading to a single room with a tall ceiling and a dusky beige carpet. There was a kitchenette to the left of us with a granite counter and two chairs tucked beneath the stone lip. A dark gray couch and loveseat were to our right with an ottoman at the center, carrying a pinewood tray with television and cable-box remotes. Another two rooms were across the apartment—a bedroom in one and a bathroom in the other.

"Nice place," Nichelle commented.

"Nicer than what we've got," Tracy said, wiping her finger across a shelf and then holding it up. "And way cleaner."

I went to the front of the apartment and peered through the windows to see our car on the street, the dogwood trees partially blocking my view. When I turned around, a jolt went through me. I saw my past. I saw so much of it all at once that I stopped breathing. "Shit," I mumbled, unable to break my stare.

"Casey?" Nichelle asked.

"There," I said, the girls coming around to see what I was staring at. On the wall adjacent to the front door hallway, there were over three dozen pictures, varying in sizes and scattered to cover the wall from floor to ceiling. Each of them had a different picture frame—some decorative metal and wood and looking antique and others borderless or framed in glass.

"Oh wow," Tracy said, stopping to look.

"That's my girl," I said, seeing pictures of Hannah, and then pictures of me with Ronald and Hannah. It was our family.

Ronald had never stopped caring about us. He'd never stopped loving who we were.

"These are wonderful," Nichelle said, commenting as Tracy held up the camera, suggesting some pictures of the wall. I gave a nod and she returned to focus on an empty space, the wall's paint darker where a frame had blocked the daylight.

The saddest pang of guilt tugged on my emotions when I realized how distant Ronald and I had become. I hadn't kept in touch like I said I would, like I'd promised him that day he'd last left the Outer Banks. I wasn't the type to keep in touch anyway. My goodbyes were made up of well wishes and empty promises. But isn't that true for most people?

My guilt was no use to Ronald now. We had an investigation.

"The property owner. She's been in this apartment," I said.

"How would you know that?" Nichelle asked.

"I know," Tracy blurted, raising her hand to answer. "Because she recognized you."

"Yes, she did," I answered, my hands perched as I studied Ronald's pictures, having no idea he'd kept this many. There was the house we bought in northeast Philadelphia. It was across from a little league ballpark where I'd imagined Hannah playing softball one day. A split-level twin with sandstone from the pavement to the roof. The house was small but warm and cozy, and perfect for the three of us. It was the lawn that had been so attractive, with Ronald insisting on the biggest yard we could afford. I'd imagined my afternoon shifts ending and coming home to play with Hannah, the two of us romping barefoot in the cool grass. And we did. For a while anyway. That is, until the day she was snatched from the very same yard.

Soon after the kidnapping, we sold the house, along with the minivan, ending our family dreams.

There were the baby pictures too. Like the one that showed Hannah's first tooth, her face pudgy round and her light-brown hair pinned up in sprouting ponytails, the camera flash shining in her baby-blue eyes. I started studying all the pictures then, searching them for clues. Did Ronald put these on the wall for a reason? I looked for anything that jumped out as being different. But I only saw what Ronald wanted to see—the beauty of what we once had. My voice breaking as I said, "Nichelle you're right. This is wonderful."

Tracy went into the kitchenette and opened the refrigerator. "I think he'd gone to the market before traveling."

On the counter was a banana tree, a handful of bananas ripening golden, their sugar spots large. "Now this is something Ronald would have never done."

"Bananas?" Tracy asked.

"He wouldn't have let them ripen that much. Hated them too ripe."

"There are meats in the refrigerator too," she said as I peered over her shoulder, seeing the shelves filled.

"In his bag we only found one change of clothes. He wouldn't have gone to the market if he'd been planning much time away." I poked my head into the bathroom, the counter clean, the mirror free of spots and dust. I looked in his bedroom next, the bed made and a desk beneath the window clear of clutter. When I returned to the kitchen, I saw how the remotes on the wood tray were placed, side by side and facing the television. It felt strange.

"This is too clean. Someone has been here."

"Maybe he was neat, he liked to keep things clean and in order?" Nichelle suggested, peering out the front window, sunlight bright on her face before cloud cover moved in. "Or he cleaned the place before traveling? I know I hate going home to a mess."

"I lived with him long enough to know this isn't him." I shook my head, saying, "He'd put things away, but he was never this orderly. Everything's lined up so neatly."

"The landlady?" Tracy asked, suggesting the property owner had cleaned the apartment.

"Possibly," I answered as I flipped a switch, overhead lights buzzing, white light shining. On the counter, a cluster of vitamins and supplements, along with prescriptions, the bottles counting many and standing side by side on a wood lazy Susan. There was a paper tablet next to it, pens and pencils tucked between the pages. I picked up the largest prescription bottle, reading, "Coumadin." Tracy typed the name into her phone as I picked up another bottle and read the name, "Lisinopril."

She glanced at me with a scowl, reading the bottle again. "It says these are used for treating heart issues. The first one is a blood thinner."

"The second one is for cholesterol," Nichelle said, picking up the bottle and shaking the insides. "My pops takes this."

"Heart issues?" I asked, my hand moving to my chest. I'd always known Ronald to be healthy. I returned to the refrigerator to see what was on the shelves again. They were filled with fruits and vegetables and lean proteins like chicken and fish. My voice sad and with guilt, I said, "I had no idea."

"You wouldn't have known," Nichelle said, reassuring me.

"I know, but we told each other we'd stay in touch." I went back to the stack of medicine bottles wondering how long he'd had issues.

Without a thought, I took the notepad, curious to see if there was anything written on it like a schedule, a doctor's appointment maybe. The page was blank, but the last page had been torn haphazardly, leaving behind ratty paper stubs, the sight of it coming with an alarm. "Guys. This confirms it. Someone else was here!"

"What do you mean?" Tracy asked, joining me on the other side of the kitchen counter. I brushed my fingertip over the torn remains of the missing page. "It didn't tear evenly. Ronald had his odd quirks. Stubby paper on the pad would have driven him nuts. While he'd never been a neat freak, I know he would have torn this clean. Someone took whatever was written on this notepad."

"The scratches," Nichelle said, her eyes darting back to the door, growing large when she glanced toward the bedroom. "Are we alone?"

"Whoever it was is long gone," I told her. "But, I am certain they were here. I believe they searched his apartment, and they took whatever he'd written."

As I held the blank notepad, angling it, I could see an impression on the surface. The letters were in Ronald's handwriting. Nichelle saw it too and handed me a pencil. "Just like the old movies," she said excitedly.

"Yeah, it is," I agreed, chipping the wood from the end of the pencil to improve the lead surface.

"What do you mean, *from the old movies?*" Tracy asked.

We both looked at her. At first, I thought she was kidding, but saw the confusion and knew she wasn't familiar with what we were doing. "When Ronald wrote in the notebook, he pressed hard enough to leave an impression on the page beneath."

Nodding slowly, recognition appearing, she said, "You'll be able to read it after you darken the page."

"Bingo," I said and gently swiped the pencil lead over the letters, the impressions deep enough for me to turn the edges dark. "I'm getting something here."

As I continued, a second letter appearing, Tracy's camera flash came without warning, making me jump, "Sorry."

"A heads-up will work." My fingers cramping, I dropped the pencil when I was done, Ronald's note complete. It read, "Rourke."

"What's a rourke?" the girls asked, Nichelle on her phone while Tracy took another photograph.

"It's not a what, it's a place," I answered, knowing immediately why Ronald had come to the Outer Banks to see me. "It's Rourke Memorial Hospital. It's also the last known location of our daughter."

"Right," Nichelle said, a spark appearing in her eyes as she recalled the hospital's name from our work with my online sleuthing team.

It was in the work with this team that we'd made an incredible discovery. One of the members posted a short video, a security camera capturing frames in the dead-still of a rainy night. In it, we saw my daughter Hannah's kidnapper placing her body on the ground in front of Rourke Memorial Hospital. Later, a woman in scrubs picked up Hannah. She disappeared after, leaving the video camera's view with my daughter in her arms. The woman never went into the hospital, ending the clue abruptly.

"Do you think Ronald saw the online video? The security footage with Hannah?"

"Maybe it was leaked on YouTube?" Tracy suggested. "I'd think Hannah's kidnapping case is still in the news. A video like that is bound to get clicks."

"So he'd been searching for your daughter?" Nichelle said. "But what did he find?"

"Whatever it was, I think it got him killed."

EIGHT

After questioning some of Ronald's neighbors, we left his apartment in the hands of Philadelphia's finest. I'd called in a favor with my old station. I connected with them, gave them the background, and asked for a fingerprint crew to work the rooms. They didn't hesitate and would help. We'd gotten started with a heavy concentration on the kitchen area, and then turned the work over to their capable hands. I strung up a yellow and black crime-scene tape across the door, leaving it to hang slack for the officers to fix in place when they were finished.

Although we wore gloves during our visit, I also had the crew fingerprint each of us, all ten digits to use in eliminating my team from the site. If someone other than Ronald had been in his apartment, we'd have a good chance of finding a print worth investigating. I had my doubts though, Ronald's place being as clean as it was, all the surfaces wiped down and everything placed just right and seeming too tidy. I'd known Ronald to be neat, but not that much. If this was a visit by Ronald's killer, what were they searching for? Did they find the notepad and take the top sheet?

We stopped by the apartment manager's officer to let her know about the other team. She was absent though, and any questions I had for her would have to wait. Curious, we took a small stroll around the room, searching for any kind of technology that could be helpful to us. I wanted to know who was coming and going, particularly who'd been on Ronald's floor the days after he'd left Philadelphia.

There was a computer on the manager's desk, the monitor made of thick glass with a plastic back that was a foot deep. It was a model and type I'd seen decades earlier, Nichelle admiring it, mentioning that it should be in a museum. Tracy joked that the manager should be in a museum too. As the two laughed, I browsed through ledger books and calendars piled on a shelf, the information in the pages telling me most of the building's management still resided on paper. The building was probably old enough for a museum as well. And while it had been immaculately restored, it lacked a surveillance system. We searched the foyer next, our footsteps bouncing off the high ceilings with an echo with us finding the corners empty. The elevator car and hallways were last, but the ceiling corners were free of security cameras as well, our finding only the occasional spider, a web drawn in wait for a silverfish or a moth to pass.

Before leaving Philadelphia for the highway drive, I had to feed my team. We'd left the Outer Banks before sunrise, some time before four. By now, the sun was sitting well past the noon hour and easing toward the west, our shadows cast short toward the east. It was time for food and then the road. Nichelle and Tracy insisted on Philadelphia's finest—cheese steaks and soft pretzels and whatever else they found appetizing. They refused my suggestion of a grab-and-go burger at a drive-thru.

Nichelle opened the maps app and saw that Ronald's apartment was within walking distance of the Reading Terminal Market. The weather fared well for the walk, and they raced ahead of me like happy children entering a park to play.

My stomach growled, my insides grinding on empty. I had to eat, but my head wasn't feeling it. The questions about Ronald and what he'd gotten into were many. I stopped on the sidewalk with city sounds raining down—footsteps on concrete, the rattle of bus

engines, a taxi honking its horn. Maybe it bothered me that Ronald
had found something about Hannah that I had overlooked. Maybe
he'd found a nugget of information that I'd failed to uncover in all
my years of investigating her kidnapping. But this wasn't just any
nugget. What kind of massive revelation must it have been? A part
of me wanted to think that Ronald was the unfortunate victim of a
serial killer. That he'd crossed paths with a killer who had liked to
play games with ropes and had used Buxton Woods as their
dumping grounds. But if I was right, Ronald's killer had visited his
apartment. In my experience, serial killers don't tend to make
house calls after you're dead.

"You okay back there?" Tracy asked, stopping to peer over her
shoulder. She noticed the look on my face and urged me to catch
up to them. I waved for them to keep going, Nichelle turning too.
When Nichelle saw I was okay, she took Tracy's hand to cross the
street, their fingers staying intertwined a moment longer than
expected, a gaze between them locking, their friendship having
grown into something more. While they'd been careful to hide it
from the team, I knew, and I thought it was great.

"I'll catch up to you guys," I said, raising my voice over a clamoring bus that spewed coal-gray smoke as a dozen pigeons took
flight in front of me, broad wings batting air with loose feathers
falling.

"See you inside," Nichelle replied as the two disappeared into
the crowd surrounding Reading Terminal Market.

"See you," I said, stopping at the corner. The foot traffic was
heavy at the intersection. A shoulder bumped mine and bounced
me like a steel ball in a pinball machine. I wasn't claustrophobic
but it suddenly felt like I'd been rushed into a small closet crowded
with bodies. I dipped into a stone doorway, grabbed hold of a small
iron rail, and gripped it hard enough to hurt my palm.

"A dollar to spare," a scratchy voice came from behind me. The
corner of the doorway was in darkness. There was a pungent smell
familiar from my days working the streets as a uniformed patrol. I
saw the whites of a homeless woman's eyes, her soiled clothes and

dirt-covered face hiding her well in the shade. "Fiddy cent maybe?"

"Sure," I answered, fishing out a couple of dollars from my pocket to leave with her before braving the crowd again. I exhaled the air from my lungs. I told myself Ronald's case was like any other.

That was a lie though.

I stepped onto the street, a horn blaring while I crossed to meet up with Tracy and Nichelle.

This wasn't like any other case. Our daughter was involved somehow. This had to do with her disappearing from that hospital all those years ago. Why else would Ronald have anything to do with Rourke Memorial Hospital? There simply was only one connection to him... and to me. It was Hannah.

I found Jericho exactly where I'd left him earlier that morning, tucked tightly beneath the sheets of our bed, his broad shoulder rising and falling steadily. He could sleep like the dead and never heard me coming home or entering the house. I'd even closed the front door with a heavy hand, partially an accident, but also because I was missing him and wanted to hear his voice.

"Hey, have you been back long?" he asked, rolling onto his back, moonlight shining through the window, its colors floating in his eyes.

The bedroom was hot, the air stiff. I put the ceiling fan on and stripped my clothes before climbing into his arms. "He had pictures."

"Pictures?" Jericho asked, scratching his chin, the whiskers noisy in the still of the house. "Like dirty magazines?"

"No, you goof. Nothing like that," I answered, nudging his chest. "They were of me and Hannah, our family."

"That sounds nice," he said. And then asked, "Isn't it?"

"But they weren't in an album. He had dozens of them framed and on his wall like a kind of shrine."

Jericho muscled his position with a groan, sitting up some to move closer. I swung a leg over his, lying next to him where I felt the most secure when out of sorts. "You had a wall too," he said, recalling what he'd seen at my old apartment—a large wall I'd worked at for years while investigating Hannah's kidnapping. "Could be the same thing. Do you think he was investigating your daughter's kidnapping?"

I shook my head, brushing my hair against his chest, where I heard his heart beating faintly beneath my ear. "It's like his wall was for inspiration. And mine was for the forensics of the research."

He kissed the top of my head, adding, "I wonder what he found?"

"I don't know," I said, sweeping my hand across his middle. "But when we find out, we'll find who killed him."

"Casey," Jericho said, the sound of his voice making me look up. "You'll be careful?"

I planted my lips on his, hard and long, wanting to rest his worries. But there was danger. I could sense it, feel it coming like an animal knowing when to run. Only I wasn't about to run. "I'll be careful."

"Good," he said. "It's late, you've got to be tired."

I kissed him again, more sensual, arching my back with my chest warming against his. "I'm not tired." His eyes grew wide with surprise.

"Oh," he answered, returning my kiss.

By the moonlight filling the bedroom, we said nothing more about Ronald's murder or about my visit to Philadelphia. Instead, we made love and rested in one another's arms, breathing heavy until sleep found Jericho and me. But it became a restless sleep, my stirring and trying to forget the day. I was awake a few hours later and crept from the bedroom to the spare room. It was where Jericho had helped me setup my virtual wall, my computers, and monitors which I used to continue Hannah's kidnapping investigation.

. . .

"Let's see what we see," I mumbled while fumbling in the dark to click on the power. The walls in the room came alive with light, the pixels on the screens growing bright. I rolled my chair out from beneath the desk, brushing the dust from the seat and the backrest. The days had been too many since I was last active online. I sat in it, stretching my legs and arms before jumping onto the forum where my sleuthing team liked to gather.

Nichelle had set me up with the anonymous group a couple of years ago. She'd done so after revealing to me one of her off-hour passions. She was involved with an amateur crime investigation team, and had been long before I even knew about it. After she'd pulled the curtain aside, I joined the team to continue my investigation as one of its members. Other than Nichelle, nobody on the team knew my real identity. Like the team, we worked anonymously as a group of true crime enthusiasts whose interest had turned into something more.

There was one team that was dedicated to Hannah's kidnapping, and I had to wonder if it was possible Ronald had approached them at some point in the past. My cursor blinking, I typed, *"Is anyone on? It's late, but I know you guys are night owls anyway."*

"Aleria?" a user called Kestrel answered with a smiley-faced emoji. I recognized the handle immediately and warmed to reconnecting with the team. But I wasn't keen on the handle they'd given me. *Aleria*, Latin for the fierce eagle. When I'd first joined, the team insisted I have a handle to go by, and I let them pick mine. So, Aleria it was.

"Yes, it's me."

"It's been a while," Kestrel answered with a sad-faced emoji.

"I'm sorry," I replied. *"Life got busy. How is the rest of the team?"*

Three sad-faced emojis popped up, my heart sinking.

"Sorry to tell you this, but they've moved on to new cases."

"Yeah," I typed. *"I had a feeling that might happen."*

"I'm still working on Hannah's case," Kestrel typed with two thumbs-up emojis. *"Ahren is still working it too, but I haven't seen Ahren online lately."*

"Maybe Ahren moved on too?" I asked.

"Perhaps," Kestrel typed with another sad-faced emoji.

"Ahren was good too. If you can reconnect, say thank you for me."

"Sure thing." Three dots appeared as Kestrel typed, bouncing like a trumpet player's fingers. *"Was Ahren's video helpful?"*

"Yes! It was extremely valuable."

Ahren had been the one to introduce the surveillance video of Hannah at a hospital. Shortly after being kidnapped when she was three, Hannah had become deathly sick. That's when her kidnapper took her to a hospital and left her on the wet pavement outside.

I could never figure out the hospital's name or where the hospital was. It was Ahren who had figured it out though, telling the online team and me, *Rourke Memorial Hospital.* It was the single biggest break in finding Hannah that I had since her kidnappers were put behind bars. Ahren's video may have changed the course of the investigation. Gratitude warmed me, a reminder to say thank you to Nichelle. It was because of her that I was a part of this group.

I didn't know who Ahren or Kestrel truly were. And I knew I had to be careful. But we knew one another well enough online to have earned the trust needed to work as a team.

"I am starting work on the hospital."

"That's great." Kestrel typed back. *"I gotta go, it's late for me."*

"Thank you again," I typed. *"I wouldn't have gotten this far without you guys."*

I opened Ahren's last message containing the video of Hannah being taken from outside the hospital as a three-year-old. My screen was frozen on the frame that showed some of the nurse's face, the black-and-white pixels a blur, but clear enough to identify

her as being Caucasian and dark-haired and of average build. I'd
yet to determine her height and thought Nichelle could help me
with it. I texted her the screenshot, asking her to revisit this one. I
also broke the news that the online sleuthing team had moved on to
other cases. Nichelle texted back,

Sleeping. I'll get started first thing.

Kestrel was gone when I looked back at my monitor. I was
alone in the forum room, my thoughts going back to my handle,
Aleria and what it meant—*fierce eagle*. I got curious and looked up
the name *Kestrel*, finding that it was a kind of falcon. There was a
theme in the names of the team: raptors, birds that hunted.
"Ahren," I mouthed, my fingers frozen above the keyboard, a dread
stirring with a truth I was suddenly too terrified to see.

I typed in the handle "Ahren" and searched the name's origin.
When I saw the meaning, my hands dropped to my lap, and I sat
back. Ahren was a male name, and it meant *enlightened eagle*. I
was sure he was meant to be the male to my female eagle, Aleria.
Wasn't it Ahren who'd insisted on the name Aleria? While I didn't
know the truth at the time, I knew it now and a tear stung my eye
as images of Ronald's face from the morgue flashed like a nightmare. Only one other person knew about Rourke Memorial Hospital. While I didn't have anything firm to say for certain, was it
possible that Ronald was Ahren? Had he been in touch with me all
this time?

NINE

Bleary-eyed, I made my way to the station's parking lot and circled a few cars amidst the empty spaces to see who from my team had gotten up with the daybreak. I was also hoping to have a message from Swales about the bones. Was it a man or a woman? How old? What else did she find? I circled the parking lot. None of my team had arrived yet, and there was no sun this morning. The day was overcast, a thick blanket of gray cloud and a fine mist hanging in the air. There were droplets on anything that stood still long enough to collect them. I parked and sat in the silence of my car, the motor ticking as I turned the radio off. I stayed that way, taking shallow breaths, my emotions mixed about what we'd seen at Ronald's apartment.

Enlightened eagle, I thought. I believed Ronald had been Ahren, a member of my online sleuthing team. Access to his laptop would confirm what I suspected. I couldn't remember who introduced who first—not that it mattered. If Ronald was Ahren, then he'd been involved in my search for Hannah. If Nichelle cracked his laptop password, we would know how deep his involvement was. While working as Ahren, he'd shared with the online team often, including the final video snippet and name of the hospital. I wanted to see what it was he didn't share. My chest tightened with a memory of our last conversation. A raging anger that came with my refusing to accept DNA results about a girl who I was certain was our daughter. I was wrong though. Was it the anger that kept him away and made him join my online team as Ahren?

I closed my eyes and saw the pictures from some of our happy times. I'd forgotten how much I liked photography. Back then, I was quite the shutterbug, using an old film-camera, a thirty-five-millimeter Pentax that had been given to me by my father. It was a manual camera, and my dad had taught me the basics of film exposure and shutter speeds and even how to pick the right type of film to use. And pick them I did. When Hannah was kidnapped, I'd forgotten all about the camera and the film—both sitting in a dusky blue shoebox which I'd filled with undeveloped rolls. It wasn't until I saw Ronald's wall that the memory of that shoebox came back.

"You must have found them," I said, my lips moving silently as though I was talking to him. For a moment, I imagined he was next to me. That it was the year before the kidnapping with an itch on my ring finger telling me I was wearing the wedding band that he'd placed there. "You developed the film, and you found my pictures."

"I found them," I imagined him saying. "It seemed such a waste not to get them developed. I wanted to see them."

On his apartment wall there were moments I hadn't thought about in years. Precious moments like Hannah chasing Ronald across the front lawn, her holding the end of a water hose as he playfully moved in slow motion. There were the pictures from a snowy Christmas Eve, a tree standing in our tiny living room, the top of the evergreen brushing against the ceiling and towering over Hannah as she placed the first ornament on a branch. With the Christmas lights twinkling in her baby-blue eyes, her dimples coming with a cheeky smile, she asked about the star and where it would go.

"I'm sorry this happened to you," I said, opening my eyelids to the screech of seagulls, my thoughts of Ronald replaced by a gut-wrenching sadness. I had always felt there was the possibility of

Hannah becoming a part of our lives again, but with his murder, the family we were once was gone forever. I cupped my face in my hands and let out the cry.

Knuckles rapped against the glass window of my door. I made like I was busy, facing away, wiping my face and picking up the coffee I'd bought at the Quick Mart. I took a mouthful, cringing at the tepid bitterness. When I was ready I opened the car door, Cheryl greeting me with a concerned look as I grabbed my things, acting like I was in a hurry. I needed to be a detective again, wear the hat of the investigator. There'd be time for grieving later.

"Hey there," I said, my eyelids wet. "Did you just get here?"

"You okay?" she asked, the concern for me staying fixed. She had her arms perched atop aluminum crutches which made her shorter than usual, the top of her red hair level with my eyes. Her days of stiletto heels and power suits were gone. At least for the time being while she recovered from the bullet that had shattered her hip.

She surprised me then, balancing herself and touching my arm. "Casey, I heard about your ex. I wanted to tell you how sorry I am for your loss."

"Thank you," I said as she forced a smile.

We moved a step, a break in the clouds coming. Cheryl faced the sun as it peered down on her, saying, "That feels good. I better get it while I can."

"While you can?" I asked. Her face was free of the heavy makeup I was used to seeing. Instead, her lips were wet with pink lip gloss and there was a light touch of mascara on her eyelashes. But that was all. She'd kept the concealer off and let the world see her freckles that made up most of her face. I'd never realized how many she had until now. "What's happening?"

She motioned to her crutches. "I'm not recovering like I'd hoped... like the doctors had hoped."

"More surgery?" I asked, trying not to grimace. She nodded, the look of disappointment weighing heavy. "How long do they think...?"

She opened her mouth to answer, her voice cracking. It was my turn to show concern, bracing her arm while she glanced up at the sun while it ducked behind a gray shelf moving toward the ocean. "A year."

"Oh, Cheryl—" I said, but lost my words.

"They warned that I might not be able to come back," she continued, heavy-hearted as she shook her head and tried to hide her tears.

"What can I do to help?" I asked, having no idea what else I could say.

She swiped errantly at a lock of red hair and shuffled her stance to reset the crutches beneath her arms. "Can we talk and walk?" she asked as we made our way to the station doors. "I've got a missing person case I just started to work."

My brow raised, I asked, "Missing person?"

"Point of contact is an older gentleman. He filed a report that his wife went missing."

"Female, older couple, wife missing," I said, rattling off the details while I held the wooden gate for her. I shouldered my bag to guide her inside the office space, making room to help. She became breathless as we walked, and I held back on more questions until she was at her desk and in her seat. "You mentioned older. Do you think his wife might have wandered off? Old age?"

"It doesn't sound like that," she answered, clicking her mouse, and tapping on her keyboard. "Could you take up the case for me?"

"Yeah sure, of course," I told her. I sensed there was a rush and asked, "When's your surgery?"

"Today," she said with disbelief. Beneath her breath, she muttered, "Can't believe this is happening." She focused on me, and then the door, adding, "I'm just here to close up shop and hand things over."

Without a thought, I extended my arm, offering it. Cheryl's gazed locked on my hand, probably realizing it was the first of many she'd see on this morning which might be the close of this chapter in her life. Rather than tell her it was nice to have worked with her, I stayed optimistic. "Let's say, until next time."

She braced the edge of her desk, knuckles white and creased. She clutched my hand tight, squeezing with commitment. "Yes, let's," she said, liking the choice of words. "Until next time."

I turned around to leave and when I reached the door of her office, I spun back and asked, "The missing person case. What's her name?"

"Ah, yeah, you'll need to know that," she said, handing me a case folder. As I took it, she said, "Violet Gould. She's a nurse at the hospital."

"A nurse?" I said, brow rising with a new question. "What hospital?"

"Uh, Roor... something or other," she said, searching a scatter of notes on her desk. She tapped her chin, unable to find anything.

"Rourke Memorial."

She pointed at me, impressed, saying, "Yeah! Rourke Memorial Hospital."

TEN

The sun had cleared the clouds. Sunlight poured through the station window where I stood, watching it form a misty haze to float on the roads and rooftops. There'd been no word from Swales about the bones we'd discovered alongside Ronald, but now we had a new connection to Rourke Memorial Hospital. A missing woman.

As Cheryl closed her office and stopped at the sheriff's office, I met with my team and shared the news about her going out on disability. As they muttered and peered over my shoulder to catch a glimpse of her, I also told them that we'd be picking up the missing person case she was working. The news was met with glances of silent concern, the additional work adding risk to the cases we had in hand. When Cheryl's visit with the sheriff was over, we watched her leave the station. As the last sight of her disappeared, none of us knowing when we'd see her again, I told them the rest of the news: that the missing person was a nurse at Rourke Memorial Hospital. There was instant understanding, the team being as intimately familiar with Hannah's case as I was.

. . .

We entered Rourke Memorial Hospital from the east side of the building complex where I knew the administration offices were located. The ceiling was fourteen feet or more, the floors and walls tiled with shades of bright and dark stone. There was a grand stairwell to the right where voices bounced off walls. On the opposite side was an elevator bay, with sliding doors made for wide hospital gurneys and wheelchairs.

Hospital staff and office workers came and went, glimpsing our badges strung from our necks and giving us curious looks as they made their way around us. Other than the hospital staff, we only saw the previous patients, papers carried in hand, bills marked "past-due" that needed to be settled with the accounting department. It reminded me of how I'd been a patient here before. Tracy was recently as well, the look on her face saying she was uncomfortable with the memory. She walked with me while Nichelle and Emanuel followed behind.

We stopped at the security desk. Guards stood at the inner entrance behind it, their eyes dead like the unmoving gaze of statues. As a courtesy, I held my badge for them to see, the older of the two tipping his hat. A receptionist behind the stone desk worked a telephone switchboard and a pair of computers. He juggled phone calls while eyeing me and the team, sun-bleached bangs moving with a puff of air from his lips.

An elevator bell rang as the door opened. A slender bald man with brown skin exited. He was dressed in an expensive gray suit and walked with a slight limp. The security guards noticed him immediately, their postures straightening while they stuck out their chests. If I had to guess, the man with the limp was their boss. In the corners where the walls joined the ceiling, I found security cameras, the kind I'd hoped to find at Ronald's apartment building. The man with the limp had recognized who we were the moment we'd entered the building.

"Good afternoon," he said, a whistle in his voice. He approached with a welcoming smile, his eyes darting from my badge to my face, and then to Tracy and Emanuel and Nichelle, his hand taking mine. "My name is Jimmy Rush. I am the head of security for Rourke Memorial Hospital."

"Detective Casey White," I said, returning his firm handshake, his skin soft. It was the grip of a man who spent his days behind a desk. The gleam in his eyes and the broad smile remained as he took to shaking each hand from the team, eager to make the acquaintances.

"Emanuel Wilson!" he said enthusiastically, taking Emanuel's hand last, using both of his and shaking vigorously. "As I live and breathe. One of the best I have ever seen play the game!"

"Sir?" Emanuel asked, brow raised.

"I thought that might be you walking into my hospital," Jimmy answered, stepping back, his hands on his hips. "I had to come down and see for myself."

"Thank you, sir," Emanuel said with a bashful flush. "Very kind of you."

"Played basketball myself! I could have gone far too," Jimmy said. He lifted his right pant leg, a ray of sunlight glinting a metal post connected to his shoe. "The war took my leg and set me on a different path."

"Thank you for your service," Emanuel said with a solemn look.

"Yes, thank you for your service, sir." I shifted to step in front of Emanuel and handed Jimmy a printed sheet with Violet Gould's picture. The nurse who'd gone missing a few days prior.

Jimmy's smile was gone. He held the sheet, taking a moment with it. The silence filled with the echo of footsteps as folks came and went. "Mrs. Gould," he finally said, handing the paper back to me. He studied us a moment, and then asked, "They send all of you for a missing person?"

"Yes, sir," I answered, having no reason to share anything more. "Mr. Rush, her husband reported that she was working—"

"Jimmy," he said, correcting me. "I hear *sir* and I think I'm back in the service."

"Jimmy," I answered. "As I was saying, Mrs. Gould was here

the night she went missing. We'd like to ask some questions of her co-workers, and the security desk staff?"

"Sure. Sure," he said with an ardent nod. He crossed his arms and eased a finger into the air. "But I have to ask it be done within boundaries and discretion."

"Of course. With discretion." I motioned to Tracy and Emanuel who left for the steps, our already having discussed a plan. They'd begin with staff interviews while we checked for security footage.

"Nice to have met you, sir," Emanuel said, passing Jimmy.

"Yeah, sure was. What a treat."

"Sir... Jimmy, this is Nichelle Wilkinson. We'd like to review security footage from the days around Mrs. Gould's disappearance."

"I can help you with that," he said, turning back to the elevators, waving for us to follow. We entered an elevator, the floors of the building numbering five with two levels beneath us. "You can view them in my office." He gave his watch a look, adding, "Looks to be about time for my lunch break anyway."

"It could be a while," Nichelle warned.

"Got all afternoon," he answered, his smile returning.

Jimmy Rush was the perfect host. He took us to the top floor of the hospital, his office a large room with a sofa and mini-refrigerator, along with a wide view of the Atlantic Ocean. From there, I could see miles of the Outer Banks. The beaches were specked with sunbathers as children and their parents played in the surf. There were boats near and far with most of them on anchor, a Marine Patrol boat driving high in the water while racing north. I couldn't tell if it was Jericho or not at the helm, my heart lifting with the thought of having seen him. The Manteo boardwalk was within sight, enough for me to see people roaming the boards and stirring in and around the storefronts. Beyond it, the landscape turned green behind a thickening haze, the place where Ronald's body was discovered indistinguishable from the places where life was enjoyed.

"One of the great perks of this job," Jimmy Rush said, his referring to the view. He offered cold drinks and his desk and computer, Nichelle taking to the seat as he hung over her shoulder and guided the mouse. They opened the video surveillance recordings folder he called his tape vault.

"This'll work," Nichelle said, his chair lifting as she hoisted the seat and made herself comfortable.

"If there is a recording of Mrs. Gould, you'll find it on one of these camera feeds," he said, taking hold of a crystal bowl full of licorice bites. He slid it across the desk and offered me one. I shook my head but thanked him. He took a stack of paperwork to a round conference table near the windows and eased into a chair with a grunt.

"We'll try to be out of your hair as soon as we can," I said, hoping to spend as little of our afternoon in his office as possible.

"Hair I don't have," he joked, swiping his hand over his bald head. "But an afternoon of timesheets to reconcile, I have plenty of." He winked at us and opened a bagged lunch, saying, "Take all the time you need."

We spent three hours reviewing surveillance recordings from the dozens, possibly a hundred cameras installed at the hospital. Nichelle worked efficiently, tiling pages of the feeds across the screen to play back at the same time, giving us a powerful and omnipotent view of the hospital's activities during the day Violet Gould went missing. We followed every minute of Gould's shift, seeing her walk the halls like a ghost, disappearing in one video feed and reappearing in another. The task was tedious and wore on our patience.

Before we finished with Violet Gould's shift, Emanuel and Tracy returned from their interviews, the look on their faces telling me they had nothing notable or anything out of the ordinary we could latch on to and use in the investigation. Before sending them back to the station, I had to offer some direction, but there were no breaks in Ronald's case or Cheryl's. My hopes of finding some revelation at Rourke Memorial was a bust. Cases can be like that. They can hide the big breaks, leaving us to waffle in triviality until something finally gives.

Jimmy had left us alone in his office, which freed us to talk openly. "Tracy, I want you to continue your work on the arbor knot and ropes. The type, find out where it's sold and used," I said. She put on a frown, which I expected since she'd worked a similar detail in a prior case. I held my hand up, adding, "I know, I know. Maybe pull your notes on the other case so you can use them as a starting point."

"I worked the stores on that case," Emanuel said. "I still have my notes, the inventory and what types of ropes they sold."

"Great, would you mind helping?" I asked. I had no idea what they might find, but I knew that clues can be like sand through fingers. We might have overlooked something. "Let's get that covered, get the checkbox checked."

"You don't mind?" Tracy asked, her frown gone.

"Nah," Emanuel said. He turned to face both of us, adding, "I'd like to research what you said about the rope, and the killer using it as a game."

"I've been thinking about that one too." I held my thumbs up, mimicking what I'd seen with Ronald. "Draw up the details of the knots and lengths used. I want to test the theory."

"Test it?" Emanuel asked, his words like a bark with surprise at my suggestion. "You mean like actually tie you up?"

"Definitely," I answered. Heads rose, the team's eyes focusing on me. "Guys, it'll be a controlled situation and we'll confirm the idea of whether or not a game was intentional."

"Okay. I'll set it up," Emanuel said, sounding convinced.

"Emanuel has that covered, what else can I work on?" Tracy asked.

"Then the DNA," I told her. "On your way back to the station, stop at the morgue for a visit with Dr. Swales."

"She has DNA for us?"

"Nothing for us to pick up, but she submitted DNA from the bones to CODIS. She also submitted it to some online services, the family-tree kind."

I was interrupted when Jimmy Rush entered his office, head gleaming with perspiration. He ignored us and plunked into his chair with a look of exhaustion. I lowered my voice, answering Tracy, "We may not have anything back, but ask Dr. Swales to share all the account information with you. We can take that off her hands. I'll leave you in charge of them."

Her dimples popped with an ear-to-ear grin. "In charge of them," she said, liking the sound of that. "Sure, I can do that."

"Casey?" Nichelle said as Emanuel and Tracy left the office. "I have something."

I returned to the surveillance videos, the tiled images giving me a headache as I narrowed my view to concentrate on what I was seeing. "The parking garage?" I asked, making out the details, the concrete floor and pillars. The video showed Violet Gould wearing scrubs, the color of it hidden in the black-and-white video. She was speaking to someone, her arms in motion, hands balled into fists, indicating she was arguing with them.

"Whoever that is, he stayed out of the view," Nichelle said, pointing at the concrete pillar. "And they certainly made her mad."

"I think you're right," I said. We had Jimmy Rush's attention, his looking up, curious to see what we'd found. "Mr. Rush, would you join us, please?"

"Be happy to help," he answered, wiping his head and then putting his weight onto the table to make up for the loss of his leg.

When he reached us to see what we were seeing, I asked, "Would there be another camera that'd help show who it is Violet Gould is speaking with?"

He said nothing as the video continued to play, the heat in the conversation we witnessed rising, the body language making up for the lack of audio. "Funny," Jimmy said, pinching his chin. "All my years here, I've never known Mrs. Gould to have a coarse word with anybody."

"Unfortunately, it looks like she did on the day she disappeared." I pinched my fingers and then splayed them, Nichelle taking the direction to zoom in on the feed so it filled the screen. "About the other camera feeds?"

Jimmy shook his head. "Even with so many installed, we still got blind spots."

"I wonder if that person knew?" Nichelle asked, commenting as we watched the argument continue.

"Look!" I said, sliding to the edge of my seat. "Look at the lower right corner!"

In the furthest corner of the video, a white lab coat flicked into the frame as the person Violet argued with moved. Nichelle saw it and rewound the video, playing it back three times to confirm the scene. "Sir," she began, and then corrected herself. "Mr. Rush, who else wears white coats like that?"

"Well, that's a lab coat," he said, continuing to pick at his chin. "Mostly it'd be the docs. Then there's the technicians too, the ones who work with the microscopes and instruments and such."

"Would all the doctors wear them?" I asked, having no idea when they formally graduated to wearing a lab coat. In my field, it'd be like the patrol officers, the uniforms of a street cop, and then promoting to ranks of detective and to plain clothes with a gold shield for a badge. I think hospitals worked similarly.

"No, not all," he answered, taking to lean on a cabinet behind us. "The new kids, the interns we call them, they only wear scrubs. Even then, some of the docs only wear scrubs."

"The residents?" I asked, recalling the term from a television show.

"Some junior resident positions like to wear the scrubs." Jimmy pulled a large binder from a cabinet, the pictures of doctors and nurses and other staff in the pages. The book reminded me of a mugshot portfolio, only this one contained all the hospital's staff. "I keep a hard copy of the issued identification badges. It's an old-school backup. We could look through them? You might find the staff who wear lab coats."

Nichelle's eyes grew large as she leafed through the dozens, possibly a hundred or more pages. "Would you have a soft copy?" she asked, voice lifting with hope for something digital. "I'll be able to work it a lot faster."

"That, I can do. In fact, I have every year since I started here," he answered. He held the binder another moment, adding, "Hard for me to give up on old school."

"Access to the identification badges would be very helpful," I said. "Would you coordinate that with Nichelle?"

"Of course," Jimmy answered. "You'll have full access."

Whoever it was in that video, we needed to find them. They may have been the last person to have seen Violet Gould before she went missing.

ELEVEN

Wednesday night at our house was junk food night, denying ourselves nothing to mark the end of the week's hump day. That meant we could ditch the healthy stuff for whatever it was we fancied. When I opened the front door, I was met by the delicious smells of some of my favorites. With the aroma and the noise coming from the kitchen, I could tell Jericho had picked up a large pizza, which was sure to have extra cheese with one half covered in the fishy anchovies he enjoyed. I think he knew I was homesick, the warm doughy smell making me feel nostalgic for Philadelphia where every corner had a pizza shop with Philly styled tomato pies, cheese steaks and hoagies. There were the side orders too, which Jericho would never forget to include—the mozzarella sticks, the fries with cheese and a dozen jalapeño hot poppers. A gnawing pang lurched in my belly, the time growing long since I'd had anything other than coffee.

With each step toward the kitchen, I shed the hours that made up the day and shed the days that made up the week. While it was only Wednesday, it felt like we'd been hard at work on Ronald's case for a month already. I suppose that's how it is when a victim is someone you know, someone you'd shared the deepest parts of your life with. Maybe when it's this personal, it means you are doing something right. That you are doing for the victim what they could no longer do for themselves.

I entered the kitchen, the look of it a century old, a design renovation Jericho had worked on before I knew him. The stone counters and the cabinets had a turn-of-the-century western vibe with appliances and gas range that were new, the stainless steel glimmering with fading daylight. The bright glow of the day's end bled through the patio doors, a white and red fire on the bay's surface, a wind turning up the surface in a ripple. Through the open windows came the call of a loon, and a second loon answering it as the soft lap of water broke against the backyard's shallow beach.

Jericho was busy working, a cleaning towel in hand, wiping the table for us to sit. He had placemats in the other hand and on the counter a stack of plates and flatware. He was already out of his Marine Patrol work clothes, having donned a pair of shorts and one of his favorite concert tops, a leftover from his twenties—an over-sized black cotton with the rock band AC/DC on the front. The band's logo was split and cracked, and the shirt's threads were worn thin to the point I could see his pale shoulders bleeding through.

"I think it might be time to retire this one," I said and leaned into him.

"AC/DC?" he asked, showing off the front. I ignored the plea to keep the shirt and pulled him into my arms and held him. "Never. Did you know they shared the same producer as Def Leppard? And did—"

"Yeah, I don't care," I told him, shutting him up with my lips on his. He took my weight into his arms, holding me effortlessly. "It feels good to be home."

"It does. I know it's been rough. I know it's not the same, but... I remember how I felt when I lost my wife," he said, his voice like a lullaby. When I let go, he made like a waiter to present our meal, saying, "I know this case has been tough, but I wanted you to know how proud I am. I love you, Casey."

"Thank you," I said, bracing his stubbly cheeks between my hand, his face handsome, his words sweet. "Love you back."

At that, a loud growl flipped my stomach. I was hungry, yet thoughts of Gould's disappearance and the hospital she worked was on my mind. I could easily continue working, but knew I had to eat first.

"Good timing, the food is hot." He opened the pizza box and handed me a slice, steam rising from the pie. I didn't care how hot, I was ravenous and going in. As I closed my mouth around that first bite, there came a knock on the front door.

"Seriously," I said, grumbling with disappointment. Chair legs rubbing across the tiled floor, I moved to stand. But as quick as I was, Jericho was closer and already ahead of me.

"I got this," he said. "You've got that *hangry* look, probably best to eat before interacting with anyone."

"You're probably right!" I said, sounding more than a little miffed. As he left, I chomped the cheesy delight and closed my eyes. It wasn't just the hunger. It was the case. We needed a break in it soon. We needed to show progress.

"Hey," I heard from the front.

"Is Casey here?" It was Nichelle's voice, her tone ringing with concern.

"Yeah, sure. We were just about to eat."

I perked up in my chair. "Come in," I yelled toward them.

"I'm sorry," Nichelle said, footsteps leading, her appearing in the kitchen with Jericho behind her. Her gaze went to the table, Jericho's food displayed in all its glutenous grandeur. "Oh, guys, sorry. I... I can come back."

"Nonsense," I said, thinking of the day, the two us together for most of it. "We've got plenty of food. Are you hungry?"

"Well—" she began and licked her lips as Jericho gathered more flatware and a placemat. He set a place for her at the table and offered a chair. "Yeah. I can eat. Definitely. Thanks."

"One rule," I said while she made her way around to my side. When our eyes locked, I said, "We must eat first."

"I can do that too," she answered, lowering her bag, and her backpack, her laptop inside. I was sure it was cued up to present something about the case. Why else would she have come here tonight? Whatever it was, I hoped it was what we needed.

Nothing goes better with pizza than a bottle of red wine. While Jericho never touched the stuff, he opened a bottle and poured a glass for me and Nichelle. We ate most everything in front of us, resting the growls and pangs that had riddled my insides since coming home. Nichelle was more than satiated, a content look on her face as the carbs from the pizza and the sugars from the wine made for a cocktail of satisfaction.

Although we enjoyed dinner, I'd rushed through it, eager to see what it was Nichelle had found. "What do you got?" I asked, picking at the last of some pizza crust.

"Ahren," she said, mentioning Ronald's online name from my sleuthing team. She wiped her mouth before swinging her backpack onto her lap. "About that night you texted, suspecting Ahren possibly being Ronald, you asked about the hospital video with Hannah."

"The blurry image," I said while Jericho cleared the table for us. He left us alone to work, and in place of the pizza box, Nichelle put her laptop, the screen on it bigger than on most desktops. I knew it would be high end, and powerful. "I picked up some new tools to help recover faces from bad images."

"The nurse that took Hannah?" I asked, biting my lip with anticipation. I could see it in her eyes. She had a new lead.

Nichelle gave me a nod as she finished her glass. I offered more, but she waved me away. She tackled the keyboard, fingers dancing over them, screens flying in from the corners of nowhere until one was at the center and showed Hannah in the arms of a stranger. "I started running the recovery tool the morning of your call." She tilted her face with a frown aimed at me. "Early, that morning I might add. Very early."

"I couldn't sleep," I said, embarrassed by my selfishness.

"It took a while, but the new software constructed a face—"

"Let me see!" I insisted, moving closer, the chair legs scraping with a grating shrill. "Please."

"Just warning you, it's not perfect." Nichelle zoomed in on the pixelated face, the magnification producing a blobby bundle of black and white. One by one, she presented new renditions, sounding each off with a count. "Iteration one, and two, and three—"

"Would you mind jumping to the last one," I asked, needing to see if we had enough for a possible identification. Nichelle clicked her mouse to show a picture of a woman in her early thirties, possibly late twenties. She had short brown hair and a button round face with a narrow nose and flat chin. But it wasn't a photograph in the way I'd imagined it being. "It looks a little artificial?"

"That's the smoothing and the varying degrees of interpolation as the AI filled in the blanks," she explained as she poured us more wine, deciding on one more, but limited it to a splash. "There's at least a hundred iterations from the original, the algorithm making work of previous images."

"And with more guessing, you end up with a softer looking image," I said, taking a sip and thinking of what we could do with the image. I tipped my glass against Nichelle's, telling her, "This is good. It's as good as any sketch artist drawing."

"It's better than that," she said, finishing her glass and setting it aside. "And we can use it. Thanks to Jimmy Rush."

"The head of security for the hospital?"

She nodded. "He sent me the link to their identification badges. I was searching for lab coats, listing the doctors who wore them, but then I found her."

I put my glass down, a tremble in my fingers. I tried to wet my lips, my mouth drying as images of Hannah's kidnapper popped into my head. My chest cramped as I recalled pictures of him placing my daughter's little body onto the wet pavement. "You found the nurse who took Hannah?"

"I did," she answered, opening a folder on her desktop with hundreds of thumbnail images, a thousand maybe.

"You searched all of them?"

"Kinda," she said, rocking her head back and forth. "He mentioned having all the security identifications since he'd started as head of security. I searched the folders from around the time the video of Hannah was made. That's when I saw the woman who looked like the picture the AI made."

"Who is it?" I asked, strength coming into my legs as I began to stand. In the back of my mind I saw the bones Tracy had stumbled upon. There were stray thoughts weaving together a massive conspiracy that connected everyone to Hannah. It was the same craziness I'd done many times before with pictures tacked to a wall and miles of yarn strung from thumbtack to thumbtack. But what if this was real? What if this time, the lead was valid? "Show me."

On the screen, Nichelle presented the identification badge, the woman's round face appearing with an uncanny resemblance to the image she rendered from the video. "Casey, it's Violet Gould."

"Gould," I mouthed, fingertips approaching the screen to touch her face. The missing person case. Was I right? Was it all linked to Hannah?

But while the name on the identification badge said Violet Gould, I couldn't place the face with the woman we'd seen in the recent parking garage video. "She looks very different now."

"This might help," Nichelle said, picking a second identification badge. "This is Violet Gould's most recent identification badge."

"Really?" I asked with a gasp.

"Really. It's dated two months ago." We said nothing a moment as I stared hard at Nichelle's screen. She asked, "What are you thinking?"

I felt myself blinking fast as if something were in my eyes. I felt somewhat dumbfounded. "My case, that is, Hannah's case, it's involved with Cheryl's missing person case. The woman who went missing this week, she took Hannah fifteen years ago."

"Seems to be," she answered.

"And somewhere, buried in all of it, there is a connection linking back to Ronald and his murder. The name of this hospital was written on his notepad back in Philly. It all comes back to Rourke."

"Do you still think it's a missing person case?" she asked, adding another splash of wine to our glasses. She saw the look on my face, adding, "Me neither."

"Whoever wanted Ronald dead, I think they got to Violet Gould too."

"But why?"

"I don't know." I drank my wine, thinking we'd just fallen fifty feet into a black hole where the earthy walls were caked in clue after clue, their brittleness causing them to crumple with every touch. I tilted my glass toward her screen. "This confirms what we suspected. This is about Hannah. It's about my daughter."

I sat back staring at the side-by-side pictures. I was blown away by how much older the woman appeared. While the pictures were taken roughly fifteen years apart, the woman had aged decades. Was it the stress of the job that aged her badly? Swirling the last drops in my glass, another thought came to mind. Perhaps it was guilt that aged her. What did Violet Gould do with my daughter?

TWELVE

It was early, sleep avoiding me at home, my night restless with nightmare images of Hannah being stolen from me. I was young and living in the city, my baby's foot between my fingers in an odious tug-of-war with a monster. Only, it wasn't a monster I was battling. It was the grainy black-and-white face of Violet Gould when she'd held Hannah outside the hospital. When I woke with a start, stirring Jericho, I decided I'd had enough.

It wasn't until I was in my car and driving that I realized why I was so bothered. It wasn't that Nichelle's techno-magic had finally revealed who was last to be seen with my daughter. It was who that person was. Violet Gould. A Rourke Memorial nurse reported missing. The team hadn't openly explored the possibility of a serial killer for Ronald's murder and the other bones, but with the ropes, the knots, and the location being the same for two victims, I had to keep the idea pinned as a possibility.

I had a missing person. If there was a serial killer at Rourke Memorial Hospital, and we'd stumbled on their dumping grounds, then that is where we needed to search for Violet Gould. We knew she'd been working the night she disappeared. We knew it was a late shift. And we knew she'd been in a heated discussion with someone before her disappearance. Could an altercation have occurred after? Something outside the camera's view? With every breath, and every mile I drove, I felt it in my bones that we should have searched the grounds some more. I glanced at the machinery Tracy brought, a new toy for us to use in this early daybreak search.

Once again, we left the safety of a trail in Buxton Woods Coastal Reserve. The ground was wet from an evening shower, a still haze hovering around our knees and sunbeams touching cobwebs beaded with raindrops. There were early morning joggers with radios strapped to their arms, white headphone cords dangling from their ears, eyeing the activity as we crossed a crime-scene tape to exit the trail. A row of parents with babies in strollers came next, slowing to pass the police car parked at the edge, the patrol lights flashing blue and red across their faces, curious to what we were doing.

Crowded with cattails and sawgrass, and the skeletal remains of trees that had died in years past, I'd learned the area flooded seasonally. The rains would come in heaviest with the hurricane season and were apt to steal anything loose, burying branches in muck or carry them when the waters receded. With a tropical depression climbing the coast, I felt an urgency as well as the heat of the day. With the sheer size of the reserve, we faced the proverbial needle in a haystack.

"Watch your step this time," I said, half joking, Tracy tilting her head with a roll of her eyes.

"We might not have found those bones if I hadn't tripped on them," she answered, her arms and hands full of gear.

"Give me some of that," I insisted, taking care as I lifted the main body of a drone, its weight lighter than I thought it would be, but its size bulky. "The batteries are charged?"

I saw another eye-roll. "Please. Now what do you think?"

"I'm just checking," I answered, sidestepping a marsh puddle, the color of it like black coffee and a stench coming from its briny bottom. "The last thing we want to do is get it up in the air only to have to recharge the batteries."

Tracy stopped, her boots sinking as she stepped over the mud.

From the green vinyl bag slung over her shoulder, she pulled two bricks, pressing the sides of them, a row of green LED lights flashing. "I made sure to bring power with me, so we can recharge in the field."

"That's smart," I exclaimed, thinking we could steal some for our phones if we needed it. "Got a plug for phones?"

From the bag, Tracy revealed a spaghetti bundle of wires, the ends showing every connector type I could think we'd need. "I thought ahead."

"Yes, you did." I looked over my shoulder at the trail, a steady flow of traffic on the other side of the crime-scene tape. The ground next to me was where Ronald was killed. The sight of it made me cold and sick.

"Casey?" Tracy asked, hesitating as she stared at the ground where my ex-husband was murdered. "Do you really think Violet Gould is out here too?"

"I'm not sure," I told her, kneeling, the tips of my fingers pushing through the grass until I touched the cool soil. "But this is where we'll start looking."

"Do you have a plan?"

I got back to my feet, pulling a clipboard and pencil I'd tucked away in the small of my back. I showed her the blank pages and started to draw. "This is what I had in mind," I said, penciling a dot at the center with circles at different diameters, extending outward until the last circle edged the trail. "This way we limit the overlap. We'll use north as twelve o'clock so if anything shows up, I'll mark it. Can we do that?"

Tracy flipped the small switches on the controller, focus concentrated as the bull-nosed body hummed with mechanical life. She turned on the remote's viewer, tilting it for me to see the screen, answering, "We can do any pattern you want. I've added a view like we have on a boat's GPS guidance."

"Perfect. With the flight path mapped, we can fill in the blanks," I said, admiring the technology, and Tracy's fast study of it. "Nichelle helped?"

Tracy grinned. "Yeah," she answered. "She really knows her stuff."

"Yes, she does." It wasn't just the tech that Tracy could learn from Nichelle, but the crime-scene investigation knowledge she could share with Nichelle. "You guys make a good team."

"Shall we?" she said, the drone's blades spinning until it was a whirring blur with air rushing across our feet and legs. Hair flying around her head, she raised her voice, "I know it's a little loud, but I liked the extra power with this model."

"You're not kidding," I said, wanting to cover my ears. I held up my thumb, eager for her to lift off. She did as asked, the drone rocketing eight feet upwards and then stopping. It hovered above, the camera capturing our upturned faces on Tracy's screen. "Wow, would you look at that."

"It's amazing quality, isn't it?" she said, the forced air tossing our hair around our faces like we were models at a photo shoot. Tracy let out a laugh, saying, "You should see your face!"

"You should see yours," I said, the lightness of the moment welcoming.

"I'll take a picture of us! Hang on," she said excitedly, wanting to show off her toy before we got to work. "On three look up at the camera."

I rolled my eyes but indulged her, put my arm around her "One... Two..."

The controller in her hand made a shutter sound like a camera, the image of us appearing. "That was easy—" I started to say, my voice stuck, my gaze locked on the screen.

I'd never seen Tracy's baby-blues look so bright. On the picture, the sunbeams made them sparkle. Something about her young face took my breath. It wasn't just that though. I'd known Tracy since arriving in the Outer Banks. And in that time, she'd grown so much. I thought of her uncle, a friend of mine and Jericho's who'd been murdered. Tracy was close to him and had struggled with his death. He would have loved to see who she'd become.

I nudged her arm, "You look all grown up. It's really something to see. Your uncle would be so happy."

"You think so?" she asked, emotion in her voice with the mention of him.

"I know I am."

"I've had good teachers," she said, nudging me back. "You and everyone else. I wouldn't have made it this far without you guys."

"Well, most of the work was yours. I've gotta give credit where due, and you're a natural at this."

Tracy shifted close to me, saying nothing for the moment, the gesture warm. When she was ready, she held the controller and asked, "Wanna give it a try?"

I took the plastic in hand, excited by the idea of flying the drone, but decided against it. "Probably best if you drive and I'll navigate."

The fans blew her hair across her face, the sunlight flashing gold highlights while she centered the drone ahead of us, saying, "We'll start at this position." She marked the screen with a dot, reading off the coordinates and flew the drone in a circle, completing a first pass.

"Marked. Extend out for the next circle."

"From center, I'm adding twenty feet to the radius," she commented, making a beeline away from us. "Can you mark it? We're now at forty feet from center."

"Marked," I told her. I added, "What's that? About five thousand square feet?"

Tracy glanced at me with a nod. "Five thousand and twenty-six."

"Close enough," I answered, the drone circling, a blur of green and brown rolling across the controller screen. "Anything standing out?"

As the drone circled, Tracy moved with it, turning in small increments like hands on a clock. She squinted when facing the sun, her brow rising with a start. She waved her hand for me to see. "Got something!"

I placed a mark on my sheet, the letter x at approximately four o'clock. The drone hovered and then spun around, the camera angle changing too fast for me to know what I was looking at. "What was it?"

"It was just there," she answered, frustration in her voice. "I think I flew past it."

"Zoom out," I suggested. "It might help. I've marked where we are so we can come back to it."

"Okay," she said, moving one of the controls, the camera's view widening until a bright jumble of pixels appeared. Something was buried in the thick of the marshy vegetation and surrounded by patches of purple flowers. "There!"

"What is that?" I asked, putting my arm around Tracy's shoulder, moving closer as I held the clipboard above the screen and shielded it.

"It's white, whatever it is," she said.

"Lower the drone as close as you can."

Tracy began the descent while I peered over the clipboard to make sure there were no bushes or tree branches in the way.

"Casey?" Tracy said with alarm.

I ducked my head beneath the shade, eyeing the screen. "Can you focus the lens?"

Tracy did as I asked, the blurry image clearing, the pixels becoming sharp.

The outline of feet and toes was unmistakable.

I saw the hands next, with legs and arms held in place by a nylon rope connected to the person's neck.

"Zooming out," Tracy said, voice turning raspy. The drone rose to bring the full body into view.

"It's another victim. Female, but is it Violet Gould?" I began, seeing the long dark brunette-colored hair, and hating that I was right to come back to Buxton Woods. The details from the drone's camera made it look as though we were standing next to the body. The victim was lying nearly flat face down against the ground, her head raised and her shoulders sagging. There was a deep crimp in the skin of her neck where I saw what could have been an arbor knot. "Another murder."

"Casey!?" Tracy said, wiping her brow. She moved the lens to focus on the rope around the ankles and wrists, the victim's hands, and feet the color of clay. "That's the same technique—"

"Yeah," I answered, stepping aside to make the call, a tremble rising in my fingers. "It appears to be."

"Wouldn't that mean we have a serial killer?" she asked while I sent a text to Emanuel. He'd kick things into motion and have the teams out here within fifteen minutes. Tracy lifted her feet in a small jump as though standing on hot coals. "If so, then this would be his dumping grounds?"

I revisited the thoughts of a serial killer—the grounds and the ropes and the approach being the same. "Yeah, this does fit the likeliness of a serial killer," I answered as I finished the text messages, the next pair going to Sheriff.

"You don't sound all that convinced," Tracy said.

"There are hallmarks of a killer playing some kind of game," I admitted. "But... these don't feel like random killings. They're too connected. And I'm convinced someone was at Ronald's place. Why would a random killer have gone to his home?"

"But the knots and the location," she argued, returning the drone to land at our feet, blades spinning invisibly. "All the victims are naked and were tied up so the ropes choked them. Classic serial killer repetition."

"That's why I'm not saying no definitively. It could be the killer, or killers are trying to make it appear like they are a serial killer." I pulled a pair of latex gloves over my fingers and headed in the direction of the body. Cattails and shrubs crunched beneath my shoes. Tracy grabbed her drone to follow. "Head back to the car and grab the gear. I'll meet you over there."

"Okay," she said, voice wavering, the discovery rattling her as she eyed the area around us.

I motioned to the red and blue lights on the trail. "We're safe,"

I assured her. "The gears are in motion, the patrol already knows and the team will be here soon."

"Understood," she answered, sounding less timid.

And as she trudged back through the path we entered, I made my way to the victim, following my nose as the smell of death got nearer. I had a rough idea of location based on the sketch made, having placed a letter x where the drone hovered.

Tracy's mention of a serial killer was still at work in my mind. I'd done my best to sound confident in my position, but some of the evidence supported a textbook serial killer.

"Uh-uh," I heard myself mutter while walking past a pair of dead trees, the wood without bark and blanched bright like bone. A vulture sat at the top of the tall one, its black wings tipped ivory-white and spread wide to face the sunlight, ridding itself of the early morning chill. It may have arrived with a feast in mind too, and I shuddered. But that was nature. Criminal or not, how the body got here was of no concern to the bird.

I waved my arms, yelling "Shoo!" It stared uncaringly, talons squeezing the branch to perch with a wider stance. I yelled again and again, the bird finally dropping from the tree limb, flapping powerfully, and lifting into the air. Unlike the vulture, how the body got here was a concern to me. With likenesses such as the location, was this a series of murders made to resemble a serial killer? Were they trying to throw the investigation? Was it a murder followed by another in an attempt to cover up a much bigger crime?

As I stepped around the naked body of another victim, my thoughts went back to Ronald and his investigation. If he had discovered something, its impact came with a rippling effect like a rock crashing into the still surface of a pond. I knelt to face the latest victim, trying to find resemblances to Gould. Her head was raised enough for me to see that her eyelids were peeled back, gray orbs bulging from their sockets, her tongue swelled and filling her mouth.

On my phone I opened the picture of Violet Gould and placed

it next to the face. The grimacing look of death was hard to stomach—it had come with certain cruelty and violence, her final minutes torturous and stealing much of her identity. But there was enough of her for me to make an identification. We'd found Violet Gould.

I had to find whatever it was Ronald found. Find the crime, and I'd find their killers.

THIRTEEN

With news of a third body, the entire team arrived at the site within thirty minutes. Another twenty minutes and I saw the medical examiner's wagon parking, then Derek and Samantha guiding themselves across the grove and past the dead trees. Behind them, cars and vans were finding places to stop alongside the police-guarded perimeter. Some of them were reporters, already with cameras and microphones in hand, while others came with communication dishes perched on the roof of their vans, spiraling upward through the trees. It wasn't long before long lenses were finding us, their snouts prying into our work, magnifying the gruesome details to help tell and sell their ink and digital stories. I clenched my jaw, knowing the types of questions I'd have to field. Thanks to Samantha, Ronald's name had been made known to a reporter, but had it been made public yet? I hoped not. For now, Violet Gould would be the priority, the missing person case having been in the public eye the last twenty-four hours.

"Hey, Emanuel?" I asked, leading him by the arm to turn us around so we could speak candidly.

"What's up?" he asked, a frown forming.

"Nothing bad," I assured him. He relaxed. "How do you feel

about meeting with Violet Gould's husband once we've made a positive identification?"

His eyebrows snapped, rising high as his lips tightened while he considered delivering the news the man's wife was found murdered. Slowly he began to nod, saying, "I can do that. I've done my share when in uniform. Just haven't as a detective."

"Good. And bring a patrol car so an officer can escort him to the morgue." I glanced over my shoulder at the team. "If you get time to ask questions—"

"I got this," he said with a smile forming, showing his confidence. "I'll go directly there after we're done?"

"Yes," I said, waving at a buzz around my head while we returned to the body.

"It's another one?" Samantha asked, waving her hands, a cloud of gnats bouncing around her head with a few landing on her face. "I thought this was a quiet place?"

"Most of the time it is," Tracy said. "I grew up here."

"You do know we work with death?" Derek asked with a spirit of snark.

Samantha scoffed, "Yeah. I know." She jerked her arms, her palms up, adding, "I meant this. The ropes and this place, these woods."

"You're right, this is not normal," I told her, showing my gloved hand when seeing that hers were still bare. Turning to face the victim, and kneeling, I said to the group, "I'd like to get started. Tracy?"

Tracy's eyelids sprang open, surprised by the call. "You want me to run this?"

"You can get us started," I answered, knowing the discussion would open within a few minutes. "It was you and the drone that found the victim."

Tracy cleared her voice and moved to the front, cringing briefly at the sight of the victim's face. "Female, possibly mid forties, cause of death appearing to be strangulation. The manner of death is similar to previous victims with use of ropes around the legs and ankles and neck."

She stopped speaking while taking a minute to assess the victim.

I asked, "What else?"

"Well, the victim is hog-tied, but with a noose around the neck." She rocked her arms back and forth to show the motion of a fulcrum. "The victim's arms and legs acted as a counterweight, pulling a rope through a slip knot which might be an arbor knot, closing or tightening the noose on the victim's neck."

"Is it an arbor knot?" I asked. Booted feet crunched against the ground as faces closed around the body. This was the first thing I noticed when I arrived at Violet Gould's body. I broadened my question, "Are the knots and ropes the same?"

"Similar, but uh-uh," Emanuel said, using his phone to take a close-up picture of the ropes. "I mean, most wouldn't notice, but the rope is different."

"And that knot?" Tracy said, a question forming on her lips. "It's really similar, but I don't think that is the same either."

"Good work," I told them. I pinched the frayed ends of the rope where an arbor knot would have been if this had been made by the same hands as Ronald's killer. Instead of finding clean lengths of rope, and meticulously perfect knots, we had a sloppy jumble of overhang knots, which were the simplest knots to use. Living in the Outer Banks and with time on Jericho's Marine Patrol boats, I had learned my share of knots and saw these were different immediately. I glanced quickly toward Samantha. She'd released details of Ronald's murder, the ropes and knots making their way into the Outer Banks local news cycle. "The structure is the same with the use of the legs and arms as a counterbalance. But some of this—"

"We could have another killer," Emanuel suggested, his glancing at Samantha and then to me. "With the news reporting so much."

"I'm starting to think we have a copycat of copycats," I said, frustration stirring with the case. "It's like there are multiple killers and they all want us to believe it's a serial killer."

"How do you want to proceed?" Tracy asked while Nichelle documented the differences we were finding.

I waved my hand. "We'll process this like we process any murder."

"Understood," she answered. Tracy moved to the midsection and lowered her face close to the body where she studied the victim's lividity, a swatch of blue and purple flesh where the blood had settled. I continued to circle, to counter Tracy's position, and studied the body to find anything different from Ronald. "What do you make of the time of death?"

"Well, the livor mortis, the post-mortem lividity begins at thirty minutes to forty hours after death." Tracy dropped to both knees and placed her hands on the body and shook her head. "The body loses one to two degrees per hour after death. But I can't tell the temperature without an instrument to assist."

"What else?" I asked. I glanced at Derek who could get a body temperature in the field, but there was more for Tracy to consider. "Without equipment, what else could you use?"

"Um," she began, getting up and going back to face the victim. When she saw it, she answered, "Her eyes. It's the corneal cloudiness, which begins two hours after death."

"That's good. What else?"

Tracy's eyes narrowed, thinking she'd covered it all. She looked to Derek, her brow furrowing. When she turned to Samantha, the girl swatting at the gnats, Tracy's expression changed instantly. She nearly yelled, "The flies! They aren't here yet!"

I gave her a nod. "They will be though," I said, assuring her. "They'll be arriving and doing their thing."

"Gruesome," Samantha muttered with a shake.

"Does that mean we have time of death that is less than a day?" Nichelle asked, her camera flash like an exclamation. She crossed us to make her way to the bundle of ropes around the victim's hands and feet.

"Without the flies, I would put the time of death anywhere from twelve to forty-eight hours ago," I answered, the timing was an estimate at best. "It does raise questions."

"Yeah, it does," Emanuel said, looking beyond the trees, the deadwood, and to where Ronald had died a hundred yards away. "Is it possible the body was here when we recovered the first victim?"

"It is," I said, motioning to Derek. He knelt next to the victim to measure the body's core temperature, the faces of the team shying away as he did his work. We were quiet while waiting, the sound of nature speaking in the absence of our voices—birds chirping, a family of deer passing, and a breeze gusting across the grove. "What do you have?"

Derek stood over the body, reading the instrument, and answered. "I've got just under fifty degrees."

Tracy looked to the sky, fingers perched in a pyramid while calculating the rate and speaking aloud to herself, "A body's temperature drops one and half degrees per hour. With a healthy average temperature of ninety-eight point six, that would mean the victim lost almost forty-eight degrees."

"Did you get that by dividing one and a half into forty-eight point six?" Samantha asked, brushing a lock of black hair away from her face.

"Correct," Tracy told her.

Samantha's lips moved as she did the math. "Then time of death is at thirty-two and half hours ago?"

"I believe that's right," I answered.

"It is," Tracy confirmed.

"The victim was killed late Tuesday evening, after the first victim," I said, with a sickening chill, hating to refer to Ronald as a victim. But that is what he was. A victim. I motioned to Emanuel, saying, "Let's mark that as part of the timeline."

"Got it," he answered, his voice low, his gaze locked on the victim's face, recognizing her as I had. "So. Is this her? Violet Gould?"

The team stopped with his mention of a name. "I believe it is," I answered, looking at the victim again, confirming some of the details—middle-aged, her hair colored brunette and styled, a recent salon visit coming to mind. "We can notify the station, but as a possible finding. Dr. Swales and her office will make the positive identification with family members notified."

"Understood," he answered, taking to his phone and wandering the ground for a stronger signal.

I shifted to the knots, finding a few were arbor knots, but the others were half attempts, ending with overhang knots. The nylon was different from Ronald's too. To me it looked like the kind used to hang clothes. It was also small enough in diameter to have torn into the victim's flesh, slicing mercilessly, and drawing blood which had dripped like wet paint while she was still alive. "This is troubling."

"What's that?" Tracy asked.

"The depth here, the bleeding." I had Nichelle photograph the victim's calves and the dried blood. "With the first victim, the binding had only caused rope burns, shallow abrasions. It indicated the knots were in place minutes before death. But these are far more significant."

Tracy took to kneeling next to me, dry grass crunching beneath her knee. "Evidence of a struggle?" she asked, carefully moving one leg. Her single motion caused both hands and the victim's head to move, the victim's head, neck and limbs wired together like a horror show marionette. Whoever had done this had successfully made the knots work together. Pull on one arm, and something else moved. Pull on the hands and feet and the noose around the neck closed, asphyxiating the victim. "What would have caused the rope to do such damage?"

An idea came to me, and I stood up and traced our steps back to the trail. "With Ronald, we think he was made to strip and then the ropes were applied. Once his ankles and wrists were bound, they placed the noose around his neck. They watched him try to escape, then watched him struggle. And then die."

"Maybe the ropes were already in place?" Emanuel lowered himself to assess the damage. "At least on the ankles and wrists."

I searched the grassy area, and it was on the second pass I found the evidence—cattails broken, the grass flattened, a small evergreen bush with a clump of branches and leaves missing. "Tracy, open the victim's fingers."

Tracy did as I asked, prying open the dead woman's fingers. A lump of crumpled leaves fell from her hand. Though they were wilted, they matched the evergreen bush.

"So she was already tied up when she was dragged here," I said. "At least partially." I searched the victim's skull, my fingers probing to find a muzzle mark like we'd found on Ronald's scalp. What I found was a bump large enough to suggest she'd been knocked unconscious, possibly concussed. I searched her neck next and found a patch of dried blood. "There is evidence she was battered with a blunt object."

"Would it have knocked her out?" Nichelle asked, appearing over my shoulder to take a photograph as I parted the victim's hair, the scalp showing with bruising and a short, deep gash. "Oh wow. From the size of that, I'd think so."

"Me too. I'd think a hospital visit would be needed. An autopsy will tell us if there was a skull fracture." The team's eyes were on me, knowing there were substantial differences from Ronald's murder. I went back to the victim's hands and feet. "With the first victim, his thumbs showed burns, which is why I'm thinking the killer is making this a game."

"But not this time?" Tracy asked, fanning the victim's fingers, the thumbs appearing without injury. "Why wouldn't they do the same with her?"

"I don't know," I answered, embittered with not having an answer. "What if she knew them? What if she knew they weren't going to let her live?"

"If she knew there was no hope, then why play the game?" Emanuel said.

"She fought back instead," I said, checking the arms and face for injury. "We may find additional defensive wounds."

"Not if she was concussed and tied up like that," Samantha said, her suggestion timely.

"Right. She never got the chance. Before she could put up a fight, she was knocked unconscious, and her arms and legs were tied. Then they brought her here... dragged her to this spot and let the ropes do their thing."

"And the other victim, Mr. Haskin?" Tracy asked.

"Ronald," I said, imagining what must have happened. "I think they must have lured him. Could be they told him there were answers to the questions that led him to the Outer Banks."

"If that were the case, he followed them willingly," Emanuel said, continuing what I'd started, the thought of it sickening.

"Willingly," Tracy continued. "Only, it was a trap and they made him strip and then played that game."

"And he played because it was the only thing he thought to do to survive." I knelt in front of Violet's face, the look of death staring up and me. "Violet Gould didn't play. She never had a chance."

FOURTEEN

Wearing a lab coat now, and with gloves on my fingers, I entered the morgue where Dr. Swales was busy at work. Her faded green Crocs made a squeaking noise as she shifted her weight atop the step stool and worked a large needle and thick thread. Ronald's chest was partially open, Swales applying post-mortem sutures she called baseball stitches. She jerked on the fine cord until it was taut as I watched from behind. Her arms moved with repetition, applying the stitches over and over in perfect symmetry.

I didn't want to see Ronald's open chest, his organs, his heart, stuffed in a bag like a store-bought chicken's giblet bag. I let Swales know I was here as she did her work and went to the skeletal remains of our oldest victim. The gurney was no longer piled with the jumble of bones as we'd found them at Buxton Woods. The pieces were in order, in their proper locations, and showing the victim in full form, telling me their height. To look at the hundreds of bones, I wouldn't know if any were missing, but to me, it appeared perfectly ordered like a picture from a medical journal.

"Five feet and two inches," Swales said, looking at me over her shoulder while finishing a stitch. "And female."

My eyes wandered from bone to bone. "Mind my asking how you know?"

"The pelvis. It's round and wide and shallow in the female," she answered. "While in the male, you'd expect to find a V-shape or heart shape."

"Shallow and wide to help deliver a baby?" I asked, my gaze falling back to the autopsy table with Ronald. Swales saw that I was staring and motioned me over.

"That's right," she answered. "The pelvis is not as distinct before puberty. However, in the adult female, it is more pronounced."

I stood on the other side of the table where Dr. Swales had just finished the autopsy of my ex-husband. The post-mortem sutures were complete, yet his scalp remained intact. There was no incision from ear to ear as I'd seen before. "Just his organs this time?"

Swales brushed her fingers over a tuft of hair near Ronald's forehead. "If I'd been searching for a neurodegenerative disorder, then I would have had a need to autopsy the victim's brains. However, the cause of death was already known."

With his body washed, the injury around the neck was ghastlier. "And you still believe asphyxiation was the cause of death?"

She rocked her head, surprising me as she held on to new details. "The rope around his neck expedited his death," she said, the tone of her voice mixed. "But it wasn't the cause."

I dipped my head, searching her face. Her ash-colored hair stood tall and cast a shadow across Ronald's body. "I guess this is why we perform the autopsies. If he didn't die from asphyxiation, what did you find?"

"To start, there was the gun-muzzle marking behind the head. I then found some bruising on his arms."

With permission, I searched Ronald's arm closest to me, my focus falling to his hand, his fingers, a memory of holding them in a movie theatre when we'd first started dating. Beneath his shoulder, his upper arm showed a bruise, the marks like fingers, possibly a handprint with the thumb and index finger, or maybe the middle finger. It was enough to take a measurement and give us the size of the killer's hand. "Were there more like these?" I asked, seeing how dark the bruising was. "How old are these?"

"To answer your first question, yes. There's another set on the forearm. The bruises are similar and I've already taken pictures—"

"Excellent, you'll send them?"

She nodded, her glasses shifting, her expression remaining absent of emotion. "To answer your second question, take a look at these," she said, showing an area around Ronald's chest and his legs, a rash that looked like what I'd seen with asphyxiation, but deeper and larger.

"Petechia?" I asked, straightening my shoulders.

"This is called purpura," she answered. "It is like petechia, having to do with the blood vessels, but these are not related to the injury to the neck. When I saw this, and saw the bruising on the arms, I became suspicious."

I was getting an idea of what she meant, an image of the prescription bottles on his counter coming to me. "Was Ronald sick?"

She gave me a slow nod, pulling paperwork from the table, a blood workup form I'd recognized from the lab. "There's evidence he was on heart medications, including a blood thinner."

"Which is what caused the purpura?" I touched his arm, the bruising with the finger marks. "It meant he bruised easily?"

"Correct," she put her hand on his chest, covering some of the baseball sutures. "The cause of death was a myocardial infarction which occurred while his arms and legs were bound, his struggling would have likely precipitated it."

"A heart attack?" I asked, catching my breath, the severity of Ronald's heart issues striking. We'd seen his medications, but I'd only glossed over them, noting them as I'd typically do when investigating who a victim was. I should have known more though. This was Ronald. My tongue was dry like paper. "In his apartment, there were medicine bottles..." Her eyelids fluttered slowly with an understanding. "Ronald, he was always very fit when I knew him. I mean, he'd never let himself go or ate bad—"

Swales shrugged and gave a slight tilt of her head. "Some people are genetically predisposed to high cholesterol that no amount of salad greens will help."

Finding the news difficult to believe, the pitch in my voice raised, I asked, "You confirmed it was a heart attack?"

"Certainly," she answered, her voice short with a pinch of insult.

"Sorry, I didn't mean to question. It's just hard to believe is all." I found myself brushing my hand on his shoulder, wanting to comfort him, but there was no comforting the dead.

"Casey, there was evidence of a previous heart attack as well. It was minor, recent, and which is why he was prescribed the medications in the first place."

The sting of tears threatened now. Ronald had been tortured, which was already terrible, but I had to ask, my words on a tumbling breath. "Did... did he suffer?"

Swales took a deep breath, gazing at my ex-husband mournfully, a useful and rehearsed response I recognized when dealing with loved ones. "It was significant," she answered, pushing up her glasses. She covered Ronald's body with the sheet, adding, "In the old days we called this type of heart attack a widow-maker on account of the severely low survival rate. In Ronald's case, the severity was significant enough to cause a rupture in the affected area. It's my medical opinion that his death occurred quickly, ruling out asphyxiation as a cause."

I pressed my palm against my chest, an involuntary move as I bowed my head. It helped to know death was quickened, that he suffered less. But he did suffer at the hands of killers, there was no escaping it. While learning of his heart condition was upsetting, it was his blood thinner medication that might tell us who his killers were.

"Do you have measurements for the bruising?" I asked.

Swales handed me two sheets of paper, splotches like charcoal indicating the positions of the fingermarks, their positions splayed for the purpose of taking a measurement. From tip to tip, she'd identified the one handprint as having a six-and-a-half-inch spread, and the other one smaller at only a five-inch spread. "I took the liberty of doing the work."

"I see," I said, admiring them. And while they looked like the hand drawings made by children during the Thanksgiving holiday, they were made with an accuracy we could use to estimate the height of the killers. "Doctor, what are the odds on a person having hands of different sizes?" Her eyes became round, a frown forming as she tried to understand the question. Her reaction was enough for me to know the chances were slim. "I'm guessing it'd be small?"

"Very small," she answered. "I mean, with birth defects the possibility is always there, but relative to the population of men who could forcefully subdue a victim this size, I'd say none. Why?"

I held the sheets with the measured handprints. "This confirms there were two killers involved in Ronald's murder."

The resin doors swung open with a clap, a gurney appearing with Derek pushing from behind, his large frame filling the opening as he tilted his chin to acknowledge me. Samantha entered behind him and spun around and exited within a few steps. I heard her complain under her breath about the cold on her return. She'd layered on another lab coat, a trick I could appreciate, the refrigerated air going through me like a breeze through tree branches.

"I'll forward you my final report on Ronald Haskin," Dr. Swales said with formality and sincerity.

"Thank you," I answered, taking hold of the gurney with Violet Gould, guiding it next to Ronald. "Mind if we take a look at this one, get your initial assessment?"

"Yes, let's," she answered, peeking at her watch. "I do have a lunch date, so we'll keep this brief."

"A lunch date?" I asked, adding a lilt to my voice to mimic the faint southern accent I sometimes heard from her.

The corner of her mouth curled with a soft grin. "A lady never tells," she said with a short laugh.

I'd get details later. For now, it was work and Violet Gould. I tugged on the body bag's zipper, Derek holding the corners. As the zipper rolled the smell of decay spilled out, the brackish air having masked much of it at Buxton Woods. "Smells stronger."

"It always does when we get the bodies in here," Derek said, the top of his cropped hair almost touching the autopsy room's overhead lights. "I think it might have to do with the colder air."

"Perhaps." I took hold of the victim's legs while Derek carefully eased his hands beneath the shoulders. Samantha positioned herself at the gurney, gripping the body bag to remove it once we lifted. "And lift."

As Violet's body was hoisted, a gush of air escaped her lungs and made me gasp and jump and nearly drop her.

"That happens when we get here too," Derek said.

"Is that normal?" Samantha barked, jerking the body bag free with a look revulsion.

"Yes, perfectly normal," Swales answered, donning fresh gloves. "When a person dies, air may remain in the lungs, and escape when we move the body around."

Samantha shuddered, exaggerating the motions, her humor and mannerisms reminding me of Dr. Swales. "I doubt I'll ever get used to that," Samantha said with a frown.

Swales spoke toward the microphones above us, dictating to transcribe later. "Preliminary findings for Violet Gould..."

As Swales dictated her notes, I took advantage of the bright autopsy lights, searching Gould's naked body for any injuries that'd indicate additional details of what happened before her death. A white female, we learned that she was in her mid forties, the death mask hiding her age. Gould had a physical build, her muscles toned, her hair colored a dark burnt red that may have been styled professionally. Her fingers and toes were swelled and a deep purple, almost black, but the fresh polish on her nails showed a professional touch. This was a woman who went to a salon a few times a month. She probably also frequented a gym or a fitness center.

"Remove the ropes or should I wait?" I asked.

Swales leaned close to the victim's neck, the thin rope slipping beneath the flesh like it had on the ankles. "With the depth of these injuries, I'm inclined to remove the ropes as a part of the autopsy."

"Understood," I agreed. "We'll need them to remain intact as much as possible."

"I can see why." Swales held the overhand knots, seeing how it differed from the first two victims. She leaned away to assess the ropes. "Someone tried hard to make it look like the others."

"That's my thinking too," I said and motioned to Gould's head to confirm what I'd found in the field. "The scalp."

"Casey?" Swales began as Derek and Samantha left the morgue, Samantha clapping her hands on her arms to shake the cold. The doctor's eyes followed until I heard the resin doors clap shut, she continued, "I am so sorry about—"

"It happens," I said, glancing up at the microphone. I'd learned Samantha had owned up and told Swales about her leaking the details of the ropes to a reporter. I sensed Dr. Swales felt horrible about it. And probably even worse about Ronald's name. I didn't want her to say anything that would be recorded, the morgue saving the audio. "The scalp. I found something in the field."

Swales slowly closed her eyelids, opening them and nodding that she understood. "Injury? Let's see what we see," she said and continued with the preliminary findings. Swales eased onto her toes for the microphone, saying, "A large contusion to the back of the skull."

"We found evidence she'd been dragged to the location." I went to the victim's legs, to where the ropes had cut into the skin. "I believe she'd been unconscious."

"This injury is significant enough the victim had no idea what was happening to her." Swales stepped down from her stool, ending the preliminary review. She eyed the clock on the wall, the second hand swinging around the bottom as the minute hand approached quarter past the hour. "I'm suggesting a brain autopsy to provide us a definitive pathological diagnosis."

"You think the blunt trauma may have killed her?" I asked, the cause of death not what was suspected. "That'd make two cases where asphyxiation seemed the cause but wasn't."

"This is true," Swales commented, her gloves removed with a snap, the latex dust floating freely through a beam of light. "First, I have a lunch, and then I'll attend to the brain autopsy and the rest of the procedure."

"I'll be waiting," I said, removing my gloves, pressing my body against the door. "Terri, have a good lunch date."

"Oh I will," she answered, a grin planted on her lips as she shooed me out of the room with a wave.

I climbed the steps leading to the main floor of the municipal building, texting the team, rallying anyone available. I told them to finish with their lunch breaks and that when I got to the station, we would have a team meeting. Gould's cause of death was questionable, and her murderer appeared to have copied the likeness of the first two murders.

FIFTEEN

I stopped on the sidewalk leading to the station, reporters gathering around the entrance. They filled the bench seats and crowded the doors, their voices buzzing like flies humming around a carcass. Only, they knew this story wasn't dead, it was just beginning. I swung around and made like I was on my phone, annoyance stirring as I started to automatically piece together a statement in my head.

As the sun warmed me, the heat reaching deep to free the cold that had settled in my bones during my time at the morgue, I pulled out my phone and prepared a few fragmented lines. They were disconnected words and incomplete thoughts, but it'd be enough for the news reel. Footsteps came from behind, shoes trampling sand swept onto the pavement. I was aware they saw me, but kept my stare fixed on my phone's screen, replacing words, editing, and piecing the lines into something resembling a cohesive statement and braced for the cameras and lights and microphones.

"Guys," I said, greeting them as they circled like a pack of wild dogs. My name was called in chorus as the reporting ensued, lights flashing and lenses poised, cameras nosing in my direction. The day's heat had turned their faces shiny. A soundman's headphones glided errantly from his bald head while he struggled with a microphone and boom arm. I felt it too, a cloudless sky, the top of my head getting hot. I shifted around so my back was to the station, the municipal building appearing behind me to add a level of formality to my statement. They tracked, following, focusing, and panning to keep me in their sights.

"Detective White, what can you tell us about reports of three bodies being found?" a reporter asked, her face unfamiliar, her approach universal as she wedged herself between two teams I knew to be from local television and radio stations. "We also have reports that all three bodies were recovered from the same location at the Buxton Woods Coastal Reserve."

"That's correct," I answered her, eyeing the parked vans and the satellite dishes on the roofs, one of them rotating, leading me to believe this was a live broadcast. I glanced at my phone, seeing a line from my statement, reading it unrehearsed, "At this time, the medical examiner's office is actively working the autopsies for three bodies recovered from the Buxton Woods Coastal Reserve."

"What are the preliminary results?" the lanky reporter with bright red hair asked, bumping shoulders with the newer reporter. He shoved his phone close enough for me to step back. I gave him a firm look of annoyance, fixing it with silence until he made room. He nodded an apology and gave me room.

"The investigation is ongoing and some of the families have yet to be notified—" A flurry of questions, words raining heavy and peppering my ears without the possibility of any comprehension. I raised my hand and shook my head. They quieted, allowing me to continue. "We are working with the medical examiner, and I can share some preliminary autopsy findings."

Feet shuffled as they crowded around to record my statement with one of them asking, "Was it a homicide?" It was a breeze of relief, hearing that the details of the murders Samantha had leaked hadn't made its way through the core of reporters yet. The orientation of the ropes had been leaked though. Nichelle had broken the news to us in the late night, sending a text with a video snippet, which showed a crude drawing of how the ropes were used to kill the victims. "On Monday, you reported that the death was suspicious. Could you expand on reports of ropes being used?"

"Not at this time," I answered, keeping the details. "However, the victim, male, forty-four years old was found dead in Buxton Woods—"

"Give us something new," one of them interrupted.

I cocked my head at the arrogance. "This is an ongoing investigation, and I don't have to provide anything," I warned, furrowing my brow with laser focus aimed at the source of the comment. "This is a courtesy, don't take advantage of it."

"Dude," the red-headed reporter said, speaking over his shoulder. He turned back, "Apologies for that. Please, Detective, continue."

"The man's death was determined suspicious for reasons that have not yet been shared while we continue to investigate." A rise of sighs, shoulders drooping with faces pulled in disappointment. They needed more. I picked the safest information, the most innocuous of details to share. "However, in the case of the forty-four-year-old, his death has been confirmed to be a result of a heart attack brought on by the circumstances. Yes. It is a homicide."

With my words there came an outbreak of enthusiastic clicking, reporters jockeying for a better view and a position to ask the next question. "There was a report that the victim was your husband?" a woman shouted from the back of the crowd. My throat closed with the words, a hush falling over the other reporters as heads turned. The lone voice continued, "The heart attack victim? It was your husband, Ronald Haskin?!"

I took a heavy breath, felt my knees go weak a moment while the reaction rippling over the crowd settled and they returned their focus to me. It was the reporter Samantha had been speaking with. I wanted to be angry. I wanted to be annoyed. But thankfully, I found that I was grateful the reporter hadn't leaked his name earlier in the week. Today was Thursday and Ronald's body had been found Monday. His family was notified Monday afternoon, my speaking to his sole remaining relative, a sister living in a suburb of Philadelphia, Bensalem Pennsylvania. His name was out there now, and I'd be fooling myself if I didn't think the reporters weren't going to ask about him.

"Detective!" the reporters said in a raised voice. A soft touch of someone's hand came to the small of my back. I turned to find the mayor standing by my side. The reporters changed focus, speaking haphazardly and without reverence. They yelled her name, voices clamoring, "Mayor Stiles! Mayor Stiles!" until she raised a hand.

"Hello all," she said, hushing them with efficiency, their expecting an impromptu press conference. "I'm sorry to have to do this, but I'll need to borrow the detective for an urgent meeting."

"Mayor—" I began.

Julia Stiles was tall and slender and dressed like an executive running a Fortune 100 company. With the sunlight beaming on her brown skin, she squinted as she waved at the reporters and took my arm in hers and led us toward the station. We walked in silence until we were out of hearing distance of the reporters.

I asked, "I have to apologize, did we have a meeting scheduled?"

We reached the station, the inside twenty degrees cooler, large fans whirring in methodical harmony, the blades batting air and lifting fliers tacked to the announcement board. The mayor waved off the question and gripped my arms, her brown eyes filled with a care that took me off guard. "I thought you could use the interruption."

"There's no meeting?"

She rubbed my arms affectionately then led me toward my desk. "I have a meeting with the sheriff. But I read about your ex-husband this morning." She noticed a frown, and added, "I get reports from Dr. Swales too. Casey, I am sorry for your loss."

With her words came the eyes, the gaze, the one that was filled with sadness and meant to be caring. I'd seen it when Hannah was taken from me and had seen it enough for one lifetime. "Thank you," I answered, trying to muster appreciation for the care. "Alice?" I muttered, seeing the station manager approach. Behind her was a man in his fifties, looking frail, maybe sick, and walking with a cane. White hair sprouted around the brim of a tweed cap. He wore a paisley plaid shirt and light blue polyester slacks, looking as though he'd just come from putting around nine holes. His eyebrows were wiry thick and bounced as he acknowledged the mayor and me.

"Wait there a moment, sir," Alice said, a hand poised like a traffic cop while he stood on the other side of the station's gate. When she faced us, she said, "I am really sorry to interrupt, but this man is insisting he speak with Emanuel and said he was also trying to reach Detective Cheryl Smithson."

Before I could answer, the man with the cane opened the gate, choosing to ignore Alice. His eyelids were puffy with pouches beneath, the blue in his eyes glazed and bloodshot. Without thinking about it, I grabbed a chair from an empty cubicle and wheeled it to him. He plopped down and wheezed a choppy breath as he removed his cap to wipe the sweat from his brow.

"Sir?" the mayor asked. "Are you okay?"

"It's my wife," he answered, lips a gray-blue and thin like lines drawn on paper. His mouth shook between his words as he continued. "She's dead."

"I can take this," I said with a nod to Alice. "Mayor, thank you for the kind words."

"If you need anything," the mayor said as the sheriff's office door opened.

"You're here about your wife?" I asked, seeing an empty chair behind Emanuel's desk. I rolled my chair and sat down across from him, knowing this was the husband of Violet Gould, the man Cheryl had told me about, the man who'd just learned of his wife's murder.

"I filed a missing person report the other day," he answered, glancing at the station monitors and then back at me. His voice trembling, he mumbled, "But was told this morning that she died?"

"I am so sorry for your loss," I said, craning my neck around the station in search of Emanuel. Surely he'd brought Mr. Gould here? "You came to the station with the detective?"

"Mm-mm," he answered, eyes glazed, his sounding slightly altered. He raised his hand above his head. "The tall detective. I told him my son would bring me."

"Okay, I understand," I told him, thinking maybe he'd come to the station looking for Cheryl.

"She's a nurse, you know. But she wasn't at work when I went to get her."

"Violet," I said.

"Yes, ma'am. Her name is Violet... like the flower," he answered. I recognized the anguished look on his face and heard the desperation in his voice. He stared distantly with weepy eyes.

"Sir, are you alone? You mentioned your son?" I asked, thinking he had to have come with somebody. He clutched the top of his cane, his fingertips the same blue-gray color as his mouth.

"I got one of my boys," he answered, chin quivering. His focus sharpened. He clapped the top of his legs, adding, "Some days my driving isn't so good. My boy is parking our car."

"That's good," I said, searching the front toward Alice. It was best to wait until the son returned. "Can I get you a coffee, maybe some—"

"What happened to Violet?" he asked, striking the butt of his cane on the floor, the sharpness snapping my mouth shut. "The tall detective said she'd been found?"

"What did the detective share with you?" I asked, wondering how much Emanuel had said.

"Not much. It's my health," he answered and began wagging a finger. "I'd just come back from the doctors and couldn't sit long enough to speak with him. That's why I came here."

A sigh slipped from my lips, my insides rattled by the part of the job that I hated. Violet's husband was only aware of her death. He had not heard any of the details. There was no easy way other than being direct and stating the facts. "Mr. Gould. Your wife's body was found early this morning in Buxton Woods Coastal Reserve. I'm sorry to tell you, but her death is a case of homicide."

"Buxton Woods?" he asked as though he hadn't heard the latter part. Fresh tears came, his mouth opening as though wanting to scream. "She always loved that place."

I put my hand on his. "Sir, I am sorry for your loss."

"And it's murder?" he said and pitched forward with a deep groan, his weight hanging on the top of his cane. I feared he'd tumble off the chair and knelt in front of him so I could brace his shoulders. "Who would do such a thing?" he asked between sobs.

"That's what we're going to find out," I answered as Alice joined me, a young man following her. It was Mr. Gould's son. College age, a baby face with wispy hairs sprouting on his chin. He had sun-bleached hair and a dark tan and smelled like sunblock. From his short pants and shirt and sandals, I'd guess him to be a lifeguard on the beach, working the summer for college money.

"Dad?" he asked with alarm and dropped to his knees to take over for me. "Do they know what happened to Mom?"

"Someone killed your mom," his father answered.

"What?" the son asked in a yell, a hand on his mouth with a look of horror.

I brought another chair for the son and motioned to Alice for some water, hoping it would help. "Sir?" I asked, getting his attention. He peered up, his face sagging with droopy eyes. "You mentioned your wife wasn't at work when you went to pick her up?"

"I went to the hospital on account of her car being in the shop," he said, wiping his face with a handkerchief. He dabbed his bald head, drying it. Thinking of the video, of the woman arguing with someone, I asked, "Where did you go to pick her up?"

"The parking garage," the son answered as he rubbed his father's back. "I dropped her off earlier in the day."

"Your name is included in the report filed?" I asked, taking a note, the report offering a timeline.

"Yes, ma'am," the son answered. "Mom was working an eleven

to seven, the night shift in the NICU. Or might have been the PICU."

"NICU and PICU?" I said, asking about the acronym as I wrote it down.

"They are the Pediatric and the Neonatal Intensive Care Units," Mr. Gould answered. "She worked in them. She also worked Labor and Delivery too."

I had three locations in the hospital, and asked to confirm, "That would be NICU and PICU and Labor and Delivery?"

"That's right. She liked working with expectant parents and the babies and little kids," Violet Gould's husband answered as he started searching his pockets. "Oh shoot, where's my inhaler?"

"You okay, Dad?" his son asked.

"Go get my inhaler." The son did as asked, leaving us alone. While the man seemed frail and relied on his cane, I noticed his breathing was fine. He stared hard and long at me while waiting for his son to exit the station. When we were alone, Mr. Gould asked, "How did my wife die?"

"Sir?" I asked, his face empty of emotion, blank like a marble statue.

He looked toward the front, making sure we were alone. "What did they do to her?"

I couldn't help but think of Ronald as I considered my words. And I couldn't stop seeing the bindings on his ankles and wrists and imagine what it must have been like for him when his heart exploded inside his chest. There was no easy way to tell the man, except to say it plainly. "Your wife's homicide appears to have been asphyxiation."

"She was strangled?" he said, eyes bulging.

"Yes, sir." I chanced taking his hands in mine, thinking to comfort him. He gripped my fingers, his strength weak, the weepiness returning. "Do you have any reason to believe someone would want your wife dead?"

"I think she was having an affair," he said, his words a surprise.

"An affair?" I asked, believing I had to have misheard him. He let go of me, and cupped his mouth, anger rising as he held back a cry. He couldn't speak and gulped water from a bottle. When he was ready, he nodded to continue. "An affair with who?"

"It's with a doctor at the hospital." His gaze fell to his legs and then his cane as he muttered, "I've been a burden too long I guess."

I saw a flash of the white lab coat behind the parking garage pillar. "What makes you believe your wife was having an affair?" I asked, the station gate slapping shut, the son returning with the man's inhaler.

"Violet didn't know I was there the one time. I seen them together," he answered, seeking out his son and gauging how much he could say. "I'd gone to the hospital offices for an appointment and saw her with him."

"Who was it, sir?" There was an edge now to his voice that contrasted with the feebleness.

"His name is Dr. Sully," the man answered, stamping the end of his cane as he'd done before, ridding his face of any anguish. He motioned to leave, his son returning in time to take his father's arm. Mr. Gould grunted when he tried to get up, my lending a hand. As he stood, he squeezed my arm, our eyes locking a moment. "I hope I am wrong about that." His voice stayed cold. "But if you have questions, I'd start with him."

"Sir, thank you for coming to the station, and again, I am so sorry for your loss."

"What do I do now?" he asked, searching around the station as if there was a place to wait.

"Our medical examiner can walk you through what's next," I said, transferring his hand to Alice's.

I stood alone near my desk and watched as the sickly man was helped by his son. They exited the station with Alice by his side. The reporters didn't mess with Alice. They knew better. From here, Mr. Gould would be contacted by Dr. Swales or someone in her office. I'd text ahead to give them notice. Violet Gould's body wouldn't be released anytime soon. We had our work to do, which might require another trip to the hospital. Mr. Gould had named who it was that might be our mystery man standing behind the concrete pillar. A Dr. Sully. I texted the name to Nichelle, asking for a breakdown of the hospital staff, an organization chart of sorts for us to understand the layout. There was more going on behind the hospital's walls than saving lives.

SIXTEEN

Thankfully the front of the station was empty of reporters. I'd left the cozy comfort of our bed earlier than usual, knowing some of the press had caught on to when I started my days. And a start it would be. The team needed to put their cards on the table and show their hands. We needed movement on the tasks given the last few days. I opened the station doors, finding a new desk officer to replace Alice on the eleven-to-seven night shift. He looked fresh out of the academy, his uniform pressed clean, his sandy brown hair combed straight. For the morning hour, the benches were clear, the evening's collection of drunk and disorderly put to bed in the holding cells.

"I've got something on Dr. Benjamin Sully," Nichelle suddenly said, popping up from her cubicle as I reached my desk. My heart jumped into my throat. With a look of surprise, she added, "Sorry, I thought you knew I was at my desk."

"Nope. Didn't know anyone was here other than me." I went to her, seeing Tracy was also at her desk, the two driving in together. I didn't see their car, but then again, I wasn't looking for it this morning. "Emanuel?"

"I'm here," he said, appearing from his desk too. "Baby had me up since four." He held up a sample of the nylon cord, adding,

"When I couldn't get back to sleep, I decided to come in and found these two already here."

"How long have you guys been here?" I asked, taking the lid off my Quick Mart coffee, wondering why I let myself drink their swill. I checked the station monitor, the early news broadcast showing it was quarter past six.

"Was it five?" Tracy asked.

"Might've been a little earlier," she answered.

"I'm guessing all of you have got some stuff for a show and tell?" I blew on the coffee's steam, careful not to burn my mouth. "Starting with Dr. Sully?"

"The hospital org chart like you said," Nichelle answered while I went to her cubicle. She'd changed the cat calendar I fondly used to track the days in the month. The new one showed two kittens sitting in mason jars, their furry paws perched on the glass lip. "Do you think Violet Gould was having an affair like he said?"

"It's our job to find out. But if they were, then that opens up the door to motive."

"Poor guy," Tracy said. "What's wrong with him?"

"I'm not sure," I said, uncertain what the man's ailments were. He wasn't more than fifty, but he looked as though he'd been sick for a long time. Was it the stress of being a caretaker that aged Violet Gould? I had my doubts. She was a nurse after all. I shifted back to the topic I wanted to discuss. "As for this Dr. Sully that Mr. Gould named. He may be the man in the parking garage video. He could be the one wearing the lab coat."

"Team meeting time?" Tracy asked, her voice pitched excitedly high, especially considering it was early morning. We turned to see her expression looked utterly explosive. She grabbed her laptop, hopping up and down while me and Nichelle watched with comical confusion. "I got something to share!"

"Yeah, no kidding," Nichelle said with a breathy chortle. "Solve the case, did ya?"

"Conference room," I told the team. "And fast, before Tracy erupts."

We settled into our unassigned seats. I took the head of the conference room table and plugged the video cable into my laptop to control the big screen at the front of the room. But before I could say a word, Tracy sent me an email message, the subject line reading, *the Bones and DNA Results*.

"You have DNA results already? From the bones?" I asked. We'd only submitted the samples on Monday. It was Friday, but I hadn't expected results for at least another week. She nodded eagerly. "That was fast."

"A special service, I think," she commented. "Like the services have a department dedicated to working with law enforcement agencies. Dr. Swales can explain it better."

"That's great." I took a chair, sitting and turned the meeting over to Tracy. "You have the news, how about you lead us off with what've you got."

She went to the front of the conference room, motioned for me to click the link she sent. I did so, opening a web page to the first family-tree service we'd submitted to. Tracy cleared her voice. And even though it was just us, there was a touch of nerves showing. "I think the other reason we got such a fast response was because the family had also submitted a DNA sample."

"Back up," I said. She'd jumped ahead, her voice shaky and fast. I motioned her to relax, saying, "Let's start at the beginning."

"Start with a name," Emanuel suggested, speaking slow to try and help.

"Sure," Tracy answered, taking a breath. "From the bones recovered, our victim's name is Janice Stephen. She is originally from Doylestown, Pennsylvania, and went missing from this area three years ago."

"Doylestown," I said, having been there many times. "That's about sixty miles or so northwest of Philadelphia."

"Philadelphia," Nichelle said, inferring a connection to Ronald.

"Location is probably unrelated given the time difference being three years," I said as Tracy showed us a picture of the victim's Pennsylvania driver's license. In her photograph, she looked young enough to have been in high school, wearing stylish glasses, her brown hair at shoulder length. But it was her shirt top that brought me to stand—a pair of hospital scrubs. "Tracy, what did Janice Stephen do for a living?"

"Janice Stephen, twenty-five—" Nichelle said, tapping her keyboard, her voice raised. "—was a third-year medical student. She was working rotations at Rourke Memorial when she went missing!"

"That's what I was getting to," Tracy added, nostrils flaring, Nichelle mouthing an apology.

"From the file, it's an unsolved case. We reviewed it when you first started here," Emanuel said, his face cast in blue light as he read from his laptop.

"Medical student?" I asked, thinking through all the cases I'd researched when I followed up on a clue in Hannah's case. "I think I remember her case."

"I'll reach out to the detective assigned the case," Emanuel said. "It might be there have been new details."

"Good," I told him. "We haven't gotten anything back on the CODIS submissions. Tracy, you said *they* had submitted DNA? How would you know that?" Tracy pursed her lips with a look that she'd done something wrong. "Did you contact the family?"

She began to nod her head, then shook it, uncertain how to answer. "Just an email about the DNA and the service. I didn't offer anything official," she rambled. "In the email, I said we were working a case and had submitted DNA to the same service."

"Emanuel, please let the detective know we've been in contact with the family." I squeezed my eyelids closed, thinking who else I might need to rope in. I wasn't sure if there was protocol broken or not, but there was a formality when it came to contacting relatives.

"Indicate that the exchange was limited to email about the DNA service."

"Sorry," Tracy said, taking to her seat.

"After the meeting, we'll contact them more formally," I told her. "Emanuel?"

"I'll pass it on to the detective," he answered.

I couldn't peel my gaze from the victim's picture. "We've got Ronald Haskin, Violet Gould and Janice Stephen. Although there's some question about the ropes, we do have one thing in common across the three. What is it?"

I went to the screen as the team answered together, their voices in unison, "Rourke Memorial."

"Can we revisit the idea of a serial killer?" Emanuel suggested. "I mean, with any other case, the evidence supporting it would be overwhelming."

"You're right. The ropes and arbor knots, and the location. There isn't anything random about these murders. There's a show of consideration and preparation with them," I said, having to agree as I went to the whiteboard and wrote the victims' names. "If we explored this being a serial killer, the mystery doctor would be a suspect. Or even the hospital as a place the killer uses to find his victims."

"What about Dr. Sully? He's a doctor at Rourke Memorial where Janice Stephen worked," Nichelle asked. "And there's Violet Gould. His is the only name that's come up with two of the victims."

"That could be," I agreed. "Either way, he's first on our list to be questioned. Let's do that at the hospital."

"Staying on the serial killer track, and the hospital connection, the killer might work there," Emanuel said, pawing at his chin.

"That also could be the case," I said, noting it on the board, underlining unknown hospital employees. "There's an issue with that and Sully."

"Ronald Haskin doesn't fit," Nichelle answered.

Emanuel sighed with disappointment, adding, "Also a hospital connection would know the victims because he worked there."

"With Ronald, there's no employment or hospital affiliation." I underlined my ex-husband's name. "But he was investigating the hospital. His only connection to it being my daughter and that Hannah was found by Violet Gould at Rourke."

Doubt formed on the team's faces. Our workup of a potential serial killer was doused with mention of Ronald and Hannah. "It doesn't exactly fit the mold, does it?" Tracy questioned.

"The hospital remains the strongest connection," I said, trying to make it work. "Perhaps Ronald accidentally exposed Janice's killer during his investigation."

"What about the evidence that there were two people involved?" Tracy added. She motioned to the back of her head. "There's the muzzle impression and handprint bruises."

I held up my hands, fingers spread wide. "From Dr. Swales, we also have two different sized handprints found on Ronald's arms."

"So... we nix the serial killer track altogether?" Emanuel asked, his hearing enough evidence to be convinced.

"I think so. I think we're looking for a killer, or killers, who have tried to disguise the murders as those committed by a serial killer." I turned back to the whiteboard, adding a second underline to the name of the hospital. "That's what we need to investigate."

"I've got the org chart," Nichelle said, leaning up and taking the video cable. She showed the hospital, a page full of boxes and lines, the different areas named.

"Zoom in on Dr. Sully." I sat against the end of the table, taken aback by the count of staff working the hospital. Finding a killer amongst them would be a daunting task. I could only hope I was right about there being two killers. With two, we doubled our chances of one of them making a mistake. We only needed to find a single slip to catch them both. "What are those departments?"

"NICU and PICU," Tracy read. "They are the Neonatal and Pediatric Intensive Care Units."

"Dr. Sully runs both?" I asked, his name in a box above them. "Gould's husband mentioned her working there."

"It looks that way," Emanuel answered. "I've got his profile page from the hospital. Says here that he has been the head of the departments for twenty years."

"Violet Gould?" I asked, hoping the org charts hadn't been updated yet. I was tense with the news Nichelle shared the other night. The news that Violet Gould had taken Hannah.

Where was Hannah? Had she been taken into the hospital?

Nichelle searched the screen, the lines and boxes flying sideways and then up and down with dizzying speed. When she landed on Gould's name, her employment record was within Dr. Sully's organization. "She worked for Sully. But doesn't confirm what her husband said, his suspecting there was more going on between them."

"Guys," Tracy said, shuffling loose paper, her notepad near her face. "In the email from Janice Stephen's family, her mother mentioned Janice's favorite place to work was in the NICU. She never missed a shift."

"Never missed a shift to work in the NICU," I commented, parroting Tracy's words.

"So the connection to the hospital got Janice killed?" Emanuel asked. "Why? Did she see something?"

"Maybe Janice Stephen saw the affair between Gould and Sully?" Nichelle asked. "You know, forbidden love, they killed her as part of a cover-up."

"Forbidden love," Tracy said with a smirk. Her face turned serious when she saw me. "That wouldn't explain Violet Gould being murdered."

"Right," Nichelle commented.

"People have killed for less," Emanuel said, regarding the proposed motive.

"The NICU and Janice Stephen. What if Ronald was investigating the hospital for more than two years? He could have reached out to Janice. Maybe she found out about Gould taking Hannah," I said, affirming a direction, a path for us to follow. "In some way, I think that's what got them all killed."

As the conference room cleared, Tracy stayed behind as I placed a video conference call with Janice Stephen's family. Emanuel's making contact with the investigating detective had an immediate response, including all the case details being turned over to our team. It was early Friday morning and Tracy had sent an email response to Janice's mother, asking if we could contact them. Our morning turned lucky when the response came back with the family eagerly wanting to speak with us.

"Hello," I said, my screen turning bright with the image of a family crowding around a computer. Janice's parents, an older couple, the woman without makeup, her hair white and combed back. Her husband wore a nice suit, appearing as though he were on his way to work. Behind them were a brother and sister if I were to guess, young enough for high school, or college students perhaps.

"Ma'am?" the woman answered, her husband gripping her shoulder. "Do you have news about our Janice?"

Most of the time, I'd want to do this in person. But with the family being near eight hours north of us, and Tracy having reached out to them, I believed it best to tell them about their daughter. If I were them, I'd want to know. Janice's father moved around his wife, his face growing big as he went closer to the camera.

"This call is about the DNA you guys asked about?" her husband followed up.

"Sir, it is." I pushed my laptop back to better frame my face. "I need to tell you that while investigating a death in Buxton Woods, North Carolina, the remains of your daughter were discovered."

The couple looked at each other for a moment of silence that seemed to stretch on for hours. It was the news they must have known was coming.

"I knew it," Janice's mother eventually said with a sob, gripping a kitchen towel and pressing it against her face. "My baby is dead. Was it murder?"

"Yes, ma'am," I answered, keeping it simple for them at first.

"Lord, I knew it. I knew it," she sobbed, her husband putting his arms around her and the siblings in the background embracing too.

"I am so sorry for your loss," I said, the tragic sadness aching in me rearing as it did whenever in this situation. When Janice's mother peered back at the camera, I explained, "If not for the DNA you submitted to the family-tree services, we might never have found the identity."

"We were so frustrated," she said, swiping at her face with the towel. "We'd kinda given up with the police and decided to do something on our own."

"It worked," I said, putting on a smile, hoping it eased the delivery of the painful news.

"We included all ours. Every one of us," Janice's brother said, speaking up.

"It was a perfect match," I said, remaining impressed with their efforts. Sensing there was an opening, I asked, "Could you tell me anything about your daughter's work at the hospital?"

Janice's mother turned to her husband, and gave each of them a hard look of confirmation. "I told you it was that place."

"Ma'am?" I asked. "Did your daughter share something with you?"

Janice's mother leaned forward, her face nearly filling my screen. "My baby loved medical school and becoming a doctor. She absolutely adored her work with them babies."

"The NICU and PICU?" Tracy asked, the top of her pencil whirling in circles.

"Uh-huh! She treated that place like it was her church." Janice's mother sat back and covered her face as a cry returned, the sound of it breaking my heart. "She loved them babies. And she knew too."

"Your daughter knew what?" I asked.

Janice's mother let out a deep sigh, answering, "We tried to tell the cops, but they wouldn't listen."

"We're listening now," Tracy offered.

"We never found out what it was exactly, except that it had something to do with the babies."

I traded glances with Tracy, the two of us confused.

"Janice never missed a shift," her father said. "Except that one when she called us and said she was coming home."

"She said she was in danger, that she wasn't safe." Janice's mother let out a cry, adding, "Only she never got home to tell us what she'd seen in the NICU."

"Trust me when I tell you, we'll do everything in our power to investigate your daughter's murder." My mind raced with ideas. The biggest of them telling me that Janice Stephen had tripped onto whatever Ronald had. "Did Janice share what it was at the NICU that made her think she was in danger?"

Janice's father leaned forward again, his glasses smudgy from the tears. "I thought she was overreacting, but when she didn't show up, well... well, it just about crushed me."

"Oh, baby," his wife said, embracing him, her words muffled as she said, "it's not your fault."

He returned to the camera, glasses removed. He wiped his face and said, "Janice told us she found something in the charts. I'm sorry, but we didn't know what that meant."

"The charts?" I asked, puzzled by what their daughter was referring to. I was expecting a big revelation, the mention of a dead body stowed behind a wall in the hospital basement, or even discovery of solicitous activities and a cover-up. But charts? I tapped Tracy's tablet, her eyes large, hungry for answers too. "From the NICU?"

"Yes, ma'am. Janice said they were doing things." Her face turned sullen then, the news of her daughter's murder reaching deeper into her soul, the first of the hardship only beginning. "I wish we'd known what any of that meant." She looked to her husband, who was nodding now. When she turned back, she asked, "Ma'am, what do we do now?"

"Our medical examiner will be in touch with you about making arrangements," I told her. "And if you can remember anything more about your conversations with your daughter, please contact us."

"We will," Janice's father said, tapping the keyboard, the screen going black before I could say another word.

"Charts?" Tracy asked. "What kind of charts was she talking about?"

"I suppose we have to think of every kind of chart a hospital uses?" I said, questioning as I considered all the paperwork funneling through a hospital. "Maybe we're overthinking this."

Tracy agreed, saying, "Well, Janice was a medical student—"

"—then the most obvious chart she'd work with are the patient charts," I finished for her.

"That's got to be it," she said, standing to leave. "We'll get on it."

I was alone in the conference room and staring at the monitor and the whiteboard and the words and names I'd underlined. When I looked at Ronald's name, the second known victim after Janice Stephen, I had to wonder: what did he find that could possibly relate with Rourke Memorial's patient charts?

SEVENTEEN

Tracy drove this time while I took to the passenger seat and Nichelle sat in the back. For all of us, there was a storm of questions stirring about the hospital and the patient charts. During Janice Stephen's time there, she'd discovered something in the patient charts. And Ronald may have discovered the same. How would he have gotten access? How good was he with a computer? Sadly, I didn't know the answer to that question. But whatever he and Janice knew, it must have been significant.

Emanuel continued his work at the station, working on a demonstration of the arbor knots for me to try. Could I escape them? Could I beat the killer's game? I was nervous, but it would either prove or disprove the theory that the killer was playing a deadly game.

I heard frustration from the laptop keyboard, Ronald's password remaining hidden as Nichelle pounded the keys with each attempt. None of the names or dates I'd offered worked. Even the combinations of what were our most intimate, like the first day we met or our wedding day and the day that Hannah was born.

"Maybe it's not from your past?" she said, asking, her voice in competition with the radio. I rolled down the volume to hear her.

"Like, a password made from words and dates that include the hospital?"

"That could be," I said, but felt unsure. I was open to trying anything. I'd been certain I would have been able to help crack the security, but that hadn't happened. "Could we look at the hard drive directly? Remove it from his laptop and mount it as an external drive on my computer?"

"That's a possibility," she answered.

"But?" I asked as she hit the enter key and sounded another grunt, Ronald's laptop locked.

"I think it will be encrypted." The look on her face told me the idea wasn't promising. "Which means the only access to his data has to be through the laptop."

"Let me think of what else Ronald might have used." I turned back around, turning the radio up, Tracy's taste in music oddly old-fashioned. She had the local station that played songs from when I was a little older than she is now, in the early days of dating Ronald. "Don't be a stranger," I muttered while staring out the car window, a steady flow of vacationers passing in a blur of beachy colors. Those were the last words Ronald had said to me, and they'd haunt my waking thoughts until we solved his murder.

"Oh snap! I think I got it!" Nichelle screamed at the top of her lungs. I spun around to face her as she showed Ronald's laptop, the desktop icons appearing. "Can you freaking believe it!"

The inside of my chest jumped as disbelief flooded my brain. I'd thought for sure Ronald's laptop was a loss. "Write the password down before you forget!" I said, demanding.

Nichelle tapped the side of her head, her golden eyes huge. "I'm not going to forget this one." Her skin shined from the day's heat, or it might have been the excitement as she waved air on her face to cool down. "Man, that was a tough one."

"Well!" Tracy shouted. "What was it?!"

"I wrote a script to build permutations of names and dates, and injected things like ampersands and commas and hyphens... stuff like that." She showed a script on her own laptop. I tried following the lines of code, and while the words made sense, most of it was beyond my comprehension.

"Ah-hem!" Tracy said with emphasis.

"The one permutation that worked was a combination of Rourke Hospital, a hashtag and the date of your daughter's kidnapping."

"The kidnapping. Same as the security code on his car door," I said, thinking it an obvious part of the password. "Nichelle, that was a great call!"

Tracy motioned to her laptop sitting next to Ronald's, and asked, "Can you make a copy of the hard drive?"

She dug into her backpack to pull out a bundled cable. It was white and beige and snaked through her fingers like a spaghetti noodle. "For sure." Nichelle dipped her head, seeing the hospital entrance ahead. She pulled battery packs from her backpack next, saying, "I'm not leaving anything to chance. I've got power and I've got access. I'll create an image of his drive."

"Good," I told her as Tracy cornered the curb, rubbing her rear tire with a scrape. "We'll do the interview while you get that done."

Nichelle wiped her brow and sucked on the end of her water bottle as Tracy shifted the car into *park*, the front of it lurching. "Just make sure to leave the windows cracked."

I wanted to go back to the station and sit down with Ronald's laptop and see what he was up to. But I played it safe, leaving Nichelle to create a backup now that we had the access. Knowing how Nichelle worked, I was sure she'd create a backup of the backup. We'd both learned to never trust hardware when a case hinged on its use. With her help, I'd have my time with his data and would see what Ronald's online persona, *Ahren*, was working on. I'd search for my name, *Aleria*, to get started, and to see if he was Ahren as I believed him to be.

The hot and humid air turned cool as we entered the hospital administrative building, our footsteps a hollow echo. We were the only visitors in the lobby, alone with the guards and receptionist. I eyed the high ceiling, their corners, finding the cameras, a red light blinking on the top of them. Something told me Jimmy Rush was watching and that he'd be down in a minute to greet us.

"It's quiet here today," Tracy said, hoisting a bag slung over her shoulder as her gaze darted around the empty space. Her study settled on the reception area, the security guards' faces unchanged since the last visit. "It feels like a museum in here."

"Or a mausoleum," I said, raising an eyebrow.

As I spoke, a burly woman in her sixties, maybe older, appeared from the elevators. Dressed in beige-colored blouse and dark slacks, she wore heavy jewelry which bordered on gaudy, but the pieces expensive. The identification badge around her front, and the way the security guards adjusted themselves mildly, told me we were meeting Jimmy Rush's boss, or possibly someone even higher in the ranks. "Who is that?"

"I don't know," I answered, extending my hand as the woman came to us, high heels tapping the granite. With her arrival came the powerful smell of perfume, a throwback to when I was younger, my grandmother suffocating me with hugs. When her hand was firmly in mine, I said, "Ma'am, Detective Casey White, and my colleague, investigator Tracy Fields."

"Welcome to Rourke Memorial Hospital, my name is Laura Stillwell," she said, her pink lipstick pasted on thick and leaving a mark on one of her teeth. "I am the medical director of the hospital, and understand you're investigating the death of Violet Gould?"

"Murder, ma'am. It was murder," I said sharply, her eyelids batting at my word like they were flies.

She looked around, making sure we were alone, her head tilting with concentration. "Yes, of course. But could we walk and talk, my office would be best."

"That's fine," I told her while entering the elevators, the doors closing. The doctor eyed the elevator panel, saying nothing as the elevator doors opened. I got the sense she'd say nothing else until we were in her office. I traded a look with Tracy, seeing she sensed the same. While I'd thought Jimmy Rush's office was grand, the medical director's office was a penthouse, complete with kitchenette and bath and the largest mahogany desk I'd ever seen. Windows faced the beaches and ocean, while shelves lined the other wall and carried diplomas and certificates and pictures of her family. In one of them, what looked like her husband and son stood dressed for the slopes in front of a snowy mountain behind them. "Snowboarder or skiing?"

"I like to ski," she said, coming to my side and taking the picture. Her expression warmed as she tapped the glass, adding, "My son there, he's the snowboarder. He was good too, went to nationals and could have made the Olympic team."

"What happened?" Tracy asked, her face bright with admiration, impressed by the woman's office.

The medical director's face emptied and turned cold. "It was a bad fall." She put the picture back on the shelf, her stare remaining. "It didn't seem like much at the time, but when he didn't move —" She cupped her mouth.

"I'm sorry," Tracy said, glancing at me with a look of feeling bad having asked.

She blinked rapidly with a shake. "Brain injuries. Awful." Her gaze went back to the photograph as she centered it on the shelf, and muttered, "He's never been quite right since."

"I am sorry to hear about your son." She glanced at me, acknowledging my comment. Her look was so familiar. I'd known what it was like to lose a child. I've known what it was like to hold on to the hope of them still being alive, and the nightmare of wondering if they were dead or alive. But I've never known what it must be like to have an injured child, a catastrophe that changes them forever, and steers them away from who it was they might have become. "The investigation," I said, eager to continue.

She dismissed the memory, her face warming again as she asked, "How can I help?"

"As I was saying, there's been a second body identified. A woman named Janice Stephen."

The medical director slowly rocked her head, gold earrings dangling. "I'm afraid that name isn't familiar to me."

With her words, Tracy handed her a sheet of paper. On it, I had printed the hospital identifications of both victims—courtesy of Jimmy Rush. The medical director's brow rose with acknowledgment. "Mrs. Gould I knew well. Many years actually." She tapped the printout, lips curving. "But as for Ms. Stephen, I'm afraid I don't recall the person or the position she held."

"We'd like to investigate the NICU and PICU where both women had worked," I said, asking without asking, my tone carrying insistence. "That would include the patient charts from the times they were working."

"Of course, you can discuss with staff in those department," she said, hands clasped tightly against her chest. "But the patient charts? I'm afraid that's not possible."

I gave Tracy the opportunity to answer. Tracy saw my gesture and stepped forward. "In working with the Stephen family, we learned Janice was a medical student, your hospital is associated with her school and she was doing rotation in the NICU as well as Labor and Delivery."

"That sounds common," she said, commenting, "this is a teaching hospital and we have medical students passing through on rotations all the time."

"We learned that Janice was fond of working late. That she sometimes worked through the night to care for the babies in Neonatal Care. Janice believed human contact, even her voice, was enough to make a difference to help the premature babies."

"And you are looking for?" the medical director asked with indifference. She flicked her fingers, adding, "I'm sorry, but I don't understand where the patient charts connect. All patient records, including medical charts, are private."

"Correct. They are considered private. However, this involves a criminal investigation—" I began to say. She waved her hand, cutting me off.

"Yes, yes, yes! I am aware," she said, annoyed by my response.

A look of resignation appeared as she understood she had no argument. She sighed. "So, you want access to patient charts. Any particular ones?"

From the corner of my eye, I saw Tracy's reaction. We had an opening to see what Janice Stephen had found in the charts. "The ones kept while the mothers are in Labor and Delivery?" I asked, playing ignorant to the internals of the hospital's workings.

"And the babies in the NICU?" Tracy added, following my lead.

"How far back?" she asked, drumming the tips of her fingers across her phone. "There's a potential problem."

"As far back as possible," I answered, offering no dates that could be used to put parameters on our search.

"Well, we used to keep the patient charts hanging on the door or at the end of the hospital beds, but we transitioned to an all-digital system a year ago and now we use tablets to keep the charts." As she explained, she shook her head. "To get what you want would require the IT staff to identify the patients you'd want to review and then filter them."

"You said a year ago?" Tracy asked. "That's when you converted patient charts to digital?"

"That's right," the medical director answered, moving to the window and staring into the sun, her face turning white and showing scraps of makeup, some of it penciled out of place.

"Ma'am, we believe Janice was murdered three years ago," Tracy said, following her to the window. "She disappeared one night from this hospital."

The woman put her hands behind her back as she regarded Tracy's words. "You'd need the old charts—" she began to say, her voice soft as she thought through it. She faced Tracy, answering, "I'm afraid they may have been destroyed due to the privacy laws and all."

"Really?" Tracy said, disappointed.

A brief look of satisfaction came to the director's face. I recognized that she was playing ignorant and had seen enough.

"Surely you have a retention policy for legal purposes—" She peered at me, an eyebrow rising. A person doesn't get to this level and this status of her career without knowing a thing or two. "—to cover defense positions for malpractice lawsuits?" I asked. She turned back to the window, the satisfaction gone from her face. "What is the hospital's retention policy?"

"Probably more than two years," she answered gruffly. "But I'd have to check with legal on that."

"In the meantime, I trust you will direct us to the location of the existing patient charts?"

The woman returned to her desk, her body swallowed by the large brown leather chair as she sat down. A gush of air hissed from the thick padding settling. With her eyes leveled on me, she picked up her phone and dialed, her long fingernails scraping the buttons. In that time, I don't think she blinked. Not even once. When someone on the other end picked up, she put the phone on speaker. "Carl!" she shouted, and explained to us, "He's older than time and his hearing has been bad since Clinton was in office."

"Yes... yes this is Carl," an answer came through the speaker.

"This is medical director Laura Stillwell—"

"Hello! Hello," he said, raising his voice. "What... what can I do you for?"

"Carl, I am sending two investigators to you—"

There was a ruckus, a clamoring, the man shuffling the phone, or dropping it. Maybe both. "Two investigators, got it!"

"Please provide any assistance they need in reviewing patient charts from the medical records storage."

"Charts?" he asked. "Are those the ones we—"

"Carl!" she said with a shout. "Assistance. Do you understand!"

"Understood," he answered, hanging up.

"Where can we find Carl?" I asked, texting Nichelle to join us. I got the feeling we'd need the help.

"Basement," the medical director answered dismissively. Her

focus shifted to her computer. Without looking back, she added, "I'm sure Carl will take care of you."

"Thank you," I said, staying cordial. I heard Tracy thank the woman too as we exited her office and went to the elevators.

"She seemed nice," Tracy commented, her naivety showing.

"She's hiding something," I told her, thumping the elevator button marked with a letter B.

"Really? You think?"

"Don't have to think. I could smell it on her."

EIGHTEEN

The elevator doors opened to a hallway of fluorescent lights and chalk-white walls and floors. Though we were in the basement, the brightness had me narrowing my eyes until they could adjust. Unlike the ever-present scent of antiseptic riddling the hospital halls, the basement was odorless—no mustiness or damp stench I'd expect like that at the station. Nichelle had joined us for the elevator ride down, leaving Ronald's laptop locked in the trunk of the car, but having brought hers along. She also brought her bag of tricks, a slew of IT hardware tools adapted for criminal investigations. Tracy stayed too, bringing her laptop to help piece together a connection between the victims and the hospital. We hoped the answer was hidden somewhere in the patient charts.

Carl was waiting for us. I didn't get a last name but didn't expect to need one. He stood over six feet, but the hunch in his back shortened his stature a few inches. With black and graying hair hanging over his ears, the top of his head was receding to a fine point. He wore blue coveralls, soiled on the knees and elbows as though he'd been crawling. His glasses were thick beyond thick, the *bottoms of Coke bottles* we would have said when growing up. And his mustache was kicked straight out of the seventies, his upper lip hidden beneath it.

"You them people they send?" he asked, mustache bouncing.

"Carl?" I asked, even though his name was written in cursive red lettering on his work shirt. "Yes, we them people."

He tilted his head back, mouth slack as he focused a moment on each of us while jiggling a large keyring slung from a belt loop. "Want the old records or the like?"

"Yes," I answered, noticing the hallway was free of eyes. No security cameras. "The records, or the like would be fine."

"Welp," he said, wiping his sleeve across his mouth. "Got a heck of a load for ya if you got the time."

"Lead the way," I said, eager to get started. We were well past noon on a Friday and I had no idea just how much work we might have bitten off. Carl waved for us to follow, his left leg shorter than the right, his shoe's sole thickened an inch to compensate. His gait echoed with a clip-clop while Tracy and Nichelle walked along looking at their open laptop screens, trading glances and making comments.

"Did you guys find something?" I asked.

Nichelle peered over her laptop. "Maybe? But I'll need to confirm."

"Can you give me a hint?"

As Carl led us down the hall, I took to the space next to Nichelle, her screen showing court documents. It was official paperwork for a limited liability corporation, an LLC. The paperwork showed it had been filed with the same county as the hospital. "This is for a company on the boardwalk. They've been in business the last twenty years."

"A boardwalk stand?" I asked, wondering how she made the leap from investigating the hospital to finding a company on the boardwalk. "What kind of business is it?"

She clicked her mouse, another court filing appeared for another business in the Outer Banks. "I found a couple of them so far. They are cash-in-hand type stores, including one of the Quick Marts where we get coffee."

"My Quick Mart?" I asked, the small shop being a regular stop on my way to the station. I touched my chest, feeling as though the case had just made the leap to a personal touch.

"That's one of them."

"What's this got to do with—" But I never finished, Nichelle scrolling to the space at the bottom where the signatures were placed. On her screen I saw the names Jeb Gould and Dr. Benjamin Sully. "Mr. Gould and the doctor."

"There might be other partners too," Tracy said, pushing her screen forward with instructions about forming an anonymous LLC. "Those are the only two names we found."

"What are they doing in business together?" I said, asking aloud. "Mr. Gould was convinced his wife was having an affair with Dr. Benjamin Sully." I spoke in a low tone. Carl was many steps ahead of us now.

"What are you thinking?" Tracy asked. "Do you think he would have lied about an affair to throw us off?"

I shook my head, unsure why he'd make up a story about an affair. "Can't say, but I think we've got an interview with him in our future."

"You guys coming or what?" Carl yelled from the end of the hallway, his hands on his crooked hip as he waited. I didn't realize we'd stopped walking midway, the three of us standing in the middle of the long hallway. "Cafeteria closing soon. Today is fish sticks and the mac and cheese."

We rushed along, feet shuffling, the rubber on our shoes screeching. "Sorry, Carl, we're ready," I told him.

From his belt loop, he jerked the keyring free, a hundred of them jangling as he sifted through them and found the key to the door. "There you are," he muttered, unlocking the handle of a gray steel door with letters painted in golden-yellow, spelling RECORDS. As it slowly crept open, a sliver of black appearing in the crack, he faced us and centered his heavy glasses. "I need to eat, but I'll be back." He made like he was hitching a ride on a highway, saying, "What's in this room, stays in this room. Understood? Them instructions come from upstairs."

"Understood, Carl, and thank you."

He headed back to the elevator, every step having a distinctive thump. Nichelle and Tracy stared into a void, the room as black as ink.

"Guys, you look like we're about to enter a funhouse."

Nichelle tipped her chin. "You go first."

"Yeah, you first," Tracy added.

"We just need some light," I told them, turning on my phone's flashlight, their nerves contagious enough to give me the willies. The room was dark, and the overhead fluorescents in the hallway were unable to shed any help for me to see the floor inside. My phone's light managed to show a bare concrete floor like the parking garage. I felt for a switch, finding a handful of cobwebs instead. A sudden scuttle of legs running across the back of my hand made me jump with a yelp.

"What is it?" Nichelle shouted.

"Small spider," I said, my fingers landing on the switch.

"Nope. Nuh-uh."

"Come on, guys," I said, flipping the switch. "Let's get to work."

I shoved the door open, the light flickering as the overhead lamps ticked and warmed until they were solid. "Oh shit!" Tracy exclaimed, the three of us entering. The room was like our station's storage where case files were archived. Gray and black shelves were assembled in rows, a dozen or more reaching the furthest wall. Each of them stood as high as the ceiling, twelve feet from the looks of them. Their depth filled up to the far wall opposite us, which was twenty feet, maybe thirty by my guess. Every available inch of shelving was covered in cardboard boxes, a single eight-and-a-half by eleven-inch sheet of paper listing a department name and set of dates on each one. There were signatures as well, just as we do with evidence to show a chain of custody. "We're going to need help. A lot more help."

"From the looks of it, I'd say the hospital's retention policy is forever," I commented, walking the line in front of the shelves, trying to do the math in my head and come up with a count of boxes. Behind me were two computer stations and one of the biggest copy machines I'd ever seen. This room must have been a temporary setup, the standing paperwork ready to add to the new system the medical director had spoken of. "Guys. It looks like they were starting to convert the files to digital."

"Whoa!" Nichelle went directly to the copiers and workstations, her face bright with delight. In true form, she went to the backside of them, finding the connections to their network so she could jack in her laptop and do what it was she did best. "These are way impressive!" She held up a cable, adding, "And they've got like fiber terminating right at the wall. There's a media converter here!"

"Okay. And that's good how?" I asked, understanding enough to tell me the network connection was decent.

"It means they're transferring seriously large amounts of data," she answered. "Like you said, they're converting these records for online use."

"Afterward, the hard copies are thrown away?" Tracy asked. She stood in front of two floor-to-ceiling shelves, signs on the endcaps. She read them, "Incineration."

"Burn bags," I said. "Once scanned, they have to make sure to destroy them and protect patient privacy."

"Where do we start?" Tracy said.

"We want to review charts dated around Janice Stephen's disappearance," I answered.

Tracy pulled a box, showing it to us and saying, "Or we could review all the NICU, PICU and Labor and Delivery files."

"Possibly. But I'd be afraid there's too many." I went around the back of a copier, seeing the fiber connection and what Nichelle called a media converter which had the network connections I was familiar with. "Nichelle, how about reaching out to Jimmy Rush, tell him about our being given access to the charts for NICU, PICU and Labor and Delivery."

Nichelle knew where I was going and plugged her laptop into

her phone to use it as a hotspot. "I'll ask for temporary credentials so we can review what's already been digitized."

"Exactly," I said. "It's an open investigation. He'll contact the medical director to clear it, and then you can plug directly into the hospital's network."

"While she's doing that, we'll search the paperwork," Tracy said, gazing around her at the boxes. "Focusing on Janice Stephen's shifts."

I fixed her a look, seeing the reservation about the work in front of us. "We go old-tech while Nichelle goes new-tech." I put my hand on Tracy's shoulder as we sized up the work, assuring her, "We only need to review a small range."

"What's Nichelle going to search in the archives?" Tracy asked.

"Good question," Nichelle said. "What do you want me to search for? Just the charts that Janice Stephen worked?"

"Start with that, but we'll want a bigger scope than that," I answered.

"How much bigger?" she asked slowly, cautious of the workload.

I clarified. "Let's work multiple angles. Janice told her parents that she found something in the patient charts. So we do need to analyze as many as we can."

"So... what are we actually looking for?" Tracy asked.

"We might not know until we see it. For example, is it possible for us to identify a hospital employee who'd worked the same shifts as Janice? Maybe even worked the same patients with her? That could lead to our killer."

"And if we don't find anything conclusive?" Tracy asked.

"Then we'd shift concentration to the patient data itself and search for anything that seems... off."

"Like... anomalies?" Nichelle looked confused. "There's just so much."

I made a suggestion that would help. "What if we compare the data to national averages? List the differences?"

Tracy nodded. "Could there be something in the patient charts that's drastically different from the expected."

"Yes. Start by including everything a hospital reports on." As I spoke, I dialed my phone, expecting the day was going to take us into the night, and possibly the weekend too. "If any of the data sticks out or feels strange, I want to know what it is."

"What are you going to do?" Tracy asked, curious who I was calling.

"I'm ordering food. A lot of food," I answered. "I'm asking Jericho to bring it, and to pick up Emanuel and your IT folks while he's on his way. We're going to need the help."

NINETEEN

In the hospital basement there were no windows and no clocks on the walls for us to see the hours and hours pass by. The work moved quickly, with us wanting to stretch the day as far as we could. I was tempted to ask the team to work the weekend, but couldn't bring myself to do it. A late Friday night was what I got, and the team rallied to work it.

Jericho joined in the evening efforts, contributing a never-ending flow of coffee, soda, and food. He also participated in the box-to-box searches for all charts involving Janice Stephen. When we came across some NICU charts with Violet Gould's initials, we extended our search. When Gould's name kept appearing, a faint hope glowed deep inside me like a warm ember. But I needed a soft breeze to fan the flame and bring it to life.

I'd started searching the PICU charts, seeing if any involved a three-year-old girl, a Jane Doe. What if one of the boxes contained a clue about Hannah, Violet Gould bringing my daughter's fevered body into the hospital? But it wasn't long before we discovered that none of the records were older than seven years. Hannah's last appearance on video had occurred years before that. The pool of charts we had to work from was too shallow to have anything about my girl. The inkling of a flame I thought was there, had gone out.

To help with the task, Nichelle's small crew from the station's IT Department joined us. It was a staff she'd been overseeing to take care of the station's daily chores while she shifted to crime-scene investigator. From the looks of them, they could have been straight out of high school—a hodgepodge of computer and glee club leftovers. But with them, they brought Nichelle's high-quality smarts and boxes of tools for us to use. There were denim bags slung from their shoulders, filled with portable scanning hardware, fused power strips, network switches and cables, and enough extension cords to light up a city block. Nichelle had trained them well, and the area around the commercial copy machines turned into a work-hub, the boxes carried in, scanned, marked as completed using a Post-it, and then returned to the shelf it came from.

While the IT team breezed through box after box, I worked with Nichelle and Tracy, the three of us using the scanned results to search for any names that occurred repeatedly. We centered on Janice Stephen and Violet Gould. While I'd already shared I had little confidence in the idea of a serial killer, we would do the due diligence to rule one out. And while we scoured the charts for names, we were building a hefty data store.

"How's it going?" Jericho asked, bleary-eyed and looking to pack it in. He nudged his chin toward the door, saying, "I've got to get up for a morning shift in a couple of hours."

"Thank you," I said, throat crackly and dry which made my voice hoarse. I looked at the table of drinks and food, appreciating everything he brought to help. "I'll see you at home in a little while?"

He planted his lips on mine, keeping the kiss short, when a knock on the door came unexpectedly. It was nearing two in the morning, and I wouldn't have expected anyone from the hospital.

Standing in the door frame was a doctor with wavy gray hair, a deep bronze tan on his face and hands. He had brown eyes and was of average height, his build small. On his lab coat, the stitching read the name "Dr. Sully," but I think I knew who he was before that. I made sure my badge was showing as I went to greet him, Jericho following. "Dr. Sully," I said, extending a hand. He offered his in return, his fingers soft with nails polished clear. "I trust the medical director filled you in on the criminal investigation?"

He narrowed his eyes as he craned his neck to see beyond me, answering, "She did." Jericho moved casually, blocking his view so that he'd have to work with me. His focus came to me, face scrunched with concern as he waved a hand, pointing toward the shelves. "These are private patient charts. But I can see you are scanning them."

"A few. It's to help us determine if there was any connection between the recent victims," I answered. Of the thousands of thin sheets of paper, there was no knowing how many would be turned over to the district attorney. There actually was no knowing if it would even come to that.

"I think the hospital lawyers might have issue with your copying privacy data," he said, arms crossing as he planted his feet, his lips narrowed. "These charts are also scheduled for incineration."

"These are now a part of a murder investigation, which is all we need to review them." I handed him a card, holding it between us as he assessed whether to take it or not. "You can have the hospital lawyers contact me directly. If needed, we'll make sure to delay the destruction of the patient charts."

Dr. Sully took my card and tucked it away in his shirt pocket. "I'll do that." His expression changed then as he raised his hands and painted me a fake grin. "Whatever we can do to cooperate with your team."

"Perhaps you have a few minutes to discuss Violet Gould?" I asked, wanting to question him about the parking garage.

He held his arm up, a stylish gold watch flashing in the light before it slid beneath his sleeve. It was the kind that said money, the same as his shirt and slacks and shoes. "I've got a shift—"

"That's fine, I'll walk you to the elevator," I said. The distance back to the elevator doors would buy me a couple of minutes. The paper shuffling and the whir of scanning motors became muffled as I led the doctor out of the storage room. "We believe we have security footage showing Violet Gould's last minutes before her disappearance."

"I told the police this already. Her last shift was with me," he answered, walking ahead of me. I purposely slowed my pace, Jericho doing the same which forced the doctor to wait without appearing rude. He peered over his shoulder with a look of impatience. "We worked the NICU that evening."

"When did you last see Violet Gould?"

The doctor pushed his fingers through his hair, the waves tumbling into place effortlessly. "That'd be the end of shift, an eleven to seven."

"You saw her last inside the hospital?"

The doctor paused to think and rested an elbow in his hand as he tapped his chin with a finger. "It was the parking garage I believe," he answered, then gave me a nod. "Yes, we had a discussion that wasn't hospital related."

"Is that right?" I said, finding something to dig into. "What was the conversation about?"

Brow raised, widening his brown eyes, he lifted his hands, answering, "I'm assuming you saw the security video, and saw that it was a, how should I say it... a heated discussion."

He knew the video I was referring to. "Yes. We did see the video," I said, deciding to make it clear we knew about the argument. "All of us viewed it. I believe we'd all agree the discussion was more than heated. To us, it suggested an argument."

He made soft kissing sounds while shaking his head and then sucked a breath through his front teeth. "Emotional yes, but I would not call it a fight."

"Was it an argument about a patient?" I asked, continuing to state they'd argued.

His face turned red, his eyelids closing subtly with a glare before returning. "Again, it was a discussion. It was not a discussion relating to the hospital which is why we decided to take the conversation outside."

"Because it would have been inappropriate to have inside the hospital?" I asked.

"Inappropriate. That is right." He glanced at his watch, gaze moving to the elevator doors. "I must leave. I have rounds—"

"Was it about the business relationship you have with her husband?" I asked, his attention snapping back to me. His gaze fell to the floor, lifting the tip of a shoe, a casual suede penny loafer. Expensive, like his watch.

When he looked up again, Dr. Sully gave me a hard look with a mix of surprise and disbelief as he considered the question. "Yes," he said flatly and continued to move to the elevator. "It was about one of the employees who'd been caught stealing from the register."

As he thumbed an elevator button, its bell ringing, I hurriedly asked, "A name, please?"

Confusion popped on his face. "Whose name?"

"The employee," I answered. "We'll want to corroborate your story."

He shook his head, his lips turning down. "I only involved myself on the business side." The elevator door opened, his rushing inside and spinning around to see if I'd follow him. Before the door closed, I stopped it with my hand.

"But you knew about the stealing?"

"Violet told me and asked what I'd want to do about it," he answered impatiently, his gaze narrowing on my hand. When he saw I wouldn't let go until he said more, he answered with a sigh, "The personnel side was always handled by Jeb, I'm just an investor. Now please, I have rounds."

"Just one more question. Can you tell us the nature of your relationship with Mrs. Gould?"

With that question, Dr. Sully lowered his head with a slow shake. He muttered, "Old jealous fool."

"What's that?"

"Jeb's been talking about an affair again?" Dr. Sully asked. He crossed his arms, adding, "In this hospital, Violet and I are co-workers."

"And outside of the hospital?"

"Business partners." He held up his phone, indicating he was getting a text. "The same as we've been for twenty years."

"We'll be in touch," I said, freeing the elevator doors, Dr. Sully rushing to text someone as they slid closed. When he was gone, I turned to Jericho and asked, "Did that sound reasonable to you?"

Jericho wrinkled his nose as though a foul stench had slapped him in the face. "I saw the video. That was no argument about a kid pocketing a few dollars from the cash register."

"Nope. I didn't think so either," I answered, jabbing the elevator button for Jericho, wishing I could go home with him. But I had work to do. I had a team to support. I gripped his arm, giving it an affectionate squeeze as he boarded the elevator. As I waved him goodbye, I told him, "But I am going to find out what it was about."

"I know you will," he said, disappearing behind the doors.

TWENTY

Though it was early morning on a Saturday, the team continued the labors of the day before. We'd collected data from the patient charts, Nichelle counting the size in gigabytes. I got the approvals to keep Nichelle's team running, fueling them with energy drinks and whatever else they craved. When scanning dates for Janice Stephen was done, they started at the beginning with the first box and scanned the next batch of charts. We broadened our search to all seven years of data. Nichelle put on her programming hat, amassing the data into a consumable form for us to analyze and scrutinize. Beyond Violet Gould and Janice Stephen, what else would we find hidden in those boxes? If there was some sort of anomaly, we'd uncover it.

Tracy, Emanuel and I left the team working that morning to make our visit to Mr. Gould. Like the volume of chart data being collected, there were questions growing, a heap of them around the Goulds' relationship with Dr. Sully. With my turn signal clicking, we turned onto a road stretching south. As we drove, the distance between the homes increased, the size and grandeur of them becoming more luxuriant. When we reached the Goulds' address, we were met by a gated entrance with security cameras and an access keypad.

First impressions aren't always correct. I'd assumed with Gould's frail state, he wasn't working. I also thought his wife's nursing salary might be low. That meant there must have been significant income from the businesses with Dr. Sully. The Goulds lived lavishly in a remote beach property that had waterfront views from nearly every window. Exactly what was the extent of their business relationship?

The intercom speaker belched a static buzz, the red light blinking above the camera, the glassy lens seeing me and my badge as I shoved my arm out the car window. The iron gates made a mechanical clack as the lock released to free them. They swung open on their own, Emanuel letting out a grunt, eyeing the estate while we rolled onto the long gravel driveway.

"Some money here," Tracy commented.

"No kidding," he agreed, giving his head a shake. "Would you look at this place. My second time here and still impressed."

"Not at all what I expected," I said, navigating the circular drive, parking my car on the other side of a fountain. I stepped onto the cobblestone, a sea breeze blowing my hair around my head while I took a moment to stretch and assess the Goulds' estate. The house was at least eight bedrooms with steepled roofs covered in cedar shingles. There were countless patios and decks and stone pillars. I walked to the side where I saw flagstone paths leading to private beaches with giant umbrellas shadowing lounge chairs and hammocks. There was a cottage next to a three-car garage with two expensive sports cars parked in front of an open bay. The Goulds' son stood next to it, watching us.

"Detective?" he asked, joining us, his gaze rising as Emanuel stood up, his height dwarfing my car. "My father buzzed you in?"

"Someone buzzed us in." The Goulds' son was joined by his brother, the two identical in every way except for the clothes they wore. "We're here to speak with your father."

The second son motioned to follow him, saying, "I've got him in the living room waiting." His voice was the same as the first brother.

"Twins," Tracy commented, making small talk with the brother I'd met at the station.

They weren't much older than Tracy, and he was quick to talk to her. "All our lives," he kidded.

"Thank you for taking the time to see us on a Saturday morning," I said as we entered the house's foyer where we saw the same lavishness. The walls were decorated with expensive artwork, the furniture pristine and made of fine wood and upholstery, the marbled floors without blemish. Crystal hung from the ceilings, and small statuettes stood in the corners. Mr. Gould raised his chin when he saw us, his standing at the center and leaning heavily on his cane. I extended my hand to accept his in a welcoming shake.

"Welcome to my home," he said and led us to the living room with the help of his son. There were chairs set up and a table with a pitcher of ice water infused with sliced fruit. He took a seat in a plush couch, his son holding his arm as he lowered himself as we sat in the chairs. Although we came to ask questions, he wasted no time, and asked, "I called the medical examiner about releasing the body. They said there's some delay?"

"It should be Monday at the soonest," I answered. Swales was working the weekend too to finalize her reports for us.

"Monday," he said sadly, jowls shaking. Emanuel and Tracy sat with me, our chairs across from a leather couch with a bottle of medical oxygen. The son strung a tube beneath his father's nostrils, dressing them behind his father's ears, and turned on the canister. Mr. Gould put on a slight frown and asked, "Seems an excessive amount of time, don't you think?"

"We need to be thorough in our investigation of your wife's—"

"And we need to bury our own," he objected and jabbed the end of his cane with exclamation. "We got a right to bury my wife, the twins' mother."

"I understand your frustration, sir. Monday."

He sighed again and signaled his son. His son left the room, leaving us alone. "You spoke to Dr. Sully."

"We did. His only mention of a relationship with your wife was their being co-workers and business partners."

"He'd never admit it," the man said and dipped his head.

"Could I ask why you suspect their relationship was more than work related?" Emanuel asked.

Jeb Gould sat back, his hand shaking as he turned the knob on his oxygen canister. He looked up at the ceiling and around the room and began to answer. "It wasn't always like this. There was a time when we barely had enough money to make the rent."

"Your businesses with Dr. Sully have done well?" Tracy asked, crossing her legs as she took notes.

"Yeah," he said with a cough, a wheeze rising and turning into a rasp. We stayed still as he cleared his throat. When he noticed we were waiting patiently, he thumped his chest and said, "My ticker is done."

"Couldn't help but notice your inhaler and oxygen," I said gently, trying not to pry, but exploring his illness since his wife did work at a hospital.

"They help me breathe." He wiped his mouth with fingers that were graying, a muted blue like his lips. I'd noticed that at the station too.

"Are you waiting for a transplant?" Tracy asked, her idea leading in the same direction I was thinking. But his wife worked PICU and NICU, along with Labor and Delivery. She wasn't anywhere near the part of the hospital involved with organ transplants. "I'm sorry. I don't mean to pry."

"Pry all you want and all you can, it's why you're here," he said and forced a smile. "Yes, a transplant. I'm waiting my turn. Just hope my ticket doesn't get punched before there's a heart available."

"Was your wife involved with the transplant committee—"

He wagged his finger, cutting me off. "Everything is on the up and up." He wiped pink spittle from his chin.

"I hope you understand, we have to explore every area."

He gave me a nod and picked up a picture frame from the end

table and turned it around. It showed him and his wife, both young, their arms around one another as fireworks exploded above their heads. Unlike the man sitting in front of us, the one in the picture was healthy, his skin a warm pink, his eyes vibrant. "Fourth of July. Must be twenty years ago."

"You and your wife made a beautiful couple," I told him. A smile crept to his lips but was nestled in an expression of deep sadness. The car behind them was a beat Volkswagen bug. Their clothes were basic. There was no money in the photograph, but from the way Gould gazed longingly, there was a rich memory that was dear to his dying heart. I glanced at the art on the walls, the fine furnishings, and out the window toward the twins who were washing their sports cars. Wherever this money came from, it was new. "So back to the business with Dr. Sully. Your partnership, it does well."

Jeb let out a laugh which immediately turned into a hacking cough, the noise filling the room. Without thought, I sat next to him and picked up one of the inhaler prescriptions from a collection of prescriptions on the table. He scowled, my picking the wrong one. I selected the next one, his agreeing as I handed it to him. "Thank you," he wheezed. I went back to my seat so I could face him. He gestured around him, as if to indicate his lavish quality of life with a cursory look, and then glared at the inhaler. There was deep disappointment in his weepy and bloodshot eyes. When his focus returned to us, he answered, "Yeah, ya might say so! Just wish I was healthy enough to enjoy it more. Doesn't much matter without Violet though."

"If you don't mind my asking," I began, "all this is from a single store on the boardwalk and a Quick Mart?"

"Oh those were just the first. Wasn't long before they started making more in a quarter than I did working as an electrician in a year. I'd spend some shifts in the Quick Mart too, but—" he stopped and shifted in his seat, his pant legs rising enough to show severe swelling around his ankles. "I never saw the kind of money that was showing on the books."

"Is that so?" I said, asking, a red flag going off in my head. "Your name is listed as co-owner. Did you ask Dr. Sully?"

"I didn't get a chance." He thumped his chest as he'd done earlier and lifted his cane. "Pump gave out by the time I wanted to dig into it. Violet was the quiet force behind the businesses anyway. I was just the name used on the paperwork."

"How many businesses do you have?" Tracy asked.

His eyelids popped open a moment before settling into their half-lidded rest. "Seven now?" he answered, questioning. "The older boy, he's a business major. His mom was showing him how to run things."

"Older boy?" I asked, it being an unusual way to refer to a twin. "The one I met at the station?"

With that question came a smirk as he corrected me. "Naw. That's Ricky. He's got his heart on medical school."

"The one I was talking to?" Tracy asked.

"Charly, but he insists we call him Charles now. He'll be running the businesses now."

"You mentioned seven businesses?" I asked to confirm, thinking we'd need a forensic accountant.

"Well that's not where the big money came from," he answered, his wheeze deepening until I heard it rattle loose. He waved his hand, saying, "I'm afraid I'm going to need to rest now."

"We understand, sir," I told him as I stood. Tracy followed, her expression confused. I gave her a short nod to assure her I'd stay on point. Mr. Gould went to stand, bracing the top of his cane. I lowered myself next to him, taking his hand. "Please, we can see ourselves out."

"Thank you," he answered with a rasp, his weight falling back onto the couch. "Would you send in my boys when you leave?"

"Certainly," I said. When we were in the foyer, I peered over my shoulder at Mr. Gould and saw he'd lain his head back. He wasn't texting anyone or making a phone call.

I believed there was something between Dr. Sully and Violet

Gould. But it wasn't an affair of a romantic kind. It was a financial affair.

When we were outside, Emanuel asked, "You've made a connection?"

"I'm not sure," I answered, waving to the Gould twins. "Your father is asking for you." I didn't wait on a reply and jumped into my car.

"What's your thinking?" he continued.

"The affair Mr. Gould was concerned about. I have my doubts it had anything to do with romance."

"Obviously with the *big* money, as he called it, you think it was about the businesses?" Tracy asked.

"Has to be," I said. "A lot of it too."

"To pay for this place, it was more than just a lot of money," Emanuel said. "What I picked up on was Gould's mentioning one of the businesses."

"I caught that. What one side business could generate this much wealth?" I said, agreeing as Emanuel lowered himself to fit into the passenger seat. He rocked it back and forth, shifting it to the maximum, his knees nearly above the dashboard. When he was buckled, I continued, "But certainly not from his being an electrician or his wife being a nurse."

"Like, how much money?" Tracy asked, the reflection of her face scrunched in the rearview mirror. She shook her head slowly, adding, "Exactly how much money is considered a lot?"

"Tracy, this house, this estate. It's worth millions. Many millions." I saw the whites of her eyes as her jaw went slack. I waved to the twins as they passed my car. "Those cars over there, hundreds of thousands."

"And then there is the cost of medical school," Emanuel said, grunting as his knees knocked against the car. "Another couple hundred thousand dollars."

"*Big* money," Tracy repeated with emphasis, her phone in hand as I started the car.

"Text Nichelle to see if Ronald has anything on his computer about the businesses they owned."

"I'm on it," she answered.

"Emanuel, look into what Dr. Sully's finances are like."

"Got it," he said.

"Sent," Tracy said, her phone sounding with a swoosh.

I followed the sand-colored cobblestones that made up the driveway's path, exiting the way we entered, passing through the gated front entrance. "Any word from Nichelle on the hospital data?"

"Still too early," she said, her conversation with Nichelle continuing. "What do you think we'll find?"

I gave her a passing glance, saying, "I think we're going to find something that sticks out enough that we'll have to investigate it." The rear of my car bumped softly as we exited onto the road, returning to hot asphalt, the air shimmering. "Whatever it is, I'm sure it helped pay for all of this."

As we drove away, I glimpsed the familiar face of the medical director in an approaching car. From the pictures on her office walls, I recognized her son who was behind the wheel. The sun was facing them, putting the sunlight in their eyes, and making them squint, the car's turn signal showing they'd turn left to enter the Gould estate. Maybe it was a visit to pay her condolences. We'd learned she'd been a doctor at the hospital a lifetime ago and had probably worked with Violet Gould. I slowed with traffic, and before they made their turn, her son caught me staring. He didn't have the nurturing eyes of his mother. Instead, they were cold and unwelcome, the kind that made me look away.

TWENTY-ONE

The remainder of our Saturday was spent working from home, catching up on paperwork and reviewing the chart data. The scanning at the hospital continued well into the late afternoon, amassing a volume of data that I'd begun to believe was more than we could handle. With Tracy and Nichelle sharing an apartment, and me and Emanuel in our homes, we communicated online, which mostly involved us asking questions and Nichelle explaining how she was going to manage the data analytics. The analysis so far showed nothing unusual. What if I was wrong? What if I was wasting our time?

I drifted off eventually and dreamt of a campfire, me and the team sitting squat around burning logs, marshmallows poised on the ends of sticks, the firewood splintering with a snap and crackle that sent embers afloat. It was an evening of warm camaraderie, our sharing stories and enjoying the time away from the deadly work that we do.

When glass shattered downstairs I woke with a start, told myself that it was a dream, and that Jericho was asleep next to me, his snoring doused by breaking sounds from somewhere in the house.

But it wasn't a dream.

My eyelids were heavy and a bitter taste of ash coated my tongue. With my breathing there came a heavy ache in my lungs, my nostrils filling with the pungent smell of smoke. Immense heat hit my legs and face and arms. I realized our bedroom ceiling was glowing with the colors of the sun, the flames lapping in fiery waves, their long fingers curling with a come-hither motion.

"Jericho!" I screamed, gagging at the noxious ash, loose pieces burning bright and whimsically floating like the firefly embers in my dream. "The house!"

He got up on one elbow, a cough crushing his voice, his eyes glazed with flames dancing in them. "Casey!" he shouted in a rasp, gripping my arm as the wall at the end of our bed turned a bright white blue, the start of a flame eking out through from the other side. Before we could say another word, the wall erupted with an orange blast. Our bedroom had turned into an oven.

"We gotta get out!" I tried to shout, shielding my face from the heat.

There was a crash from above us, the ceiling bowing with a sad sag that threatened to crush us in the bed we'd made love in hours earlier. "It's the roof trusses!" Jericho yelled, squeezing my arm as we dropped to the floor closest to the window.

We slinked closely together, crawling skin on skin, wearing nothing but our underwear. From on a chair that had yet to be touched by the fire, I snatched hold of a concert T-shirt, one from Jericho's collection. As I draped it over my head and shoulders, I could only hope it wouldn't be the only survivor. I could only hope we'd survive too.

"Fire trucks," I yelled, a flash of red shimmering in the window's glass.

"Smoke detectors!" he said, coughing horribly, his eyeballs bugging from his head. "They never—" There was an explosion on the first floor and a crash of glass shattering. I peered into Jericho's face, black soot on his chin and beneath his nose, his expression wild with fright. The heat became enormous, our bedroom an inferno. "The back door. The firefighters might be venting—"

Part of the bedroom ceiling suddenly gave, plaster and lath slats crashing onto our bed, collapsing the brass frame. We crawled to the eastern wall, the hot air choking us, the thought of burning alive looming like a waking nightmare. "Jer—" I said, but couldn't finish, couldn't cough, the flames licking its lips and devouring the air. The bed erupted next, turning into a bonfire, singeing my hair and toasting my skin. Tears came with the pain, and a voiceless scream escaped as my feet and legs burned. I scurried against the wall beneath the window with thoughts of death looming.

"Cover your face!" Jericho screamed. He took the unscathed chair and heaved it against the window. I heard the glass break, saw it erupt and fly outward, the shards like bullets. The bedroom's flames seemed to disappear then as though someone had turned them off with a switch. I got to my knees. Were we saved? A sudden noise came like the sucking of a vacuum as Jericho's face emptied. He screamed, "It's a backdraft."

Without warning, he jumped on me, covering my body like a blanket, his weight crushing. The flames came with a vengeance as if seeking us out. I knew I was screaming but heard nothing except the fire's rage. The flames hunted us. They devoured the room like a tornado leveling everything in its path. I peered over his shoulder for a split second as the fire drove over us and imagined this must be what Hell looks like. I gripped Jericho's shoulders, holding him tight, my fingers scorched by the heat. I should have felt terrified, scared out of my mind. But I could only think of getting out of the bedroom. The fiery wave seemed to last a lifetime.

"Jericho!" I screamed when the room emptied, the sharp scent of char mixing with air from the window. A spotlight from outside shone through the broken glass as black smoke crept like a thief across the remains of our ceiling. "Let's get out of here!"

He moved, but it was slow. I dared to touch him and felt the first of the bubbling skin on his shoulders and back. Terror knifed my insides. Jericho was burned. In protecting me, he'd taken the heat. His voice a mere croak, he answered, "You first!"

The fire was almost gone from the bedroom, water pouring in

through the roof. The damage was done. There was nothing salvageable. That is, nothing except our lives. "Babe!" I said, forcing my voice. "We need to get you out of here!"

"Gimme a hand!" a voice shouted above us. As I helped Jericho there was a firefighter standing in the window, the top of a ladder cradling the sill, the paint on the wood blistered.

"Him first!" I said to her, demanding. I carefully pushed onto Jericho's chest, helping him back to his knees. I couldn't see well in the dim light but saw enough to want to scream. The back of his legs and shoulders were tar black. "He got burned."

She eyed Jericho, assessing him. And then her focus went to me, my hands, and feet. "You both got it bad. The ambulance is on its way," the firefighter said as she took Jericho's hand. "Sir, I got you."

"And who's got you!?" Jericho asked, trying to joke, a sign he was going to be okay. I cried a laugh, the emotions slamming into me like a bullet. I bit my lip and told myself to keep it together, afraid at any moment the fire was going to come back and finish what it had started. When Jericho was on the ladder and turned around, his eyes were wet as he gave the house he'd helped build a long look. He must have seen the look on my face and took hold of my shaking hands, saying, "Casey, we're okay."

"We are," I said, gently squeezing his in mine, my fingers burned like my toes. I took a heavy breath, inviting the humid sea air, but my lungs cramped with smoke. "Lungs hurt. We were breathing in that stuff."

"Possible smoke inhalation," the firefighter said. She tipped her helmet, water dripping. "That was a fast burner. You guys are lucky."

"Fast burner?" Jericho asked, climbing down the ladder as I joined them at the opening.

She lifted the plexiglass shield to let us see her face. "Looks like the fire burned itself out by the time we turned the hoses on it."

"A gas leak?" I asked and dared to look down, the height

playing with my head, the metal rungs digging painfully into the arches of my bare feet.

I saw the firefighter's helmet shake back and forth. "That's not for me to say, but from my experience this fire had some help."

Some help? Her words struck me like lightning. I stopped my descent and searched the street, unsure of what I was looking for. Crisp blue lights skipped across the wet pavement and brightened the trees lining the road as an ambulance and patrol car arrived. Our neighbors were dressed in their bathrobes, ogling with shock on their faces as they stood on their lawns and driveways, some huddling in groups. I looked at the parked cars, searching for anything out of the ordinary, the burns on my skin urging me to move faster. As I reached the bottom rung and planted my foot onto the wet lawn, the coolness of grass soothed me instantly.

In the distance, I heard a motor roar, the engine sucking in fuel and spitting fire from its tailpipe as it raced away. Nobody else seemed to notice it, but the noise made me shudder with the thought that this was not an accident.

Our wounds were minor. And like the firefighter on the ladder had said, we'd been lucky that the fire had burned itself out in the bedroom. We both had suffered burns, but Jericho had gotten the worst of it from the flashover in the bedroom charring his shoulders and the backs of his legs with second degree burns. That meant ointments and struggles with sitting and showering and wearing loose clothes for the next couple of weeks. But he would heal.

The physical scars would be superficial. It was the scars on his heart that might never mend. As we leaned against the back of the ambulance, Jericho hunched to guard his back, we watched the firefighters do their work, we held hands, tender and with care as first aid was applied. He said little while watching the men and women rip through his home and douse the remaining flames. I could feel the pain coming off him like heat. This had been a home he'd built with the love of his life—his first wife who'd been murdered. Thankfully, it was only the two of us and Jericho's son wasn't visiting from college. I was fortunate to have found love with him but could never replace what this place must have meant to him.

"Do you think we could rebuild?" I said gently, trying to sound encouraging. Before he could answer, a wall tumbled inward, a row of roof trusses collapsing with enough force to feel the shock cross the ground and make Jericho flinch.

"I don't think there'll be anything left," he said, choking up. He tried to hold it in, but his face was wet with tears.

"I'm sorry, babe," I told him, feeling completely empty and helpless. Every inch of the house was touched by fire, leaving it charred like our skin with heaps of tinder and shelled furniture piling onto the front lawn. One by one, firefighters carried our burnt belongings to throw them onto a smoldering grave of smoke and ash that spat into the early morning sky. It'd take the day to suffocate the last of the embers while we relocated, cleaned up, and got some fresh clothes on our back.

"Your place?" he asked, wheezing a rattly cough. He spat a wad of black phlegm onto the pavement and swiped the heel of his palm against his quivering lips. He had the face of a coal miner and looked at me harder than I'd ever seen. He wasn't just sad, he was angry, and the rage I sensed was frightening.

"Yeah," I told him. "At least we have the apartment. There's another month left on the lease."

The harshness softened then, his brow lifting with the corners of his mouth. He carefully squeezed my hand, saying, "Then I say that we extend the lease a year and go shopping. We're gonna need... aw shit, Casey, we're going to need everything."

"Clothes first?" I joked through tears, tugging on my shoulders to show him the concert T-shirt I'd grabbed.

His eyes went wide when realizing what I'd used to cover myself—a black concert shirt from Def Leppard's *Pour Some Sugar On Me* tour. "Oh, Casey! I love that one."

It smelled like fire and the hem on the bottom was singed

where the flames teased the fabric. "Mostly saved, I think we could fix this—"

Jericho wasn't looking at the shirt though. With a tender touch, he lifted my chin until our eyes locked. "I don't really care. I'm just glad you're okay." I was without words and put my arms around him, the adrenaline from the fire making me shaky. At my touch, he jumped with a shout, "Easy!"

"Crap, babe, sorry," I said, bracing his face in my bandaged fingers. I found his lips with mine and kissed him as softly as I could. "Jericho, we're okay."

"Could've been out of there sooner with some smoke detectors," a froggy voice said, interrupting us. It was the fire chief, his face familiar to me, having worked with him in a past arson investigation. A tall, older gentleman his face was creased and red and his chin came to a point. He was clean-shaven and was dressed in the formalities that came with the position. Tonight, he'd worn the gear to ready himself for a firefight if the call to Jericho's house warranted it. Through his tough exterior, Chief Brady had the gentlest green eyes. "Jericho, I'm sorry for this."

"Brady," Jericho said, the two knowing one another for years. "I'm diligent about the smoke detectors. They're powered by the house wiring and I make sure fresh batteries are in them."

"Them?" Chief Brady asked. He motioned to the smoldering pile of siding and wall struts and roof shingles. "Didn't find a single smoke detector."

"No smoke detectors?" I asked, believing I understood what had happened. Jericho shook his head, staying silent, his understanding too. Someone had gone into the house while we weren't home. They'd taken the smoke detectors. "Do you know the cause of the fire yet?"

The chief glanced at his wet boots while he thought through a response. "Think so. Back of the house. The fumes were immediately noticeable."

"Gasoline?" Jericho asked.

"There was more in the basement too. Between the yard and

basement, there was enough accelerant to burn down two houses. That's why it burned so fast and as hot as it did. We've opened an investigation, calling this suspicious," he added with a single nod.

"You need more evidence?" I asked, surprised with his mentioning suspicious. Jericho placed his hand on my leg, easing the tension.

Brady regarded my words, hands raised. "It's a formality. We know what we know, but still have to go through the process."

"The neighbors," I said. "I heard something when we were escaping through the window."

"We're already scheduled to canvas the neighborhood," he said, twisting to see onlookers still gathered on their lawns and driveways, gawking at the remains. "With video doorbells and surveillance cameras, we'll have a picture of your street painted fairly quick."

"Thank you, sir," I said, feeling bad for snapping.

He slowly blinked, a spark in his green eyes shining from a patrol car's lights. "But listen. You two are fortunate. You got out of there alive. You're going to be okay."

But we weren't okay. A dark notion stirred deep inside me with the news that this wasn't an accident. Was it someone from Jericho's past? Someone he'd put in prison when he'd been the sheriff? Or was it someone close to me? A criminal from my past, someone within recent years perhaps... or maybe in recent days? Whoever it was, they wanted us dead.

TWENTY-TWO

We smelled of soot, of ash, of spent campfires and smoldering logs. The fire and its aftermath had stamped itself onto our skin and hair and beneath our fingernails. I didn't think we could ever be clean of it. When we reached my apartment, an extra set of keys in my car, we locked the door behind us and made our way to the bathroom. I'd kept the place rather than cancel the lease, which gave me time to move my things into Jericho's house at a pace I wanted, instead of rushing and doing it all at once. I was almost done with my move too, with just a few boxes remaining packed with old clothes.

The apartment bathroom was exactly as I left it—nothing had been packed. We had soaps and shampoos and brushes and combs, even nail clippers to sweep the grime. Everything we'd need to wash the nightmare from our skin. The burns would remain though, reaching deeper than the layers of soot, lying like a cancerous seed in our souls that came with an understanding someone had tried to kill us.

I worked the facecloth and lathered soap across Jericho's bare skin, being careful around the bandaging. It was important to keep them dry. When it was my turn, Jericho soaped the washcloth and gently brushed it over my skin, across my back and down my legs. The water around our feet turned black while we washed the night down the drain. I think we'd become too tired to speak as we toweled dry and held each other until we made it to a half-inflated air mattress in the living room.

My head was heavier than I thought possible. I dared a look at the clock on the wall, a funky cat Nichelle gave me with eyes that darted back and forth with the passing seconds. It wasn't moving, its stare fixed on the patio doors. The cat's eyes must have gotten stuck at three in the morning, the batteries dead.

Waves crashed outside the apartment, which was on the beach —another reason for keeping the place a little longer. It was the middle of summer when sunrise was at its earliest in the day. With my head finally resting on a cool pillow, and Jericho's arm around my middle, I saw the first shine of the sun rising.

Sunlight arrived from across the ocean as the day warmed the horizon and chased away the moon and the stars and the black of night. We'd sleep in one another's arms, but it would be a restless sleep, the two of us tossing and turning with night-terrors that woke us every half an hour. As the first of the sleepy dreams found me, my eyelids popped opened with a question. Did whoever it was that burned down Jericho's house know where my apartment was?

I woke with a start again. I opened my eyelids just enough to see wispy smoke crawling across the ceiling of my apartment and heard the crackle of a fire. He'd found us. Whoever it was behind the flames had found us and he wasn't done.

"Jericho!" I screamed, lunging forward, my muscles straining.

"Casey! It's okay," he answered, kneeling next to me. I rubbed the sleep from my eyes, the sun shining through the curtains and casting lacy shadows across his face. He wore a Marine Patrol uniform left behind in the apartment, a short-sleeved shirt he always complained about, and the forest green khaki pants with the Velcro pockets. Seeing him dressed for work, I thought the night must have been a terrible nightmare. He braced my arms, bringing his face close to mine, saying, "I'm here."

"Jericho," I mumbled, gingerly touching his face. He was here. He was with me, and on him I saw the evidence of the night before. It wasn't a dream. I saw his burns again in the cold light of day. The side of his face was raw with pink burns, the skin blistering, a gauzy bandage covering one area which oozed and turned the white material yellow. His graying wavy hair had been touched by the fire too, especially the back, making it curl from the heat. "Oh, babe," I said, taking it all in.

"I'll be fine," he said, taking my fingers, checking the bandages on them. He kissed the top of my hand and asked, "Are you hungry?"

I looked toward the kitchen where the source of the smoke was coming from. But it was a good smoke. The kind that came alongside bacon and sausage and pancakes. This morning it also came with Tracy and Nichelle standing behind the range. I put up a hand and waved through the door, my voice caught in my throat when I saw the boxes and bags piled on the kitchenette's table. "Hi, guys—"

Pinching the tears that came, I saw Jericho wiping his eyes. "There's more in the other room," he said, inviting me to stand. Every muscle screamed at me to stay on the air mattress. I got up, hurting, and saw what he was talking about. Cardboard boxes and plastic bags were everywhere. We had food and clothes and pieces of furniture. "They just started coming... and there's more on the way."

"How did I sleep through all of this?" I asked with a mumble.

"Jericho made us stay quiet—" Tracy said, a worried look on her face. She couldn't finish and hugged me. In a whisper, she continued, "We all love you guys so much."

Goosebumps flashed over me in a wave, my heart swelling as

Nichelle joined in the hug. "I love you guys too," I said, barely able to stand it. Nichelle pulled back with an expression on her face that screamed she had news. "You look like you're going to burst."

"I think she is," Tracy said as she put a hand to her hip and wagged a finger. "And for the record, I was a part of it."

"Coffee and breakfast first?" I asked, my stomach flipping as the smell of food woke me in a way that only a morning breakfast can do.

"Already brewed!" Nichelle blurted as I grabbed a pair of sweatpants, tucking my nightshirt into the waist. She led us to a table that was set with four places, complete with flatware and juices and coffee. "It's about the hospital charts."

"What did you find?" I asked, stuffing my mouth with a piece of toast, the butter dripping onto my chin. I didn't know it until that first bite, but I was ravenous. Jericho was too, his head down and saying nothing as though he couldn't eat fast enough. "Was there a connection to Gould and Stephen?"

Tracy gave a slow nod, Nichelle joining her, the two sitting in a pair like an old married couple. It wouldn't be long before they started completing each other's sentences. They may already have started, I just hadn't noticed. "It's an anomaly, like you told us to look for," Nichelle said.

"We almost didn't notice it—" Tracy said.

"Until we checked against the statistics for the state," Nichelle continued.

"—and then nationally," Tracy finished. They served pancakes with sides of toppings, the serving bowls a donation with rings of red and orange and green. "They're from Emanuel," she added, nodding at the bowls.

"Wow," I whispered under my breath, beyond grateful for their kindness, and drank my coffee. "So this anomaly. Something in the hospital that doesn't match the national stats?"

"Pretty much," Tracy answered, eyeing Nichelle, letting her tell me what it was. She took a deep breath.

"Stillbirths. The Labor and Delivery Department at Rourke Memorial has a crazy high count of stillbirths."

I stopped eating for a moment, thinking. "How long has this been going on?" I asked, wondering if there was something environmental. Could the water in this part of the country somehow be tainted?

"We were only able to go back through the years that were stored," she answered and raised a hand to quickly add, "but that was enough to see the elevated counts."

I was silent while I poured more coffee, the heat of the pot stinging my fingers.

"Here, let me," Tracy said, offering.

"Thank you," I told her, thinking of the high stillbirth rate. "What if there was negligence on the part of the hospital and they were keeping it quiet?"

"That might explain the lawsuit," Tracy answered.

"What lawsuit?"

Nichelle rocked her head, her hair swaying with the motion. "Her name is Claudette Robbins. Only in high school we called her *Cloudy* on account of how much pot she smoked."

"And she suffered a stillbirth?" I asked.

"I called her," she said, voice edging on uncertainty since the information we were researching had come from private hospital records.

"It's part of the investigation," I said, resting her worries, even though I wasn't all that certain myself where the line was. We were in murky waters, but the truth was more important. My fork poised with another bite, I asked, "So she told you about a lawsuit? It wasn't something you found."

"Correct," Nichelle answered, filling her plate. "Apparently, there are a bunch of women that have filed complaints against the hospital."

"It's got to be negligence," I said, thinking there had to be a cover-up for the Labor and Delivery Department. Was it simple carelessness?

"Another interesting metric was about the women who had the stillbirths," Tracy said.

"There's a type?" The idea of a type was a surprise, a consideration I'd overlooked. After all, negligence wasn't blind. "What kind of type?"

Nichelle grabbed her laptop and opened the lid, a report already in the making with a chart dating back seven years, the count matching the boxes in the storage room. "The blue line is the national average for reported stillbirths."

"The red line is Rourke Memorial's average," Tracy said, the red line elevated substantially higher than the blue line.

"What about the green line?" I asked. "I can see a yellow line spiking behind it too."

Nichelle hit the keyboard, removing the blue and red lines. "The green line is the women's status. In this case, it indicates women who've entered Labor and Delivery who were alone, a single parent. The yellow line is the couples in Labor and Delivery."

"All those women were alone?" I asked, thinking the data analysis had to be wrong. "The elevated stillbirths only applied to women arriving at the hospital alone? No partners?"

"That's right," Tracy answered.

"If it were department negligence, we'd expect the metrics to be the same for single or married or couples," Nichelle added.

"And the complaints?"

Tracy leaned over and hit a key, peppering the screen with bright pink dots, their aligning to the graph's green line. "It's the women who were alone that are filing complaints."

"Did the data show anything else?" I asked, thinking there could be a higher dosage of drugs. "Something to validate the findings relating to stillbirths?"

"Postpartum psychosis," Nichelle answered.

"This line here, the gray dashed line," Tracy said, pointing to it, "see how it follows the stillbirths?"

"Almost point for point," I said. As I gazed at the chart, I realized a link. "And I'm guessing..." I said slowly, "that those post-partum psychosis cases were all diagnosed by Dr. Sully."

"Every case," Nichelle answered.

"He's an obstetrician. Were there any other doctors?" I asked. They shook their heads as I reviewed the data. What they'd achieved was more than I considered possible with basic hospital room medical records. "You guys got all this from the charts?"

"Well—" Tracy began.

"We got some help," Nichelle finished for her. "Casey, this data is solid."

My confidence in Nichelle was strong. If she said the data was good, then it was more than reliable. That meant we had an accurate recording of events that raised big questions. There was a high count of stillbirths amongst single mothers at Rourke Memorial's Labor and Delivery Department. But why? And how did any of this track back to Hannah and what Ronald was investigating? Did he come across the same data? "I need to speak to these women," I said.

Tracy nodded as she sipped her drink, cringing and muttering, "Ew, hate pulp in my juice."

"I told you to get pulp-free," Nichelle told her. She looked at me and asked, "Are you up for a walk?"

"You've got a name?" I asked, knowing she'd been in touch with one of the women. "Claudette? I mean Cloudy?"

"Nah, Cloudy moved to D.C. or somewhere close to it." Nichelle let out a muffled laugh. "Would you believe she's a politician now."

"Who else?" I asked.

Tracy looked at her phone, reading, "Her name is Maureen Henson."

"And she's agreed to speak with us?" I asked, wiping my mouth, eager to learn more.

Nichelle and Tracy nodded together, following my lead with Nichelle closing the lid to her laptop as Tracy tucked her phone away. "She works in a shop along the beach. We'll need to walk though."

"I can walk," I said, standing to take my dishes to the sink. The muscles in my legs quivered with the strain, the night having done more than put burns on my feet and my hands.

"How you feeling, babe?"

Jericho, who'd been silently taking in our conversation while he ate, sat back in his chair and pushed his belly out so it bulged as he patted the top of it, a gluttonous look of satisfaction appearing on his face. "I'm feeling full. A really good full."

I motioned around my own eye, telling him, "Get some rest, and put more ointment on that burn."

"You'll be careful?" he asked as the three of us started to clean up. "Don't overdo it today."

"We've got her," Tracy told him.

"How long ago were these lawsuits and complaints?" I asked while washing a dish.

"Maureen's was three years, and the lawsuit was sealed," Tracy answered. "But I got the sense Maureen Henson wants to talk to us."

"Me too," Nichelle agreed. "She said it was her lawyer who pushed to settle."

"What was the filing?" I asked. "Whatever the parties agreed to would be sealed, but not the original court filing."

"Wrongful death," Nichelle said as I grabbed my things to clean up in the bathroom.

As I brushed the sleep out of my hair, I commented, "With negligence, that sounds open and shut."

"It does," Tracy said, her voice carrying through the hallway. "That's when we searched deeper."

I gripped the door frame, poking my head out to see them. "What did you find?"

"About a month after the settlement, Violet Gould filed a restraining order against Maureen Henson."

"Now that is something," I said, returning to face my reflection in the bathroom mirror. "I'll be there in a minute."

With a court settlement, why would Violet Gould need to file a restraining order? Maureen Henson wasn't just a victim of negligence. She'd just leaped to the top of the list of suspects in Violet Gould's murder.

TWENTY-THREE

It was a Sunday afternoon, a day to recover from a nightmare. It was a wreck of a weekend by anyone's measure, and no amount of resting would help. I was antsy, unable to stay still, and anxious to work, especially since Tracy and Nichelle had found Maureen Henson.

The timing was perfect. Before leaving my apartment, Dr. Swales stopped in to check on us. She'd always be a doctor first and brought her black bag of medical tricks and concoctions, changing Jericho's bandaging while inspecting the burns on my hands and feet. She'd also brought me a brand-new pair of Crocs to wear, saying they'd help keep my toes comfortable while they healed. How she knew my shoe size, I'd never know. I suspected Jericho was behind it, the two trading a wink when they thought I wasn't looking. Emanuel was the last to stop over. His arms cradled a hundred pounds of goods, all donations from his friends and family. He wanted to join us in our afternoon work venture but had other obligations. Fleeting guilt came when he left to be with family. I told Tracy and Nichelle we'd push the work off until Monday, but they insisted on seeing Maureen Henson, knowing full well that I'd go without them anyway. They'd also mentioned that this was better than the Sunday matinee they had planned.

We drove a few miles north on Route 12, the Currituck Sound's rippling waters to our left, the traffic bumper to bumper at times as vacationers nabbed the last hours of the weekend in Duck, a popular Outer Banks town for tourism and shopping. Once parked, we found the boardwalk with its waterfront stores and view of the bay. The stores were inviting with their canopied entrances that put the doors in shade. The roofs were steepled with graying cedar shingles, and the siding was covered with the same. There were potted plants and trees growing six feet or more, some of them covered in flowers, the colors brilliant and attracting yellow and gold butterflies. The bay edged the boardwalk, with one end bordering tall marsh grasses. There were couples walking hand in hand, and families gobbling ice cream and other delights. Others passed the time relaxing on the alcove benches as the water's shallow surf lapped softly beneath them.

"It's this one," Tracy said as we passed a gazebo that hung over the water. I covered my eyes to read the wood sign above the entrance, the planks from an old boat painted white and blue and yellow. Tracy read aloud, "Wicks and Stix."

I pulled on the door's handle, a bell clanging as heads turned to see who'd entered. From the name on the storefront, and from the smell of melting wax, I guessed it was a candle-making operation. The store was filled with the fanciest candles I'd ever seen. The shelves were lined with the decorative wax, along with candle-making kits and hardware. There was a small gathering at the other end of the store, a woman on a platform speaking to a crowd as she dipped the beginnings of a candle into a cauldron, lowering and then raising it, the hot liquid dripping. She saw us enter, her gaze finding my badge which I'd made sure was present. She was in her early twenties, a smock covering her clothes, her hair pinned back into a tight bun, a row of small diamonds and gold across the lobes of her ears. There were matching stones sparkling in the corner of her upper lip and on the side of her nose. I turned around, saying, "Let's wait outside while she finishes."

We exited the store and sat on one of the benches, Tracy asking, "Was that Maureen?"

"I'm pretty certain that's her, name tag on her smock had the name."

"Yeah, that'd be her," Nichelle commented. "I wonder if she owns the place."

Gulls circled us, wings batting the air while they searched for a bite, waiting for a scrap of food tossed from our hands, thinking we were tourists. A small boy obliged, running from his father, coming up to us and tossing a doughy chunk of pretzel. He laughed giddily when a seagull swooped and nabbed the prize. "Nice day," I said to the boy's father, his smile interrupted when he saw my badge. I tucked it inside my blouse for the time being, the door opening, the class ending, a row of older men and women exiting. Maureen was last to leave the shop, her face scrunched with the sun beaming down from its midday climb.

"You're the ones who contacted me?" she asked.

"We are," I said, reaching to take her hand and forgetting about the bandages on my fingers. She hesitated, and then eased her fingers around my palm. "Got burned."

She rocked her head and showed off a few of her own, patches of scabby marks still healing. "Yes, I'm quite familiar. It comes with the territory." She sat at a seat next to me, Nichelle and Tracy gathering behind us to lean against the boardwalk railing. "Look, I haven't been around Violet Gould, not since being served the court order."

"Violet Gould is dead." I spoke with a flat tone, offering no emotion. Maureen covered her mouth, her shoulders slumping. "What was your relationship with her?"

"She—" Maureen started but stopped. Tears came as the young woman swayed and moaned, showing more of her emotions than I expected. "She... she was my nurse."

Trying to understand the reaction, I asked, "You were close?"

Maureen reeled back as though I'd struck her in the face. "God no!" she said loudly. Her expression softened as she sought the calm on the bay and began a breathing exercise I recognized—in through the nose, out through the mouth.

"Why don't you start from the beginning?" I said after a moment, offering her the opportunity to tell us her side of the story. "Tell us how you came to know Violet."

"I'm not sure we have that much time." Grabbing the back of the bench, her gaze still fixed on the bay's surface, she continued, "I was alone when I went to the emergency room. It was three years ago, I was nine months out of high school and my water had just broke."

"So you met Violet Gould in the Labor and Delivery Department?" Tracy asked while taking notes on her phone.

Maureen looked up and shaded the sun so she could see Tracy and Nichelle. "Yeah. I wasn't in the emergency room long. I guess it was because my water broke and I was already pushing." Her gaze returned to the bay where she followed a squadron of brown pelicans gliding, the lead scooping up small fish, the others following. "I was just a kid then. Shit, I'm still a kid."

I took a chance to show compassion, touching her arm softly.

Her stare broke, her focus returning to us. "I was alone. My parents didn't know, and Chet, well... he'd already left for college."

"Did the hospital call anyone for you?" Nichelle asked. She would use the information as a datapoint and reconcile it against the records.

Maureen shook her head. "I was eighteen, an adult. I told them not to call my parents." Her posture changed, shoulders firming. "I was contracting, about to give birth. I knew I was close. They gave me drugs, pain relief medications. Like, lots of them. I said I didn't want any, but the doctor insisted."

"Do you recall the name of the doctor?" Tracy asked.

"Sure, it's Sully. He's named in the complaints I filed."

"He actually administered the drugs?" I asked, noticing people slowing as they walked by. I took my badge from around my neck and stuffed the lanyard in my bag. We didn't need to look like anything more than friends having a talk. I wasn't speaking with a murderer. An investigation would show it, but I already knew who I was speaking with. She was a mother who'd lost a child. I knew her because she was just like me.

"No, that was Gould. The nurse. She did everything the doctor told her to do," Maureen continued, her voice rising. "It was like they were a team."

"They worked together a really long time," Tracy said, adding to the conversation, supporting Maureen to help her open up to us.

"I know," she agreed, eyes growing. "Something like twenty years."

"What happened after they gave you the drugs?" Nichelle asked.

She flailed her hands, arms raised. "I don't remember much, I was so stoned from whatever it was they gave me. That's why my lawyer couldn't do much with my case."

We weren't interested in the settlement or a lawyer's legal speak. "How about telling us what you can recall."

Her face went stone cold with a look of sadness I recognized at once. "It... it was all over. I don't remember what happened, but they told me my baby died."

The three of us were silent, giving Maureen a moment as she looked into the distance again.

"And I knew—I just knew—it was impossible. My baby was a little gymnast, constantly on the move. Even after my water broke, I could feel her inside me wanting to come out. I never understood."

"Your baby was a girl?" I asked, a tug of emotion pulling the questions from a motherly place, and not at all important to the investigation. "I had a little girl once."

"Once?" Maureen asked with understanding.

"But go on. They told you that your baby had died."

She sniffed. "They told me she died... inside me. Before she could even be born. They said that I'd no choice but to deliver her.

That was when they gave me more drugs. My head was in such a fog."

"That must have been frightening," I said, recalling when Hannah was born. It had been a fast delivery, too late for strong painkillers. I felt waves of pain, every contraction, every push, but it was for a life I was giving. My heart broke for Maureen. "I am so sorry."

"I just wish I'd been more clearheaded," she said.

"Thank you for sharing with us," I said, knowing what I had to ask next and hating that I had to bring it up. "Now, Maureen, we need to ask you about the restraining order Violet Gould filed."

Maureen paused, her breathing shallow, the color on her face matching the sun. She didn't answer my question. "She took my baby!"

"You believe Violet Gould took your daughter when she delivered her?" I asked, wanting clarification.

Maureen looked at each of us, a fierceness in her eyes as she repeated, "She took my Abbie!"

We were silent again for a moment, giving her time to tell us more.

"She... she just took her. I felt her come out of me, felt the life in her little body. The doctor cut the cord and when I reached to hold my baby, Gould snatched her up. I was woozy, I was out of it, but I know that much."

Playing the devil's advocate, thinking we had a teen pregnancy, and there was the possibility there were complications that would be difficult for a young mother to see and to understand, I asked, "Is it possible they were trying to protect you? That your baby had died of complications? A birth defect perhaps?"

Maureen responded with a hard shake. "Not with all the ultrasounds. I would have known by my second trimester."

A mention of ultrasounds was enough to tell me she was engaged with her pregnancy and with her unborn daughter. "What happened then?"

"I started to scream for my baby, but they kept saying they

were sorry, but she'd died." Maureen let out a cry, a startling cry, a vicious memory clearly taking hold of her. I gripped her arm to comfort as she wiped her face. "That's when I heard her. I heard my baby crying."

TWENTY-FOUR

"But what about the body?" I heard myself asking, the fact of Maureen hearing her baby crying taking me by surprise.

Maureen gave a hard shrug, her face filled with bewilderment. "They insisted my baby was dead, that I was imagining things."

"So... did you ask to see Abbie, later on?" I continued, knowing mothers and fathers will often sit with their child when stillborn. "What did they say?"

"That's when they called me crazy and ignored me." A fierceness came, a cold look filled with hate. "They told the department that it was me that insisted they take my dead baby away. They said it was too late to see her. But I never said that!"

"Not everyone could ignore you though?" Tracy said, questioning. "What about the charge nurse? The head of staff in Labor and Delivery?"

"Violet Gould was the charge nurse and had told the staff I was delusional." Rage beamed from Maureen's face as teardrops ran to her chin. "Dr. Sully put in a diagnosis of postpartum psychosis."

We watched as a group of older women walked past us and entered the Wicks and Stix candle shop, their stealing Maureen's attention briefly. What she was saying tied directly to what Tracy and Nichelle had found, a higher than average rate of postpartum psychosis at Rourke. Maureen might not be alone. I could almost feel Nichelle and Tracy tensing behind me, and I was sure Maureen noticed.

As the group entered her shop I asked, "Tell me what happened after they put postpartum psychosis in your chart."

She crossed her arms, defensive about the subject. "Nobody would help me. Nobody would listen to what I was telling them. They treated me like... like I was a nuisance." Abruptly, Maureen stood, telling us, "Listen, I've got another class starting in a few minutes."

I handed her my card. "We're listening," I said, locking eyes, assuring her we would find the truth. "And we're going to find out what happened."

"Thank you," was all she said, brushing our hands with hers, shaking them before leaving us. Before entering her shop, she turned back to say, "I heard my baby crying. They know I did."

The three of us were silent for the moment. The afternoon was wearing on, the winds picking up enough to make the cattails sway. Whitecaps formed on the bay, the chop increasing with the threat of an afternoon thunderstorm. It'd blow out the humidity and clear the boardwalk, but I wasn't ready to leave. "Let's walk," I said, Nichelle and Tracy agreeing as they considered what Maureen said. "Emanuel mentioned he'd come across another business venture he was investigating. Did he share any findings or what it was with you guys?"

Nichelle had her phone in hand and showed us Emanuel's face, his baritone voice sounding clearly. "I'm on. I think you'll want to hear about this," he answered.

"Do you have time? Sorry to bother you on your day off, but we could use the help," I said, the three of us lining up at a Shake shack stand.

"I can join," he answered. "The baby is asleep, and I've got chores, which I'll gladly skip."

"Well, don't let me get you in trouble," I said and ordered a malted milkshake, handing over a few crumpled dollars I'd found at the bottom of my bag. "What do you have?"

"One second while I grab my laptop," he answered, the video frame jumping, the connection spotty. We sat at a round table, a red and white beach umbrella adding shade.

When he returned, his head filled the frame of the phone. His eyes were big as he answered, "There's one business that tops all the other ventures between Gould and Sully. It's an adoption agency."

"Adoption?" I asked, nearly choking as my heart leaped with a spike of adrenaline shooting into my brain. I plunked down my milkshake, ideas forming with a sick understanding of what was going on in the Outer Banks. "So... Maureen's baby *was* alive. I think there were others too. A lot of babies."

"Like the data showed," Tracy commented, reading my mind. "They were all alive."

Nichelle waved her milkshake at us, saying, "You two have got that freaky psychic thing happening again. Care to share?"

"Big money," I said to the team. "I think this is what Mr. Gould was referring to."

"If I had to guess—" Emanuel began, a cry heard in the background. "I bet it paid for that house and medical school."

I could barely sit still, an idea of where to go with this making me bounce in my seat. "What do you guys think is going on here? What do you think Ronald and Janice Stephen stumbled on?"

From Nichelle's phone, Emanuel's face showed in full frame. He answered what was at the front of my mind, "They're selling the babies."

"Yes they are!" I answered in a near shout. "That's what happened to Maureen's baby."

"They stole her baby?" Nichelle asked, the straw between her lips, with a look of disgust.

Tracy said, "Nichelle, think about it. And then add the data we have."

"She was young. A single mother. Maureen came to the emergency room in labor. And the most important part, she was alone. She didn't want her parents to be told."

"Alone," Nichelle muttered. "These women... they were all vulnerable."

"That makes them the perfect candidates," I said, tipping my shake in Nichelle's direction. "Dr. Sully applies an overabundance of drugs, putting them into an impaired state."

"Once the drugs take hold, that's when they start talking about complications," Tracy said, continuing as she opened her laptop. She pointed to the patient chart data, adding, "We can use that as a data marker. It'll help to identify a pattern. I just need to write a query to specify the time between Dr. Sully's order for drugs, and another one for when the delivery complications are first noted in the patient's chart."

"I can help with that," Nichelle told her, the enthusiasm adding to the momentum of the meeting. She eyed the sky, her mind working through the work. "We'll have to normalize the data first though. With it reorganized, the query should be straight-forward."

"Good." I wasn't following exactly what they'd do, but if it meant more for us to use, then I'd get behind it. "Any reports you can add will support this if we take it to the district attorney."

"Once the mother is made aware the baby will be stillborn, they deliver the child," Tracy said, continuing with our summary. Her eyes were big with disbelief, the motives behind the murders involving the sale of human lives. "People pay to adopt a baby?"

"I've known couples that mortgage homes, even go into bank-ruptcy to have a child," I told her. "Black market babies. Only, Violet Gould and Dr. Sully have been able to hide their crimes behind the businesses."

"Cash-in-hand businesses," Emanuel said.

"Couples wanting a baby, desperate to make a family, pay or donate to the adoption agency to make it look legitimate. What else do you have on the adoption agency?" I asked Emanuel.

"It's called the Adopt Me Agency. It was incorporated

twenty years ago, the Goulds and Dr. Benjamin Sully as partners. There is a third party also, but they are listed as
anonymous."

"Anonymous?" I asked, thinking all partners had to be listed.
"Is there any way to find out who it is?"

"I'll look into it, but limited liability corporations can provide
anonymity to prevent it." Nichelle propped her phone against the
umbrella base, Emanuel's head jumping in and out of the view on
the screen. "There's the cash stores that were mentioned, and also
a notary public."

"They own a notary service?" I sucked on my milkshake,
thinking through the connection, the cold touch feeling good on
my fingers.

"They own a notary public office which is going to employ a
public officer to handle matters concerned with anything non-
contentious."

"You mean things like financial forms, deeds, real estate?"
Tracy asked. "Their job is to authenticate signatures for legal
forms, right?"

"Yeah, and that would include paperwork for adoptions. Let
me show you something," Nichelle said, bringing out Ronald's
laptop from her bag, the sight of it a sad reminder of where this
case began. When the screen came on, she turned it around. "Look
at the bookmarks he made."

Tracy read them aloud, "There's Adopt Me Agency, Rourke
Memorial and GSS Notary Services."

"GSS," I said, picking up on the name, and thinking the
acronym could be initials. "That might be from Gould and Sully,
along with one more partner, the anonymous one?"

"S for Janice Stephen?" Emanuel asked.

"Seems she would have been too new a colleague to be in business with them," I answered, quickly dismissing the idea. I was
certain she'd stumbled on what we'd found in the data, or
suspected something was happening on the maternity wards.
Maybe she'd asked what happened to the babies. I know I would

have. "The timing doesn't work either. These businesses predate when Janice Stephen worked at the hospital."

"Also, about the Sully family," Emanuel said, continuing to brief us. "They're loaded like the Gould family. Dr. Sully's income is in the top five percent for the state. That's high, even for a doctor. Real estate records show he'd paid for his house in cash. There's no mortgages. He has three children, they're all going to the same private schools as the Goulds' boys."

"Well doesn't that make for a tight group," Nichelle commented.

"Let's review what we know." I lifted my shake, rattling it and giving it a stir. "Janice Stephen. A medical student, worked for Sully and Gould, Labor and Delivery, along with NICU and PICU."

Nichelle held her milkshake, following my lead to take a turn. "Ronald Haskin—" she began, pausing with the sensitivity of his mention. I motioned for her to continue. She tapped the top of my ex-husband's laptop, saying, "Ronald Haskin, we have evidence he was investigating the businesses owned by Violet Gould and her husband, along with Dr. Sully and one other party presumed to have an initial beginning with an S."

Tracy sat up, a grin telling me she liked the round of review we were performing. She lifted her milkshake like it was a talking stick in a group meeting. "Violet Gould, Rourke Memorial Hospital nurse, worked many years alongside Dr. Sully. She also worked the same units as Janice Stephen, including being a charge nurse in Labor and Delivery."

With mention of Labor and Delivery, it was my turn again. I repeated the words of Maureen Henson. "I heard my baby crying... the Goulds and Sully used the notary for the paperwork, probably a trail of it involving other countries, fake orphanages overseas where they pretended the babies came from." I had an idea of how to proceed, but asked the team. "What do you guys think we should look into next?"

From Nichelle's phone, Emanuel's face showed in full frame.

He answered what was at the front of my mind, "Investigate the businesses? Particularly the money behind the adoption agency?"

"How about the FBI?" Nichelle asked. I gave her a nod as she typed up the email.

"These are cash-in-hand businesses. They must be accepting cash under the table and then laundering it through the boardwalk businesses."

"To make the income look legitimate?" Tracy asked.

"Correct. Nichelle, have the FBI bring in a forensic accountant to dig into all the businesses," I said, wondering how deep they'd have to go to unravel the tight ball of tricks that had been woven. I hoped they'd only need one loose thread. "They'll need more than one. Ask that they bring a team."

"Got it," Nichelle answered, typing to her contact at the FBI. She'd remained close to them since a previous case. I'd heard they made an offer to her too. I'd hate to lose her from the team, but she was that good and could do a lot working with the FBI. She tapped her keyboard, saying, "Sent and sent."

"What about the website?" Tracy asked, seeking a task. She didn't want to leave our Sunday afternoon workday empty-handed. That's one of the things that made our team what it was. We all wanted a hand in the investigation. "I could dig into the Adopt Me Agency's website, search its previous iterations."

"Previous iterations?" I asked, thinking I understood.

Tracy fixed a brief look toward Nichelle, answering, "Nichelle's been teaching me. Every website has different versions, older versions, dating back to the original implementation. There might be something in the past that could help."

"I like that idea," I said, thinking of the corporate side, the *About Us* pages that are often filled with pictures of the owners. "Might be the anonymous partner of their LLC wasn't always anonymous."

Tracy wrote the note down, adding, "I'll do the same for their notary business too."

"The Wayback Machine is a good tool," Nichelle said, offering a reference. "It'll have every version of the website, dating back to the first."

"Already got it," Tracy told her.

I took hold of Ronald's laptop, asking, "The drive is backed up?" Nichelle nodded. A thought of Hannah in Violet Gould's arms came to me, my asking Tracy, "When you're researching the web pages with the Wayback Machine thing, try to go back fifteen years or more."

Surprised understanding crossed Nichelle's face. She put her hand on Ronald's laptop. "Ronald thought Violet Gould did something with your daughter and the PICU?" she asked.

"I don't know. But he knew something that we don't know."

Emanuel cleared his throat. I turned the phone to face him, his saying, "Might be that we never find out what he knew."

I searched the bay, the brown pelicans returning, their formation tight as they swooped down and grazed the surface. "I know that, but we got to try."

"Or it could be that he never found anything," Tracy said, with a look of concern. When I didn't react, she continued, "It could be that he just asked the wrong people the wrong questions."

"Then we owe it to him to find out what those questions were and who it was he'd asked," I said with a commanding tone. Jaw clenching with frustration, I stood up to wring out the tension in my shoulders and back while walking to the edge of the boardwalk. A gust of sea air blew my hair around my face as the team continued the discussion, carrying the meeting into the late afternoon.

"What about arresting Dr. Sully?" Emanuel asked, his voice grating with new urgency.

"Yeah, like now!" Tracy added with raised voice. After hearing Maureen Henson's statement, hearing about her baby, the team wanted blood. I could sense it.

"We could arrest him for what Maureen said," Nichelle commented. "I mean, her baby was alive. That's kidnapping, right?"

"Guys," I said with insistence. I turned to face them. "We'll question him again for sure. But we need indisputable evidence for an arrest, and we're not there yet." When my statement was met with gazes of doubt, I added, "Think much bigger. What if he's the killer? We definitely don't want him knowing what we know." With those words came the looks of understanding I wanted to see.

"Absolutely," Emanuel agreed without questioning. Nichelle and Tracy gave a nod, following his lead, saying, "Understood."

I'd given them the tasks to move on but had left my plate empty. With the sun beaming atop the water, its sharp light bouncing into my face, I dared a look at the burns on my hands as a painful throb swelled in my feet. I knew what I needed to do next.

I had to go home to my apartment and tend to healing, the physical and the mental. And I had to do it for me and Jericho. Together, we'd check in with the fire chief to see what more had been learned about the arson investigation. Like Ronald, I feared it was my questions that burned Jericho's home. They were also the questions that were going to lead me to finding out what happened to Hannah on that rainy night when Violet Gould came upon her. Did they bring her through the adoption agency? If so, who was Hannah now calling Mom and Dad?

TWENTY-FIVE

The sun was barely a glint of light on the ocean side of the Outer Banks when I stepped outside the rear of our apartment. There was enough red and orange to light the first tip of the sky, but it kept the crashing waves in shadow as I gulped a mouthful of warm coffee. The bottom of my feet were covered in cool sand, our apartment edging the beach, giving us a year-round view of each day's sunrise. From behind me, I heard Jericho's low snore, my worries of his recovery from the fire fresh in my mind.

I shuffled my toes in the sand, the cold touch a relief on the burns which had started to heal quickly. Jericho wasn't healing as fast. The physical burns were coming along though. Less bandaging needed. Less care. But since the fire, he'd been unusually quiet. There were the phone calls with the fire department and the insurance companies and the bank. The stresses were mounting and I could see the way it was eating at him. The case of Ronald's murder complicated things. Whenever it came up in conversation, he changed the subject. It might be that it was just one more thing he couldn't stomach along with everything else that was going on in his life. I gave him room and didn't press, knowing we'd get through this. Still though. I was worried for him.

As I finished my coffee and thought through the plans of the team meeting, I felt thankful we had the apartment to fall back on. It saved us. The station and the friends we had on the barrier islands, they saved us too. This morning's meeting was my test. I was going to let Emanuel tie me up like Ronald and Janice Stephen had been tied. With the thought of it came the nerves, and the screeching call of an osprey hunting the shallow surf made me jump. If I managed to escape the ropes as I believed was possible, then my theory about the killer making this a game was true. But if I couldn't escape, would that mean I was wrong? Or would it just mean that I'd experience the same fate as Ronald? Unlike Ronald, and like the sudden move to our apartment, I'd have my team to save me.

The ropes were slack as I lay face down on the station's floor, my belly pressing against the thin carpet. I could feel the ropes draped along my back, the nylon cord somewhat tight around my ankles and wrists. The one around my neck was loose though like a necklace. Only there wasn't a charm dangling at the end of it. Instead, an arbor knot was at the base of my skull, the noose connecting my arms and legs. I held my chin up and saw the station through the conference room's glass walls, saw the feet of co-workers traipsing by without any idea of what was happening behind the conference room table. I am sure I was breaking a dozen regulations, but the test had to be done. My team surrounded me with Emanuel acting as my lifeguard in case I fell unconscious.

"You got this, Casey," Tracy cheered, the tempo and tone of her voice reminding me of my early days in school when I wanted to be a gymnast and was practicing a new vault. "Do it just like you said."

"You ready?" Emanuel asked, his long fingers holding my hands and feet behind me.

I shook my head, the cord scraping my neck. I couldn't answer yet. My hands turned clammy and my breathing was too shallow. "One second," I mumbled as my body began to shake.

"Take your time," he said, squeezing my hands and feet. "Let's talk through this."

"Okay," I said, finding his voice soothing. "Explain what you've done. It'll help me visualize."

Nichelle passed by me, my recognizing her ankle bracelet and the scent of lavender moisturizer she used. She sat cross-legged in front of me and placed her face near mine. "I'm here," she said, touching my cheek gently. She slowly nodded, adding, "I'll monitor your breathing and won't let anything happen to you."

"Thanks," I said, feeling suddenly frightened and excited all at once. "Go on, Emanuel."

"I followed my notes exactly as we recorded, what we found on the first two victims. Essentially, you're belly down and hog-tied." He tugged on the main part of the rope leading to my neck, the pull causing it to go tight. With the noose closing, my pulse ratcheted and a frantic wave swept through me, and made me kick. He let go at once, asking, "Casey? Are you sure you want to keep doing this?"

"I got this," I answered tersely, the franticness replaced with embarrassment. "I just wasn't ready. Please?"

"All right, I'll warn you next time," he said, rubbing my back where he'd pulled the rope. "The major difference from being simply hog-tied is that there's a noose around your neck. The main rope to the noose is sleeved through an arbor knot and connected to your wrists and ankles."

"Which you're holding for me," I said as he squeezed them again.

"Right. So, when I let go, you'll need to keep your hands and feet in this position so the rope around your neck stays loose." Emanuel had the arbor knot and the arrangement of the ropes memorized. He'd referred to his notes just once as he carefully arranged my arms and legs exactly as Ronald's had been. "Tell me when."

I took a deep breath and thought through the strategy I had in mind, the same one I believed Ronald had thought of. "I'm ready."

"On three," he said, Nichelle's eyes larger than I'd ever seen. She gave me an encouraging nod as Emanuel counted, "One, two... three!"

I sucked in a breath as my hands and feet were released. At once my arms fell to my side and my legs fell back. The weight of them jerked the rope leading to my neck, closing the noose. I reared upward until my chest stuck out, the response immediate, the first moments of being strangled filling me with terror.

"Shit!" Nichelle yelled, horror appearing on her face as she waved her hands to stop the exercise. I couldn't breathe, but shook my head, telling her I was okay. I bent my knees to bring my feet back to the center, and raised my arms until my hands were closer to them. The move returned the slack to the main line enough so that I could take a breath.

"You okay there?" Emanuel asked, the conference room lights throwing his shadow in front of me. I could see his arms outstretched and ready if I got stuck. I nodded and saw the shadow arms retreat. "You got this, do it like you said. Use your thumbs."

I thought of Ronald as the tips of my burned fingers brushed the heels of my feet. I wasn't able to take hold the first pass. I lifted my front upward, the crook of my back bending with a pop as I arched my body into the shape of a bowl. My fingers touched my feet again, boosting me, encouraging me to bend further and take a firm hold of the rope on my ankle.

"Casey was right," I heard Tracy say. "She's going to escape this."

Blood pounded in my skull, the pressure behind my eyeballs so fierce I thought they were going to explode. Nichelle was on her knees, putting her face near mine. I could still smell her lavender moisturizer which meant I was breathing. "Come on, Casey," she said, cheering for me.

"Mm," I grunted when I managed to get my thumb between the rope and my ankle, hooking it to take the weight and relieve the strain in my leg. But it wasn't enough. The noose tightened again as my other leg fell.

"Casey, you've gotta get both of them," Emanuel said with voice raised, his shadow arms appearing across the floor again.

But I couldn't do it. I'd lost too much time trying to get hold of one leg and hadn't considered the mechanics fully. I had to hook both ankles with my thumbs to relieve all the weight pulling on the noose.

"Emanuel," Tracy said with heavy worry.

There were starlights in my peripheral vision, flying by Nichelle's head like sparks. I pinched the rope with the tips of my fingers holding it and then saw the bottom of the conference door swing open. The floor rumbled with heavy steps, the reverberation drumming into my belly. I tried to say something as the view went black and the touch of familiar hands were on me, turning me, taking the slack from my neck.

"What!? What is this!?" I heard Jericho yell. "Casey!"

The sight of him was gray like clouds, the features of his face thin as though he was wearing a veil. The strain of trying to breathe lifted and I sucked in the air as though I'd been drowning. In a way, I had been. I'd been suffocating like Ronald, and had just experienced what he must have gone through before seeing the light of day on this earth a final time.

"I'm okay," I said, uncertain of who was in the room. My head was dizzy as I felt my front lifting up, Nichelle holding me while fast-moving fingers removed the bindings from my body. "Did I get out?"

"That's a negative," I heard Emanuel answer.

"What the hell were you thinking?"

"Jericho?" I asked. When I opened my eyes again, I saw his face, his lips tight, his eyelids narrowed in a deep frown. As I regained consciousness, I understood what had happened. I hadn't gotten free but had blacked out. I had no idea Jericho was coming to the station this morning. I went to touch his face, assure him I was fine, but he stood up, the team dispersing and leaving the two of us alone. "Babe, I'm okay—"

"You push things too far," he said, raising his voice. He'd never used this tone with me before. Never. I felt immediately defensive. I got to my feet, bracing the back of a chair, the room tipping sideways as I rubbed the ache around my neck. "Casey—" he started, but only fixed a hard look on me and then on the ropes lying across the floor.

"What?" I asked, annoyed by his objection. "Listen, I am doing my job!"

"Are you?" he countered. He peeled one of the remaining ropes from my wrist, throwing it past me like it was a dead snake. "Or are you trying to understand what Ronald went through?"

"What's that supposed to mean?" I asked, rubbing the welts forming on my wrists. Jericho clapped his eyelids shut to hold back what he wanted to say. I yelled back at him, "Tell me!"

"He's dead," Jericho answered. "It's okay to investigate his murder, but to relive it?"

"That's... that's not what I was doing!" I answered.

Only, I wasn't sure. Was that why I wanted to try the ropes? Was it to experience what Ronald had gone through? "We needed to understand if the murderer—"

"Was making it a game!" he said, interrupting. "Yeah, I know. You've told me about it a dozen times."

"I have?" I asked, not realizing that I must have been discussing the case more than I thought. I pulled the chair out from the table and sat down, guilt taking some of the strength from my legs. Jericho sat down too, rolling his chair near mine. I dared to place my hand on his, wanting to diffuse things. He didn't pull away and retuned the touch, rubbing the welt which broke the skin. "Look, I didn't mean to carry on about the case as much as I have been. I didn't realize I was doing that."

"You always carry on about your cases," he said, half joking as he delivered a criticism. "But I love to hear you talk and listen to you figure them out."

"What's different this time?" I asked, thinking Ronald being the victim must be what was gnawing at Jericho. I dipped my chin until our eyes locked. In his blue-green eyes I saw the emotion, a mix of jealousy and shame. I understood the look, it was the same one I felt whenever Jericho picked up the picture of his first wife. She'd been dead a few years now, but the love he held for her was still there. "He was my husband once. He's also the father of my child."

"I know," he said, a tiny amount of jealousy in his voice. "I guess it's because I don't know that we could ever have the same life you had with him."

Without warning, I punched his arm hard enough to move him. "Are you serious?" I asked, putting on a smile. "It doesn't matter what I had with him or what you had with your wife. It's what we have today."

He sighed with understanding. "I think when I saw you on the floor like that, it got me so—"

I touched his lips, stopping what he wanted to say. I knew the anger that'd come with it would stalk the words I'd respond with. "I'm sorry, Jericho. That can't have been good for you to see."

"Did it work?" he asked, curious of the outcome. He grimaced, adding, "From the looks of it, you didn't get the results you thought possible?"

His gaze lifted to outside the conference room. I turned around to see Nichelle and Tracy staring from just above their cubicle, gawking at us like we were show animals at a circus. The sight made me chuckle. "Like kids wondering what their parents are arguing about." I stared at the floor then, the ropes and noose sitting unfinished like the last breath I took before I blacked out. "I got my answer. The ropes are escapable."

TWENTY-SIX

Sitting across from Jericho, the slight rope burns around my neck causing a sting, I'd barely caught my breath when a call that shots had been fired rifled through the station. Radio dispatches were like ambient noise in a police station. They were a constant that went unnoticed after a while. But this time there was a name and address that I heard in the call. And it was enough to get me to my feet.

"I've got to go," I told Jericho, his stubbly face between my fingers as I kissed his lips. "We'll talk more later?"

"Yeah, of course," he answered, standing with me and following me out of the conference room. "Casey, be careful!"

"Always!" I yelled and rapped my knuckles against the tops of the cubicle walls. Tracy and Nichelle stood, their having heard the same dispatch and already packing gear for Dr. Sully's house. What waited for us there was unknown. "A patrol is already on their way!"

"I thought we were going to wait on Sully?" Tracy asked, arms elbow deep in a bag of gear.

"Until we had more evidence?" Nichelle added.

"We were," I said with surprise. "This isn't us. This is Sully. I just hope it isn't what I think it is."

We said nothing else as we exited the station and ran across the parking lot's wet pavement, the daybreak coming with dark clouds and warm southerly winds. Rain swept across my head and face as we dove into my car, got seated and left as quickly as we could. We turned right onto Route 12 and headed south past Avalon Pier to turn west when we reached First Flight Airport.

My windshield wipers grew cranky, scraping the glass when the rains slowed, the sound grating as we wove through traffic and then cut across a quiet neighborhood. There were big houses on one side and smaller ones on the other, but then we entered onto a street with a crooked sign marked "Private." The property was at the edge of Blount Bay. We knew the neighborhood, having been there just recently. Sully's residence was a couple streets from where Violet Gould and her husband called home. I drove past the gated entrance and parked my car on a crescent-shaped drive, recessed lights glowing brilliantly around a centerpiece fountain.

"You guys stay here," I instructed, pulling my badge and gun before exiting my car. One patrol was already parked and another car followed me, the officers waiting for my command. It was quiet outside the house with only the sound of running water from an ornate fountain. Red and blue patrol lights flashed silently, the officers' eyes locked on me, our guns drawn, the source of gunshots unknown.

"Anything?" Tracy asked, exiting the car, staying below the window.

"Nothing yet," I said, rainwater dripping from my chin, a distant thunder rumbling. Beyond the gated entrance was the main house with a two-story arched entrance, the indoor lights shining through windows that spanned from the ground to the ceiling. Inside, I saw every inch of floor and furniture and a stairwell leading to a second story, but there was no activity. Then came the clopping of feet on stones, footsteps of someone running toward us. I braced my gun, fingers wet. "Hold on, Tracy!"

Next to the front entrance, a woman wearing a champagne-colored silk gown and evening shoes with short heels ran toward me. Her clothes were soaked, her skin showing through the thin material, the evening gown clinging tightly, her hair draping over her eyes as she screamed, "Inside!" Tracy took hold of her arm and pulled her back to behind the safety of our car, raindrops on her long eyelashes as she repeated. "Inside! My husband's study. I heard the shots!"

"Did you see anyone else other than your husband?" I said, trying to keep panic from my voice while taking cover. The officers followed my lead, our standing behind our vehicles while another two patrols rolled up behind us. My eyes flicked over what I could see of the inside of the house, its walls and floors painted by the flashing red and blue. "Ma'am, did you see anybody?"

"No one. I was in my bedroom," she cried, pointing toward the upper level of the house, her tears mixing with raindrops. "I heard the shots coming from his study."

"Where's the study?" I asked, wanting the lay of the house before entering.

"First floor, to the right and toward the bay." Her face froze in a grimace as the fright and shock bore into her. "My husband?"

"We have you," Tracy told the woman as she continued begging us to help her husband.

"Stay put behind my car!"

I ran to the entrance, shoes kicking ivory stones between the pavers, the glass front giving me full view as I slipped through the front door quietly. The air inside was chilled for summer, my wet face and clothes making me shiver in an instant as I crossed the foyer and went to the right and rear toward the study, following the woman's description. An officer followed, his hand shaking with nerves or adrenaline, the tip of his gun swaying. I motioned for him to border the wall and cover me, his shoes making wet squelching sounds against the floor tiles. He hugged the corner of the wall leading to the doors of the doctor's study. "I'm going in."

My arms were stiff, my gun gaining the weight of a hundred pounds while my muscles trembled. I couldn't get warm, but felt the heat rise from beneath my shirt. I entered the room using the tip of my foot to shove the creaking door.

The doctor's study could have been something out of an old English bookstore. The walls were shelved and lined from floor to ceiling with books. Across the floor there were six or more bronze-colored statues standing on marble pedestals, the closest one nearly becoming a victim of my gunfire, it's figure like that of a man. When I saw the room was clear, I lowered my gun. Across from me I found Dr. Sully.

He sat in a large chair, his eyes half-lidded, his right eye drifting off-center, and both eyes filmed over with death. Though he was dead, his rich bronze tan remained. A revolver on the desk was cradled loosely in his hand. On his forehead there was a single bullet wound.

"Clear in here," I told the officer outside. "Check the rest of the house and the property."

From the look of Dr. Sully, he'd committed suicide. He'd been business partners with the Goulds. At the hospital, he and Violet Gould had been co-workers. At home, they'd been close neighbors. We suspected they were co-conspirators. And now, both of them were dead.

A flashlight in my hands, I joined the officers in clearing the residence and the accompanying building. The remainder of the team, along with Dr. Swales, arrived as we swept the grounds. There were two more buildings on the property: a four-car garage, the doors open and showing three of the bays empty, a classy Mercedes Benz in the last bay closest to the main house. The other building bordered the shore and was home to a cruising boat, the hull navy blue, the deck an ivory-white. An officer motioned with his flashlight as he peered inside the cabin, calling out that it was clear.

Inside the main residence, I saw officers mulling about, guarding as they spoke with staff. Dr. Swales's assistants, Derek and Samantha, stood outside the doctor's study by a gurney with an empty body bag. Dr. Swales was in the room waiting for me to return and join her.

"I only need to go inside and change, grab some clothes," I heard the woman in the champagne gown demand, her voice deep with a southern accent. The officer with her tried to gently coax the woman away from the house. "But they won't allow it!"

"I understand, ma'am. Can you tell me your relationship with the deceased?" I asked, navigating the conversation gently, believing she was the doctor's wife.

"Beverly," she answered, her name breaking with a sob. "Beverly Richardson Sully... I'm Benji's wife."

"Ma'am, I am sorry for your loss," I said, glancing through the tall windows to where the doctor's study was located. "Is your bedroom on the second floor?"

"Thank you," she said with relief in her voice. She followed my gaze, seeing Swales's team. "Yes. It's on the second floor and I can take the kitchen entrance."

"That way?" I asked, pointing toward the garage bays. "There's a back staircase?"

"Yes, yes," she said, shaking her head between a wave of sobs. She turned to face the officer with her, saying, "She can join me."

"Tracy, could you check the back entrance before Mrs. Sully enters?" I asked.

"I'll take them," she answered, grabbing a crime-scene kit to inspect the door to the kitchen entrance.

"Officer, please escort Mrs. Sully upstairs to get a change of clothes," I said. The patrol officer gave me a nod as a sigh came from Sully's wife. "Ma'am, we'll need to ask you some questions—"

"Of course!" she said, her face scrunching as a fresh cry came. She held out her hands, damp tissues balled between her fingers. "I... I just can't be here, you... you know what I mean?"

My heart hurt for her, the pain of her loss preventing any questioning at the moment. "Do you have someplace you can go?" I asked. I thought of the station and Alice, our station's desk officer, thinking she'd be on shift soon. "We have a place at the station you can stay and get warm if you'd like."

Mrs. Sully swiped at her face, a lock of hair flopping loose from behind her head. "My sister lives up in Kitty Hawk, I called ahead."

"We'll speak later," I said, touching her arm briefly as I faced the entrance, seeing a flash of Swales's hair in the doorway leading to Dr. Sully's body. I went to the door, meeting Emanuel as he exited his car. He'd changed since the test with the ropes this morning and was dressed in slate-colored slacks and a shirt and tie to match. He slipped his arms through a business jacket, an interview coming up later in the day, his next step in his career around the corner. I'd almost forgotten what day it was and felt a tinge of nerves for him. Nobody likes to interview, but they had to happen. "Nervous?"

"Thank you," he said, ignoring my question. "I know it was you that put me up for the promotion."

"Emanuel, you did this," I said, wanting to assure him that it was deserving. "Let me see you." I faced him and brushed his shoulders and straightened his tie. "You are going to do great. What time? Later this morning?"

He breathed heavily, eyes flashing wide. "Interview is at ten thirty," he answered. "But I thought I could help you guys here first."

"I appreciate it," I told him as we entered the main house, Derek and Samantha motioning a wave when we reached the room. As we slipped booties over our shoes and sleeved our hands with gloves, I noticed the smell of death hadn't come yet. The air from the vents was still crisp and chilled as we stood at the two-door opening to get our first impressions. I nudged Emanuel's arm before entering, telling him, "I'm glad you came. I can use the help."

"No problem," he said while I gazed into the room. "What have we got here?"

"We won't be getting that interview with Dr. Sully," I warned.

"Yeah, I figured as much." He hung his thumb behind him. "I saw Tracy with a kit."

"We need to rule out someone entering the residence."

He began to shake his head, asking, "So this isn't a suicide?"

"You tell me," I said. We entered the study. All of the lights had been turned on and the break in clouds brightened the room to show the walls covered in shelves made of dark wood, mahogany perhaps. There were iron rails carrying a sliding ladder to reach the highest of the shelves. Emanuel stepped around one of the bronze-colored statues, eyeing the figure. His gaze went up to the vaulted ceiling and a thick iron chain carrying an immense chandelier that looked to have been crafted hundreds of years ago for use in a castle.

Dr. Swales waved for me to join her next to Sully, Emanuel saying, "Look at the bullet wound."

"I know," I said. The placement of the wound was close to the center of his forehead. Usually, in suicides, people place the gun's barrel on the side of the head, nearer to their own temple. "I wondered if it was a conscious decision?"

"Conscious decision?" Swales asked.

"I mean, he is a doctor, and might have seen failed suicide attempts where bullets enter and exit the temples, leaving the victims blinded but not dead."

She regarded the question a second before answering, "Could be?"

"But then I saw enough to make this suspicious." There was a bullet hole behind the doctor in the glass wall facing the bay and the other rich estates near the water. "The window didn't shatter?"

"Tempered glass," Swales answered. "Building codes require it when the bottom of the window is close to the floor."

"That's lucky for us then," I said. "If it had shattered, it would have been harder for us to tell there was a second bullet."

"That is suspect for sure," Emanuel commented as he moved to the far side of the room to study the scene. "I'm not seeing how that hole in the glass could happen from where he's sitting."

"It can't," I answered. The doctor's shoulders were slumped and the chair he sat in had a high back. In his right hand was the snub-nosed .38 revolver. It was a hefty piece of hardware with a powerful kick given its pocket size and .357 caliber bullets. "From the doctor's position, that hole in the glass isn't possible."

"Dr. Swales," I began, moving close to the large antique desk. Its corners were handcrafted with the head of lions engraved, the surface of the desk inlayed with marble. There was a single computer screen, a keyboard and mouse, but from the dust on them, my guess was the doctor was old-school, preferring to use paper and pen for much of his work. And work there was, stacks of medical folders, their field's equivalent to our case files. In all that was on his desk, it was the revolver cradled in his hand that I couldn't break my attention from. "That's a serious weapon."

"A .38 special," Emanuel said. He came around the side of the desk.

"There's no exit wound," I commented, expecting one if the muzzle had been held against the head. I looked at the gun Emanuel carried, adding, "Even with the lower velocity over your nine-millimeter, I'd expect an exit wound. And look at his hand."

His fingers were loose, relaxed and open as though the gun had been placed there. I was suspicious of it because that's what I did: I questioned everything until there were no more questions to ask.

"This isn't a suicide," Emanuel said with firm disagreement.

"It was made to look like one though."

"Detective," Swales said, her eyes looking biggish behind her thick frames as she worked a measurement of the bullet wound. As I'd thought, behind Dr. Sully's head the soft leather chair was clean of any blood. Not a single drop to blemish the black material. She eyed me over her glasses and then Emanuel. "Confirmed. There is no exit wound."

"Didn't think so." I went around the desk, taking care where I stepped, searching the floorboards for blood or anything that struck me as odd. I lowered myself when I reached the body. There was one gray eye staring at me, the other staring at Emanuel as he worked the doorway with fingerprinting dust.

"Fingerprints?" Swales asked, stepping down and backing away from the desk. "I guess this suicide isn't as open and shut as I thought."

"Not with that bullet hole in the window behind the chair," I told her. She held her glasses to clean them. The early rain cleared, the sun reaching a height to reflect off the bay and turn her face and hair a warm pink color. "I don't believe this wound was inflicted at close range. Not with that caliber."

"Single gunshot to the forehead," she said, giving me a wink, coming to the same conclusion. She stood behind the body, and raised his head, straightening the shoulders. "This is most likely the position he was in before being shot."

I spun my finger in the air, Swales moving to the left until I showed my palm. "That's it," Emanuel said. He held a laser pointer and aimed at Sully's head.

"Derek," Swales said, her breath rapid. Derek took over for her, holding Sully's dead weight, lining up the injury with Emanuel's laser pointer. "I know the gun's caliber. There'd be far more injury if the gun had been fired with the barrel next to his skull."

"Bet a beer that barrel is not the same as the impression found in the back of Ronald's skull," I said, taking a picture.

"I'd owe you a beer," Swales answered. "This is a different weapon."

"It is," I agreed with a stir of disappointment.

She stood between the desk and Emanuel, her hands on her hips as I looked at the paperwork on Sully's desk. There was a medical file open, his handwriting and signature on the sheet facing him. Swales commented, "Do you think he'd commit suicide while in the middle of doing work?"

"No. No I don't think so," I answered, taking a picture of the top of the desk and focusing on his signature and a few lines of what he'd written down. "And not many suicides by handgun are accomplished using the right hand when being left-handed."

Her expression showed surprise, Derek muttering, *"No shit."* Swales and Emanuel looked at the handwriting, the angle, the hard slant and the way the page was turned so the heel of his hand wouldn't smudge the fresh ink. "Well, if that isn't telling then I don't know what is."

"I'm thinking that someone entered the house, the kitchen entrance perhaps," I began, surmising what happened. I went to the corner of the room where the bookshelves ladder sat at rest, thinking it was the location from where the gun had been fired.

"The killer was someone he knew?" Emanuel asked with a suggestion. "Someone he was comfortable enough to stay in his chair?"

"Or, he was too terrified to stand," I said, adding my opinion. "Whoever it was, they already had the gun."

"But it wasn't somebody familiar with guns," Emanuel said, suggesting why we had a bullet hole in the window.

"Exactly. Maybe they argued? Maybe the killer came here with this intention. Whatever the reason, they produced a gun, fumbled one shot, but then got a second one off before Sully could do anything."

"A lucky second shot," Derek commented.

I went to the desk, miming what the killer had done next, explaining, "They made it look like a suicide, placing the gun in his hand, only it was the wrong hand. That leaves us to question what they came here for."

"We can check surveillance videos," Emanuel said.

I gazed at the office, the expense of it, and saw there were no cameras. "I'll get Nichelle on it, and any phone conversations."

"He may have his cellphone," Emanuel said as he searched Sully's body.

When I knelt to search the other side, patting the pant leg, I saw the books on the shelves— and what shouldn't have been there. "What is that?" I asked, returning to the corner. The bookshelves ladder had been shoved into the corner for a reason. I climbed the first three rungs, my feet aching from the burns. On the third shelf from the ceiling sat a set of medical encyclopedias, twenty volumes, maybe more. "Do you guys see that?"

"Yeah," Emanuel answered, coming to stand next to me and hold the ladder. "Those binders aren't right."

"That's because those aren't books. It's a façade," I said, carefully prying one of the edges with the tip of my gloved finger. With a snap, four of the encyclopedia binders lifted, opening in a swing toward my face and revealing a steel safe, a dial at the center. "Whoever came here, they didn't leave with what they came for."

TWENTY-SEVEN

The investigation at the Sully residence continued into the afternoon. We found no forced entry or fingerprints on any of the doors and windows. As much as I disliked it, I left the Sully house with more questions than answers. We didn't arrive back at the station until well past the late afternoon shift, the sun nearly gone in the west, the sky already turning dark again with the moon and stars appearing. While it was late, I'd called for a short meeting, our chance to convene and review our findings.

What we knew without doubt was that Dr. Benjamin Sully had not expired from his own doing. He'd been murdered. The .38 Special handgun with two rounds fired was particularly telling. Another find was that the gun was missing its serial numbers, a metal scab in place of where it should be. The weapon was unregistered, the numbers filed, the gun purchased illegally and made untraceable. And the biggest find was the placement of the gun in the doctor's right hand, despite him being left-handed.

There were multiple suspects. My thoughts weighed heaviest on the anonymous partner in the businesses shared by the Goulds and Sully. Other suspects made the list too. But these were textbook suspects, the ones we'd question as part of the process, and then weed through them when the alibis came forward, or when new evidence surfaced. The person at the top of the list was Sully's wife, his partner in life and in marriage.

"Did you find anything else about his wife?" I asked Nichelle, my elbows perched on the cubicle wall separating us. My head was filling with typical ideas of money or jealousy. Maybe she shared the same ideas of an affair going on between Violet Gould and her husband? Or had she known about the adoption scam?

"I got a financial report but haven't reviewed it yet." Her fingers gliding across her keyboard, she clicked her mouse, a look of surprise forming as she mouthed, "Wow."

"What is it?"

"The chick is rich," she answered, raising her hand above her head. "Like old money. As in family money. She's an oil baroness from Texas."

"Is that right?" I said, interested. I looked to Tracy's desk, seeing her stooped over, her face inches away from the monitor. I'd stop in on her next to ask about the Adopt Me Agency. "Sully's wife didn't need money. So nothing to gain there?"

Nichelle gave a slow head shake as she tipped a bag of chips and shook it before emptying it into her mouth. Small crumbs danced on her lips as she added, "She is one rich lady. Her husband looked downright poor next to her."

"How about Violet Gould's husband? He's already listed as partner, did we validate his whereabouts the evening his wife went missing?"

Nichelle thumbed through notes on her phone, swiping up to throw it onto one of the larger monitors. She answered with a soft voice, speaking to herself, "He'd gone to pick her up as he'd told us —" when she'd finished, she answered me, "Other than that, he's clear. Afterward he was with one of his twins—"

There came a commotion. A tumble of a chair. A screech and holler, the sound going through me like fingernails on a chalkboard. I dropped slightly, lowering my center of gravity in anticipation of an attack. But it wasn't an attack. It was Tracy. Nichelle standing beside me as we went to her cube. "What is it?"

"This!" she yelled, but couldn't say more, her mouth open and without a voice. She eyed her chair lying on its side, shame showing briefly. I dared to enter her cubicle, seeing her arms up and guarding, rage and shock on her face, a look I'd never seen before.

"What is it?" Nichelle asked, ignoring Tracy's guarded look. Nichelle was shaken by the sudden outburst, her lower lip quivering. Nichelle offered her arms, daring to touch Tracy's hand, asking, "What is it, baby?"

"No!" Tracy yelled. "Don't touch me!"

Before we could say another word, Tracy clutched her bag and ran from her desk, leaving us confused and concerned. I heard the gate slam shut and felt my legs and feet sticking to the floor, uncertain if I should follow. "Let's look at her laptop," I suggested to Nichelle, thinking it'd tell us what got her so upset.

"I've never seen her like that before," Nichelle said. She ran her fingers through her hair while I flipped Tracy's chair over. We went to the screen, finding a page from the Adopt Me website. Only the page looked different from what I'd seen. "This is an early version."

They'd mentioned looking up web page history, their archives. "You mean an early iteration of the website."

"Yeah, different iterations get archived," Nichelle answered, scrolling the page's details, a list of testimonials from parents. "This version of the site is from fifteen years ago, but it's in pieces."

"What do you mean pieces?" I asked, feeling confused by what was on the screen. I could make out portions of it, quotes and people's names. But mixed between the quotes was what looked like computer code and blank boxes, their insides with a red X and a number 404. "What does that number mean?"

"The archive, it's incomplete which is breaking the web page. The browser is trying to show it as it was when it was new, but some of the pieces aren't available. Like the pictures." Nichelle opened a new window, the label in the dropdown listed with *show sources*. She copied the contents, the code looking like gibberish to me, and then pasted them into a new window. But it didn't help, the page rendered the same. "It's the distribution network where the images were hosted. The original doesn't exist anymore."

"Isn't it on a cloud server, backed up?" I asked, wanting to see the pictures. What did Tracy see?

"Not from fifteen years ago," Nichelle answered, her fingers a blur as she tried to build a view of the archived page. "It wasn't the missing pictures. Casey, look at this."

Nichelle highlighted the unaffected testimony of a young couple. She pointed to the names, Jessica and Michael Fields. "Fields," I muttered, dropping to a knee, my insides weighing heavy with what it was that Tracy had discovered. "Fields. That's Tracy's parents."

We stayed silent as we read the broken words, the half-completed paragraphs, Nichelle hunting the archive to piece it together. We read about their years of trying to have a baby, the words of their painful struggles, and about the sheer joy and gratitude of finally having a child of their own.

That child was Tracy.

Nichelle stood up, panic in her eyes as she clasped her hands, unsure of what to do. "Tracy was adopted?" Nichelle asked, voice quivering. "Oh my God! Casey, I don't think she knew!"

"She would have been what? Two, three?" I asked, recalling conversations with Tracy's uncle, his telling me how special she was, about Tracy graduating with college degrees when she was in her early teens. "If she was three, she might not remember anything."

"I don't remember being three," Nichelle said, searching blindly around Tracy's desk. "This has got to be horrible for her. We've got to find her!"

"Okay, we'll find her," I answered. My mind was racing with Daniel Ashtole's words, Tracy's uncle who I'd come to know when I moved to the Outer Banks. At the time, he was the district attorney, and then he became the mayor. But that only lasted a short while before he was tragically murdered. There was something he'd said about his niece. It was a small conversation, words he'd muttered more to himself than to me. "Almost all of her life."

Nichelle looked at me with questions sparking in her eyes. "What?" she asked, her voice tense. Without waiting, she grabbed a bag hung from the back of her chair, asking again, "Casey, what's that even mean?"

"It was something her uncle once said to me," I told her, keeping my voice calm, hoping it would help settle Nichelle's worry. It didn't. She pushed past me and went to the station's gate, flinging it open, the wood hammering the railing. We made our way out of the station and toward my car, shoes scraping the asphalt, loose stones crunching beneath heels as we hurried. "He said that to me when I'd just met Tracy. She was working our first case together."

"You're talking about the Reynolds case. That was my first case with you guys too. I'd just started working here."

"Right. The Reynolds case. One afternoon we were talking and Daniel told me Tracy was special. I'd asked if he knew her—"

"Well, he did!" Nichelle answered impatiently as we buckled our seat belts. She waved her hands, telling me to drive. I jammed the shifter, the car lurching forward, tires chirping. She wiped her eyes, fingers shaking. "Listen, sorry, I'm just really worried about her."

"Nichelle, I understand. I'm terrified for her." And I was. My heart ached with what must have been shocking news to read. "When I asked Daniel how he knew her, he'd told me he knew Tracy her entire life. But then, he corrected himself."

"Almost all of her life," Nichelle said, repeating and understanding the comment Daniel made. An uncle would have known his niece her whole life, not just "almost" like Daniel had said— that is, if she'd been born to her parents. We exited the station parking lot, turning north. "Where do you think she went?"

"Her parent's house?" A truck flashed its headlights, its bumper on top of mine as it followed us closely out of the station parking lot. "Let's try there first," I told her, pulling ahead to put distance behind me. The truck followed, speeding up. Panic rose in the back of my throat like bile, the bitter taste scaring me. I'd been followed before, the results ending with my car in ruin. Nichelle's face was filled with worry. "She'll be okay."

"I hope so," she answered, tears brimming.

As partners, I wasn't sure how much Tracy shared with Nichelle. During a recent hospital stay, I remembered Tracy had discovered that her blood type wasn't what she'd always believed it should be. "Nichelle, remember that thing about her blood type?"

"Yeah! Tracy asked her parents about it."

"What did they say?" I asked, squinting as headlights filled my rearview mirror.

"Her mom kinda skated around the question—"

"Nichelle," I said, the rumble of the truck's motor rising as it stayed closed. "I think we're being followed."

"What?" she asked, voice breaking. She turned around to search over her shoulders. The trucks headlights beamed through the back of my car and turned her face white with light. She sat back down and faced forward. "Make a left turn up here. We can take the back roads to her parent's house."

"Let's see if he follows." My hand was on the turn signal as we approached a minimart, the gas pumps occupied, people filling up their cars. I took my hand from the signal, leaving it off and swung the steering wheel hard to the left, the car tires pinching the curb sharply, squealing as I entered the turn. The truck drove past the turn, slowing at the intersection, and then stopped in the middle of it. A large car behind it honked and flashed its lights before jumping ahead and driving around the truck. But the truck didn't follow. It eased forward, disappearing from our view. I let out a shaky breath. Hard, walloping thumps batted my chest and made my brain pulse. My adrenaline was pumping high. There was a laugh buried deep though, it threatening to burst out. For a moment, I felt stupid, as if I'd let my paranoia get the best of me.

"Is it gone?" Nichelle asked.

"Nichelle, I think we're fine—" But I never finished what I was going to say. The crash came without warning. I saw another car for a split second, saw its 1970s style, the grill of a Lincoln Continental, a row of long steel teeth barreling through the next intersection of the backroads where we were hiding. And I recognized it. It was the same car behind the truck, the one with the round, decorative windows. It must have sped ahead and made the next left, tracking us with another left turn, speeding up to catch us.

The metal strike was a punishment for having gotten away, my car's size and weight no match for the tons of machinery behind the Lincoln. Glass blasted around us, raining inside my car, covering us with pellets, their edges like razors. We rolled, tipping over with a bounce, the heavy thud on a back road concealed by the backside of stores and trash dumpsters and the dark of nightfall. The calamity of it lasted less than a few seconds, but the damage inflicted was stunning. Gasoline fumes circled my face, the motor ticking, my car's tires spinning. I choked on the smell and called out, "Nichelle?"

"Got to get out," she groaned, her body upside down, scratches and bloody pockmarks on her face. "Are you hurt?"

"Uh-uh," I said, managing to release my seat belt buckle and let gravity take hold. It dropped onto the ceiling of the car, giving me room to roll over and crawl. Nichelle followed, a whimper turning into a cry. In the daze, there were footsteps coming. My gun was in the glove compartment, but the fumes were powerful, as was the fear of fire. Again.

They'd light a match. They'd smell the gasoline and wouldn't think twice about setting us on fire. They'd tried once already with Jericho's house, and now they were coming again. My insides turned to jelly with the thought of burning to death. I squirmed on my chest and stomach through the window, broken glass shredding my bare skin as I got to my hands and knees. The streetlights were on, the white of them in a blurry halo. In the distance, I saw the main road, the cars coming and going from the minimart, my focus drifting but my hearing keen. Then came the voices.

"Get a hold of her!" one of the voices demanded. It was enough for me to drink in the mounting adrenaline like a magic elixir. I climbed to my feet, facing a man wearing a black ski mask. There were holes cut out for his eyes and mouth. Through them, I could see he was smiling, satisfied with what they'd done. "We got you now!"

Nichelle screamed. Only, it didn't last. Another man was on her with gloved fingers pressing tight against her mouth, his arm wrapped around her chest, squeezing hard enough to stifle her shouting as he dragged her to the rear of the Lincoln. I pivoted my back foot, planting it for a fight. That's when the blinding light came, a bright blue spark that blew up in my face like a bolt of lightning. A hard jolt of electricity jumped through me and dropped me onto the ground like the dead, the smell of burnt ozone filling my nose and mouth. The man with the mask knelt to show me a stun gun, triggering it with a laugh, electrical pulses bouncing across the metal posts. Without warning, he shoved it against my chest and shocked me a second time, my muscles tensing, turning rigid and seizing full control. My attacker was right. They had us now.

TWENTY-EIGHT

It was the tree frogs that woke me, singing in the night. Or maybe it was the whispering in my ear—and a gruff, menacing laugh. There were mosquitos the size of bats, or at least felt like it. They landed on my sweaty cheeks and forehead and buzzed a thank you in my ears for the quick drink. It was nighttime, the air thick and wet with humidity, the ground mushy and stinking of bog mud. It was the smell that rang alarms inside me, triggering fright like the electricity that had jumped through my body. We were back in Buxton Woods. And we'd been brought here to die.

I knew it was Ronald's killer who'd taken us, the touch of rope against my skin whispering a deadly secret. I tried moving, tried wriggling free, my stomach flat against the ground and my legs and arms pinned behind me, and found my feet and hands sticking straight up. With my moving, the nylon bindings cut into my wrists and ankles while a noose around my neck hung loose. But that was different to Ronald. The noose on my neck should have gone tight.

Confused, I pulled harder, my efforts coming to a halt when I heard Nichelle's stifled cry coming from behind me. Nichelle cried again, gasping and fighting to take a breath. I felt her arms and legs next to mine and then felt her scramble, her movements jerking my head suddenly, the noose closing until I couldn't breathe. Without thinking, I began to kick. Her screaming cries went quiet, my movement strangling her.

"Whoa!" the killer said, his grip like a tool, tightening with powerful strength. He yanked my arms and legs behind me, straightening them so my hands and feet were back in position. Nichelle's gasps and coughing were muted, the night stars fading with threats of my blacking out. The noose around my neck came loose enough for me to breathe. I fell forward, the killer holding the weight from crushing our necks. Fright filled me as the touch of his hands became a reality. I dared to look behind me, straining to move to see what he'd done.

"Easy. We're not ready to play yet."

I saw him then. Saw his black stocking cap, his face blending with the night, stars twinkling above the tops of trees. It was a full moon, but it was tucked in behind a cloud, turning us grayish like ghouls. Nichelle's bare feet were with mine, our toes cast in the faint light. Our hands were together too, bandages on my fingers loose, dirtied gauze in a dangle. I kept my muscles tensed, my arms and legs motionless. The darkest of thoughts came to me, a terror-stricken understanding of what the killer's game was this evening.

He'd pitted me against Nichelle.

If I moved my arms and legs, if they so much as swayed a couple of degrees from center, Nichelle would die. And the same fate was mine if Nichelle wasn't able to keep the same position. The killer had bound us in a way where one of us had to die for the other to live.

"You," I coughed, deciding to say something, say anything while figuring a way out of this. "You can't get away with this."

"Casey?" Nichelle cried, her knees knocking against mine with our bodies facing away from one another. "What's happening?"

"I'll tell you," the killer said. "I got a game for you two to play."

"No, please!" she begged. She'd seen firsthand what had happened to the victims. She'd seen what happened to me when we tested my theory of escape. And she knew it was happening to us. "Oh God—"

There was movement, a subtle motion coming from the corner of my eye. "Come here and help me with this!" he demanded. With his words, someone else knelt slowly. He wore gloves like the killer, his fingers wrapped in leather. The killer cursed the gloves as he worked the last of the knots while his partner held our feet and hands in place, keeping them straight to prevent any strangling before the game was to begin. "I've almost got this."

"This is bullshit," the killer's partner said. When the moon escaped from behind a lumbering cloud, I saw its light glint from a steel post running into his shoe. It was Jimmy Rush, the head of security for Rourke Memorial Hospital.

I shut my eyes and took a breath, wondering if I should say anything. The game came with a slim chance of escape, an idea I'd had when first seeing how Ronald was killed. But if I spoke, if I said Jimmy's name, could that be enough to finish us early?

"Man, this is sick," the killer's partner said.

"Nichelle," I whispered, her whimpering softly, her body quaking.

"Nichelle, I need you to listen to me!" I thought through every step I'd taken when testing the escape from the ropes. Dread settled like a dead person's blood though. This wasn't the same arrangement. "Nichelle?"

"No talking!" With the killer's voice there came a violent blow, the strike deadening, the air in my lungs gone. The shallow moonlight disappeared briefly as he spoke, "We haven't started playing yet."

"Man, this just isn't right," I heard Jimmy Rush say again. I felt his hands tremble as he held us. He let out a grunt as he struggled to keep his balance. When he began to mutter something, I stretched my neck to see his face behind the knitted mask. His yellowing eyes darted between me and Nichelle, stopping when he caught me staring. His lips continued moving, the frayed threads around his mouth moving silently. I couldn't tell if he was trying to tell me something though. He broke our stare to look at the killer, and continued, "This ain't what I signed up for!"

"You already got blood on your hands, boss!" the killer answered in a nonchalant voice. "You're committed now!"

"Uh-uh," Jimmy said, shaking his head. "Not me. I ain't got nothing to do with any of this. Just the records—"

With Jimmy's words the killer swung, lashing out, striking him hard enough to knock Jimmy's head sideways. Jimmy's grip was gone, our arms and legs falling at the same time, the slack in the nylon rope tightening like piano wire around our necks. "Help!" I heard Nichelle wheeze.

Straining, I dug my knees into the soft earth, and straightened my lower legs to add slack. Nichelle did the same as I arched my back so my hands were near our feet. For the moment, we could breathe, but the position was impossible to hold.

"Excellent," the killer said. "You guys understand how this is going to work."

"Relax!" I tried to yell to Nichelle, ignoring the killer. She couldn't control her arms or legs though. My words cut short, a puff of air slipping from between my lips. There was a brief relief, but it wasn't from our doing. The killer had taken control with both of his hands, holding our arms and legs in place.

"Hmm. Rope burns—" the killer began to ask, his face in mine. I could see a smirk behind the mask as I sucked a mouthful of air, the smell of his arrogance turning my stomach. "Were you studying my work?"

"Breathe!" I told Nichelle, concern jumping in leaps and bounds. "Keep your arms behind you and your feet up."

"I can't—" she coughed and gagged, hysteria gripping her like a rag doll. "Casey! I can't hold them."

"I can't be a part of this!" Jimmy Rush said as he waved his hands with disgust. He stumbled to his feet. "Man, you on your own!"

The killer peered up, his grip tightening to hold the ropes. "I don't think you're understanding me when I say that you *are* committed!"

Jimmy Rush leaned forward with a fierce rage in his eyes.

"Naw, man, I don't think you're understanding me." He slowly lifted his shirt, revealing a bowie knife tucked in his belt. He didn't wait for the killer to respond and turned his back to us. He began to walk away, leaving us alone. Was he running to get help, or saving himself?

"Shit!" the killer muttered. He narrowed his eyes, his fingers like claws. "This was going to be such a good game."

"Hold on!" I yelled to Nichelle, knowing what he was going to do. "Grab your feet if you can!"

"I have to go finish him. That means I have to let you two go." There was a pause as he shuffled onto his feet, his shoes crunching the trampled sawgrass. He swung his finger in the air, saying, "One of you might live. Maybe even be both of you for a while." Abruptly, he released one hand, the slack in the rope tightening, Nichelle screeching. From beneath his shirt, the killer produced a gun, a revolver like the one we'd found with Dr. Sully, a black Ruger 9mm. I knew the type to be popular for its compactness and ease of use. Seeing the end of the barrel, it could also have been the gun pressed against Ronald's scalp.

"Casey!" Nichelle cried. "I can't do it!"

He looked down at me, saying, "Never bring a knife to a gun fight."

That was the last of his words as he let us go to run after Jimmy Rush. Without a moment wasted, I reared up, bending back as far as I could, and took hold of Nichelle's hands, her fingers slippery. She was quick to react and pushed the top of one foot around my ankle. It wasn't much, but we'd manage to gain enough leverage to keep the ropes slack.

"Casey," she said, her body shaking terribly, the fright becoming too much. "I... I think I'm going to be sick!"

"Breathe!" I said, raising my voice, listening to the clamor of parting brush and breaking branches. Jimmy Rush was being hunted and he had no idea. But who was his hunter? "Nichelle, I want you to take a breath through your nose and let it out through your mouth."

"Casey, I'm so scared," she said, voice shaking. The trembling in her arms and legs grew rapidly. "I don't know... if... if I can hold on."

"Listen to me," I said, sweat stinging my eyes. An idea stirred— a dangerously risky idea. But it was the only one I had. When the killer was done with Jimmy Rush, he was coming back for us. Game or no game, there was no way he would let us live. "Nichelle. Do you trust me?"

She froze. The shaking stopped. "Trust? What do you mean?"

"I can get us out of this," I told her, sweat trickling down my back. Like we'd studied with Dr. Swales, the killer had made fulcrums to pivot leverage in the ropes, which tightened and loosened based on the distribution of weight. I only needed to eliminate the weight to free us both. But to do what I had in mind, I'd first have to take all the slack in the ropes, which meant strangling Nichelle.

I couldn't see Nichelle's face, but felt the motion of her shoulders, the rigid shaking of her head. "No. Casey, nobody else escaped—"

"This knot, this game, it's the same as the others, even though there are two of us," I began but didn't have time to explain. There was a crash in the darkness, a flash of light shining in our direction. In the distance, there were guttural sounds of men grunting, of fighting, and of one begging for their life. "Nichelle, you'll have to trust me!"

"Casey, please—" Before she could finish, I let go of her hands and cleared my feet from hers.

When I dropped my legs, the tips of my toes hit the soft earth, the rope sliding through the noose around my neck with a burn as the one around Nichelle's neck tightened. It was the noose that had been used as the fulcrum, pitting one against the other. I took all of the slack I could, Nichelle's body rearing up as she strained to breathe. My time was short as I took hold of my wrist and slipped the tips of my burned fingers beneath the nylon. I only needed one binding removed to free all of them, to free us. "Hold on, Nichelle."

"Ca—" she tried to say with wet sucking sounds as she pushed air through her lips. The muffled choking urged me to move faster. Nichelle's breathing was labored, but she held her arms and legs. I had seconds to finish what I started. "C—"

The ground felt hot, the sandy grit clinging to me as blisters opened, the rope grating on raw skin. Nichelle's legs wobbled. Her hands dropping, she moaned with a gasp as her limbs fell limp. The rope around my neck went tight. Blood stopped flowing and my heartbeat felt like gunfire in my brain. My head and face dripped wet, panic raging as I freed the first inch of rope. It was enough to gain another inch and I removed the noose from my neck. "Almost there, Nichelle!" The nylon ropes fell as Nichelle's front tumbled forward, her face hitting the ground.

As I shed the ropes that bound her, I rolled Nichelle onto her back, her bronze skin a deathly pale color, her lips already a dank blue. She hadn't just blacked out, she'd stopped breathing altogether. The shrubs around me blew up, feet stomping the ground, trampling with threats as though an army were on the attack. I fell backward onto my bottom, my arms up, guarding myself when I heard Emanuel's voice, "Casey!"

I had to be hallucinating. I glanced at the ropes, thinking I must have died, that I must have lost the frenzied battle to survive. When my gaze fell on Nichelle, I snapped back and put one hand over the other, driving them into her chest and recalling the count, the cadence we were told to use when applying CPR. "Breathe!"

"How long?" Emanuel said, appearing out of the bushes, his dark skin glistening with sweat and blood from cuts across his forehead. He swiped errantly at them and dipped over Nichelle, pushing his lips onto her mouth and breathing. He looked up at me with crazed fright, yelling, "How long has she been down, Casey!"

"I don't know!" I cried. And I didn't know. I couldn't think. I couldn't distinguish rage from fright from reality. "The killer! He's hunting Jimmy Rush."

Tracy appeared from the darkness and fell to her knees, taking over for Emanuel while he produced his gun and asked, "Which way?"

I nudged my chin in the direction where I heard the fighting, my arms stiff with ache and seeing Nichelle's eyes glazed with death. "Come on, girl!" Tracy's expression spoke the nightmare I was feeling, the worst-case scenario of my gamble having come true. I hadn't been fast enough and it was going to cost Nichelle her life. "CPR!"

"No, Nichelle," Tracy cried, brushing her hand across Nichelle's face, cleaning the dirt and grime. She began a keening wail that drove a chill through me.

"Tracy!" I yelled. "She needs a breath!"

Tracy shut up, put her lips to Nichelle's and blew into her lungs while I held on with the compressions. I lowered my ear to Nichelle's chest and listened for the miracle I needed to hear. I covered my other ear, driving out the tree frogs' incessant chirping. That's when I heard the faintest sound of a heartbeat. It was slow, but it was there. I was sure of it. I got up and found Tracy's wide eyes filled with hopeful tears. "Anything?"

"Breathe!" I demanded again and resumed compressions. In the darkness of Buxton Woods, I heard Emanuel's yells, his hollering to *halt* and to *get down*. There was a shot, and then another. I stopped for a moment to hear what was to come next. Nichelle moved beneath my hands, the suddenness startling. A wave of relief came when she let out a cough, a raspy breath following. Then came the swing of her arms and the kicking of her legs, her fighting us. "Easy. You'll be okay."

Tracy took hold of Nichelle's face so she could look at her. "It's us," she said, blubbering with a mix of laughter and tears.

"He's handcuffed," Emanuel said, appearing from the bush, blood dripping from his chin, spilling onto his shirt.

"Are you shot?" I asked, getting up to tend to him. "Is that old blood or new blood?"

"It's from the branches," he answered, wiping his face. "We ran through the woods."

"How?" I asked as patrol officers joined us. There was a damp fog, but through it I saw the patrol lights on the trail. "How did you guys find us?"

"I'm going to secure the guy." Emanuel motioned to the ropes. I handed them to him, his answering, "It was Tracy that found you."

"My keyring?" Nichelle asked, her voice sounding with a croak. Tracy shoved her fingers into Nichelle's front pocket and pulled out a set of keys. On the ring, an ivory-colored badge with a symbol that looked like the signal bars for WIFI or a cell tower. "She kept losing her keys."

"That thing is a locator?"

Tracy nodded as she hugged Nichelle. I fell onto my back, sweat stinging the cuts around my neck and wrists and ankles. Staring into the night, a million stars staring back at us, I reached over to take hold of Nichelle's hand. Her fingers closed around mine and the emotions I'd held back came forward. I struggled to say it, but managed to tell her, "Nichelle, I'm sorry. It was the only idea I had."

"Casey," Nichelle said, returning a weak squeeze. "Remind me to never ever get kidnapped with you again."

TWENTY-NINE

Our killer was quickly identified as Jerry Stillwell: son of Laura, the medical director at Rourke. On his arrest, I recognized the eyes of the man I'd seen driving with his mother into the Goulds' estate. They were a far cry from the eyes I'd seen in a photograph back in his mother's office, of a happy young man on the ski slopes with his family.

For Stillwell, there was no interrogation, no sitting in an interview room at the station, where we'd offer a soda pop or coffee. He'd tried to kill me. He'd tried to kill Nichelle. And we'd caught him in the act of murdering Jimmy Rush. It was the holding cell for the man. Our station had two, small boxes made of cinder block and iron, each with a steel cot, a toilet and sink. There were no other amenities, the cage serving the same function designed a hundred-plus years ago in the old west. It's truer purpose was born centuries before that, maybe longer—confinement and the breaking of a person's will.

I dragged a folding chair behind me, the cell we'd placed Jerry Stillwell directly ahead to my left. There was nobody else around, no one in the other holding cell, nobody to bother me. I gave the police officer standing guard at the door permission to allow my team to enter, but that was it. The chair legs scraped the unfin-

ished concrete, metal rubbing against the coarse cement, the uncer-
emonious sound enough to stir the two legs I saw hanging off the
end of the cot. As I neared, Stillwell stood and came to the iron, his
fingers wrapping around the bars like a raptor clutching a branch.

"You got something for me?" he asked as I positioned the chair
outside his cell. I stayed far enough back to safely sit without his
being able to grab me. When he saw that it was me, his hand went
to his neck, his gaze locked on the rope burns around mine. It
wasn't until I saw the look on his face that I realized he didn't know
if I'd lived or died.

"Jerry," I said, my voice scratchy, a present from the damage of
his torture. I eased into my seat, crossed my legs and sat back. I had
no laptop. No pen and paper. Just me—a conversation.

"I wondered if you lived," he said, his gaze searching my feet
and hands, looking hard at my ankles and wrists. When his focus
returned to my neck, a sporting smile on his lips, I could see he was
getting pleasure from seeing what he'd done. "The other one?"

Nichelle lived, but she'd almost died too. Neither of these facts
had to be shared. "Let's talk about you."

A look of disappointment showed, but didn't last long.

"Just so you are aware, we have you for attempted murder.
There's no escaping those charges. But let's talk about what else
you've done."

"You mean who? Don't you?" he answered, trying to sound
smart. His words, his confidence, even his voice was a lie. On his
face, dark pouches carried Jerry Stillwell's brown eyes, his sandy-
platinum hair jutting from the tops and sides of his head to give
him a wild look. He combed his fingers through it but it didn't help.
There were a few days of growth on his chin, and the clothes I'd
seen when he'd tied me and Nichelle together had been replaced
with the county jail's yellow coveralls.

"How many?" I asked, beginning with the easiest of them.
Some killers liked to brag. They liked to throw their numbers
around as though it were an indication of strength or measure of
their ruthlessness. I just thought they were sicker than others. And

I was certain I was sitting across from one of the sickest. Even if he didn't know it.

"Can I get some aspirin?" he asked, his hand on his knee and rubbing it. What was it his mother had said about skiing? There'd been an accident. A bad one. He grimaced, the pain continuing. "That Bigfoot cop of yours jumped on my leg and wrenched my knee."

I held up my phone to suggest I could place an order for him like there was pizza delivery around the corner. His eyes widened. "I'm sure I can find some for you," I told him and made like I was texting. "Coffee with that?"

"Some pop?" Stillwell asked, face lighting up. "Anything with sugar."

"Okay, but before you get your pop and aspirin, tell me about the ropes. Why do it this way? Why the game?" While there was no evidence, no fingerprints or anything found in Ronald's car or his apartment, I was certain that I was sitting across from his murderer. And although the game with the ropes was all Jerry, I was sure selecting Ronald was a decision made by someone else.

Stillwell grabbed the side of his head and squinted at the bright lights. It was a head injury, brain trauma, that his mother had mentioned. She'd also said he was never right after that. "The ropes and game?"

"It's about decisions," he said flatly, his eyelids closing as the pain inside his head clearly worsened. "Left or right. Tug or give."

He quieted, and sat down at the end of the cot facing the aisle where I sat. I didn't understand what he meant, but he motioned as though he had the ropes on him, tying and untying. It was probably something he'd done a million times, practicing the arbor knots and the labor of perfecting the trap for his victims to escape. I gently touched my neck, his following my fingers as I said, "Pull on the wrong lead and the leverage disappears and strangles you. Tug on the correct one and it loosens the noose enough to escape."

With my understanding, he fought through the pain enough

for his eyelids to spring open. "You figured it out. You made the right decisions."

"Did you make the right decisions on that hill?" I asked, believing I understood his motives. He frowned at the question. He might have been instructed by someone to murder as part of a cover-up, but his approach, his style was like that of a serial killer playing a game. I touched the side of my head to clarify what I was asking. "When you were on that hill, did you make the right decision? Left or right? Speed up or slow down?"

There was rage on his face, his scowl harsh, eyes narrowing. "Fuck do you know about it?"

I'd hit what was behind his motives, why he enjoyed watching. He wanted his victims to experience what he experienced on that hill where a wrong decision nearly cost him his life. It had also changed him forever. Uncrossing my legs, texting Emanuel and Nichelle to come in, I answered, "I made the right decisions."

The door opened, Emanuel carrying two chairs, Jerry watching him, the grimace on his face like stone. "What are you staring at, you big fucker?" Emanuel didn't reply as he sat down. "I should sue you and your bosses for fucking up my knee."

An officer entered, carrying a can of soda pop and tiny paper cup, two aspirin inside as I'd ordered. "I'll monitor," I told the officer, assuring him we wouldn't leave the aluminum can alone with the prisoner. Nichelle followed and used her leg to hold the door open as the officer exited. She carried two laptops, mine included, the questions about who ordered the murders mounting in my mind. "You remember my associate?"

"Oh yeah," he said, his gaze traveling from her toes to the top of her head. "I never forget a looker." Nichelle ignored the killer's comment as she sat down. He looked to me then too, adding, "You're not so bad either."

"Well, I guess that's enough of the small talk," I said and opened the top of my laptop. I turned enough for Jerry Stillwell to see the screen, a thin white line flashing before a map appeared with a highlighted route tracing from the Outer Banks and Rourke

Memorial Hospital as the starting point. The route ended at Ronald's apartment. "Do you know what this is?"

Stillwell chomped on the pills, chewing voraciously before sucking them down with the cola. He rubbed his knee as he did and then studied the map. "Yeah. I know what it is."

"What was your business in Philadelphia?" I asked. When he shook his head, I showed a table of data, the cells included his license plate numbers, along with dates and times. "We have you traveling the toll roads to and from Philadelphia. There's you crossing the Chesapeake. And then taking 95 through Williamsburg, up through D.C. and all the way into the Old City district."

He sucked more cola, perched his chin on his hand, answering, "I was hungry for cheese steaks and soft pretzels."

"Pat's or Geno's?" I asked. Stillwell frowned. He didn't understand the reference to the two places in Philly tourists will go to get a taste of the city. "Do you like your steak served chopped or sliced?"

"Chopped," he answered unconvincingly. A shallow grin appeared with the lie, but then was gone. Frustrated with the questions, he asked, "So what, I went to Philadelphia. That doesn't prove anything."

I leaned forward, asking, "Do you know who I am?"

He didn't answer immediately, his gaze jumping from Emanuel to Nichelle and then back to me. He touched his neck, his fingers stretching across the area where the ropes had burned me. "Should I care?"

From the case folder Nichelle brought with her, I pulled a picture of Ronald, the one taken by Dr. Swales in the morgue, days after his death. The sight of it made me shudder inside as I showed it to him. Stillwell's eyes opened wide, the sight of Ronald's face taking him by surprise. "His name is Ronald Haskin. Maybe you'd seen him on the news?"

"I don't watch much television," he answered, his gaze locked on the face, on death. He pawed at his mouth in an unconscious reaction.

"We know you were at his apartment," I said, fibbing slightly, my evidence being circumstantial only with a combination of dates and times that reconciled to Stillwell's travels to my hometown. "But you didn't find what you were looking for."

He raised his hands briefly, asking, "Is there a question in there?"

"Why?" I asked. He remained silent, his lips pressed tight and barely visible. "Jimmy Rush will have plenty to say once he's recovered."

"That gimpy geezer is dead," Stillwell scoffed, cheeks flushed bright, the conversation wearing on him.

"You're sure about that?" Emanuel asked him. On Stillwell's face there was a look of worry.

"We might be able to help you," I offered. I showed him Ronald's picture again, asking, "We just need you to help us fill in the blanks."

"My mom's sending her lawyer—" he began.

"That's fine," I said. "We've already got you for arson and for kidnapping and attempted murder."

"Arson?" he asked, sounding obstinate. He was unaware of a search warrant for his truck and apartment which turned up evidence that he'd been the one who'd set fire to Jericho's place. The officers also found a supply of rope that matched the ones used on Ronald and Janice, as well as the ones used on me and Nichelle.

The supply of rope also confirmed it was different from those found on Violet Gould.

I raised my brow and dipped my chin. It was enough to convince Jerry Stillwell that I wasn't lying about the arson charge. He emptied his face, the conversation becoming dull. His voice edgy, he asked, "What's your point?"

"Do you know who I am?" I repeated. There was a reason he and Jimmy Rush attacked us. If he didn't produce an answer immediately, it confirmed for me that he was working under someone's direction. I stood up and put my face in his. "Who am I?"

He reared back from the iron bars, mumbling, "I dunno."

From the case folder I showed him a picture of Violet Gould holding Hannah, a still image of the black-and-white surveillance photograph. There was instant recognition. "But you know what this is, right?" He said nothing but told me everything when his eyes went to Ronald's picture in my other hand. "That's right. The man in that picture was investigating the kidnapping of his daughter. That's why you killed him. That's why you killed Violet Gould and Dr. Sully."

"I didn't kill her," he answered, shaking his head. "Didn't touch the doctor either."

"But you know who did," I said, raising my voice.

He shook his head, "Uh-uh. Never touched either of them." His response gave me pause, the ropes found in his apartment confirming the likelihood he was being truthful about Violet Gould and maybe Dr. Sully's murder too. His voice became a whisper, his surprising me, saying, "And I don't know who you are."

I gripped my neck and asked, "Then tell me who did know me and ordered you to do what you did."

Jerry Stillwell looked at Nichelle, his saying, "I didn't know who you were either."

There was a flash of sadness, of remorse perhaps. The sight of it made me roil with anger, a hot tension that reached into my toes. There was no room for atonement.

"Who did?" Nichelle asked him abruptly.

His gaze fell back to Ronald's picture, lips moving, "It was about the money."

"Okay," I said, controlling my tone, trying to work with him. "You were told to protect the money?"

He was silent for a moment. "How long will it be?" he asked, his jaw slack, his shoulders slumped. It was a look I'd seen many times. He knew he wasn't going to leave. He knew he was going to prison. "How much time am I facing?"

The answer would be life, possibly multiple sentences served consecutively given the heinousness of his crimes. I didn't want to put a number out there though since I needed his cooperation. "I suppose that depends on how much you are willing to help us. It's all negotiable."

"Negotiable?" He pursed his lips while regarding my words. "So we could make some sort of deal?"

"Could do," Emanuel said, hearing an opportunity to work with Jerry Stillwell.

I added, "I would have to take it to the district attorney. She'll work it out with you."

"What would I have to do?" he asked, his guarded look gone. He looked up and down the narrow iron bars in front of him and ran his fingers over them, jerking his hand away as though they were burning. "I can't spend the rest of my life like a caged animal."

"It's time for you to make a decision then," I said, choosing his words. I turned my phone around showing my intent to record his answer. "Would you like a lawyer at this time?"

"Nah," he said, copying my tone. "What do you mean a decision?"

"It would mean you would sign a confession," I answered, seeing he was caving to save his own skin.

"And you'd need to tell us who placed the order to kill us," Nichelle said.

He drank the cola, the aluminum crinkling as he upset its smooth surface. When he was done, he motioned to the picture of Violet Gould with my daughter. "It all started because of that picture."

"Hannah?" I asked, taking a breath when saying her name. I clarified quickly, holding my phone to ensure the recording was suitable. "You are confirming the murders began because of the girl in the picture."

"Yeah," he answered, and then pointed to the picture of Ronald. "That guy must have figured it out and was going to expose it all."

Even though Jimmy Rush was indeed dead, I'd planted a seed

of doubt in Stillwell's mind, and so I asked, "Jimmy Rush. He placed the order? He was in charge of the murders?"

With that, Jerry Stillwell let out a short laugh like a cough, but then wiped the spittle from his mouth. "Jimmy didn't know anything. There was only one person who knew everything."

I had to hear him say it and moved to face the bars, standing within arm's reach, sweat beading and stinging the cuts around my neck. "Listen. The district attorney will work with you," I said, assuring him. He eyed the high window near the ceiling, a beam of sunlight easing over the windowsill.

"It was my mom," he answered simply. "She wanted them all dead."

"Violet Gould and Dr. Sully too?" I asked, needing confirmation of every victim in the case. I was hoping the barriers had come down enough that he'd confess to their murders too. Deep down I held a doubt. As he'd said, he knew nothing about them.

"I'll make a deal with the district attorney, turn over my mom and confess to the other victims. But I had nothing to do with them." He shook his head and winced, pain returning. Slowly a sneer appeared. "You got somebody else to catch."

THIRTY

You got somebody else to catch. Jerry Stillwell's words rang in my head like a bell. He was right about there being another killer. It was his mother, Laura Stillwell, her small frame in shadow as she was led to an interview room by two FBI agents, one on each side of her. She gave me a hard look, her pink lipstick bright in the dim light as she cocked her chin in my direction. For a second, I thought she was going to say something, but turned and entered the room, scoffing with a grunt as if annoyed by the interruption in her day. What she didn't know was that the district attorney was already working with her son to help collect his confession, which included his providing evidence of his mother's participation. Specifically, Jerry Stillwell placed his mother as the person ordering the murders and the arson attack that nearly took mine and Jericho's lives.

"You have a lot of nerve doing this," she yelled at one of the agents. "Do you have any idea who I am in this town?"

"I do," I answered and took to leaning against the door frame and watching while the FBI agents sat Laura Stillwell into a chair.

"You're behind this?" she asked, lips wet as she licked at them feverishly. "This... this stunt is your doing?!"

"Yes, I am," I answered, a tiny gush of satisfaction warming me.

Those search warrants we worked had done some amazing things. They opened doors and brought the FBI to the Outer Banks, who came with a dozen or more of their own warrants. With those, we opened Dr. Sully's bookshelf safe. The leather-bound books hiding it were as fake as the business empire he and Violet Gould had built. Inside the safe were years of handwritten accounting ledgers. A team of forensic accountants also arrived to review the businesses and scrutinize every ledger entry Dr. Sully made. "Your son has been very helpful."

For the agents, she played up her age, crooking her back, complaining that she was an aching old woman and pleading with them to help her. The woman she acted for them was a far cry from the medical director we'd met at Rourke Memorial Hospital. When they didn't buy into her drama, she straightened her shoulders like a sprouting weed and sneered at me. "Detective, my lawyers are on their way."

"Good," I told her. "Given what your son told us, you'll need them."

She held up her fingers, the knuckles knobby, and said, "Two hours. I'll be out of here in two hours."

"That's fine," I said, turning to walk away. "Enjoy the conversation with the FBI and our district attorney."

When I reached my desk, the team was waiting for me, Nichelle and Emanuel returning from the holding cell while Tracy was deep into the work of scouring through the Internet's history and trying to piece back together the fragments of a past website that held the testimonies of adopted parents. She'd stayed away from the station since discovering she was adopted, but had returned this morning. It was good to see her jumping back into the case. I knocked on her cubicle wall, her attention difficult to steal. She brushed back the hair in her eyes enough for me to see them. "Got a minute?"

"Sure," she answered, voice lifting as she rolled her chair toward us. "How are the Stillwells?"

"A full confession?" Emanuel asked, holding his thumb up for encouragement. "Full cooperation?"

"I hope he rots." Nichelle rubbed her neck and arms, the look on her face making me nervous for her. The injuries would heal, but it was the experience that had me afraid for her. A cold look in her eyes, she looked at me and asked, "It's not over though, is it?"

I shook my head, biting my lip. "The ropes used on Violet Gould are confirmed as being different. Stillwell is adamant about not having anything to do with her murder."

"And Dr. Sully?" Tracy asked. "Did Stillwell confess to making Sully's murder look like a suicide to cover up the baby-stealing?"

"Said he had nothing to do with it," I said, hating to break the news. "The good news is Jerry Stillwell is working with the DA. He's going to testify against his mother."

"The medical director is here?" Tracy asked.

I pointed toward the interview room, adding, "She's being interviewed by the FBI as we speak."

"But the DA isn't including Sully and Gould?" Emanuel asked, seeking clarification.

"No. She's not," I answered, the team groaning. I raised my hands and sighed with them. "Listen, I'll do the paperwork and close the cases on Janice Stephen and Ronald while the FBI manages Dr. Sully's ledgers."

"But that means we still have two murders to solve," Emanuel said. His face brightened with an idea and he snapped his fingers, the sound popping loud enough to startle Nichelle. He touched her shoulder, telling her, "Sorry."

"It better be a damn good idea," she warned as she laughed at her own reaction.

He faced the team and proposed, "We'll want to revisit Gould's husband."

Nichelle answered first, saying, "About the affair he claimed Violet and Sully were having?"

Tracy stood up, perching an elbow on the cubicle wall and wrinkling her nose with doubt. "We didn't find a single piece of evidence to support an affair. I mean, like nothing." She began counting off the reasons with her fingers. "No receipts. No secret rendezvous. No nothing."

"I know," I said, agreeing. "But jealousy is the earliest motive we had. Let's not forget, he came to the station to discuss it with Cheryl."

"You want us to take that angle in the investigation?" Emanuel asked.

"Correct." I waved my hands, adding, "Like I said, I'll button up all of this, close whatever needs closing. The case for Sully's and Gould's murders remains open."

"Do you really think that sickly man had the physical capability to do that to his wife?" Tracy asked, her brow staying furrowed.

"Of course not," I answered, the faces on my team filled with confusion. I'd purposely misled them. "I don't think Mr. Gould knew anything about what his wife was up to."

"Wait, but you just said—" Tracy began, her tone sharp. "You *don't* want us to investigate Gould's husband?"

"That's right," I answered. "I want to speak to Dr. Sully's wife, Beverly Richardson Sully."

"But Nichelle said she was some rich oil tycoon," Tracy objected, her tone remaining short. "Way richer than her husband."

"You can't put a dollar value on jealousy," I answered. "I'm suggesting the first motive we looked at. But from the perspective of a different scorned lover."

"We'll get on it," Emanuel said, clapping his hands to leave.

The team had their next tasks, and we still had another killer to catch.

· · ·

By the time the morning was gone, the FBI had a high-level over-view of what Gould and Sully had been doing. They'd brought to the station the contents of his safe—reams of pages of financial transactions that dated back more than two decades. Informally, they confirmed with me the mystery partner in the LLC was not Beverley Sully. Instead, their focus was on Laura Stillwell. They assured me it was only a matter of time before they validated Still-well as being the S in the GSS Notary Services business. When asked what it was they were doing exactly, the FBI said it was one of the largest, and oldest, baby-selling rings they'd ever identified.

As a courtesy, we gave the FBI access to our station, their taking over the team's conference room where I stood on the other side of the glass wall, a cold cup of coffee in hand, the team of men and women moving a hundred miles an hour. They were a machine of mechanized bodies, a blur of arms and legs in constant motion. The ledgers were their hub of concentration as they earmarked entries, noted them on whiteboards, connected a hundred Post-it notes that spanned from floor to ceiling. They were recreating the baby-selling enterprise using every entry Dr. Sully had kept in his deep paper trail which included all the cash businesses and the notary, along with the Adopt Me Agency. The conference room table had been repurposed too. At the center of it was a growing stack of pages, each carrying the names of the single mothers who'd been told their babies were stillborn.

Maureen Henson was one of the women in there, my thoughts of her and her baby a constant. I knew the day-to-day angst she felt. I knew the pain too. Like me, it was an ache in her bones, an open wound riveted to her soul. If she knew what we'd discovered, she'd demand we find her baby. While the dead don't speak, Maureen had told us that she heard her baby crying. And she was right. The FBI confirmed that Maureen's baby had been taken, and where she had been sent. An illegal adoption was made to look legitimate, a six-figure payment funneled through the businesses, placed by a married couple in Akron, Ohio. For the adoptive parents, the FBI believed they had no knowledge of the illegalities. It would be the FBI's work to reunite mothers and their babies, some of them already grown, some of them students in high school or college perhaps.

The other sections of the table were marked for paperwork found in the Adopt Me Agency, along with the medical charts from Rourke Memorial Hospital. We were able to help there, turning over the database Nichelle and the team had built. Nichelle stayed busy the evening after our abduction. She'd also stayed busy all of Tuesday, working directly with the FBI as a member of their team. The FBI knew her well from previous work interactions.

With the medical chart data, Nichelle helped the FBI stand up the computers they'd need, which were many. When the data began to flow, the monitors lining the far side of the conference room churned through the data like machines harvesting an endless field of ripe crop. And ripe it was. There was enough data to triple the charges. But of course, that would have to be the case when selling babies for more than twenty years. This was a big case, a national case with international ties, and it belonged to the FBI now.

While the commotion in our conference room escalated, the accumulating agents like worker bees around a hive, a touch of guilt hit me. Ronald was the spark that had ignited this fire. If not for his investigation, none of this would have happened. His laptop confirmed what we had discovered, the GSS businesses being a front. We'd also found an anonymous tip had been emailed to him, telling him to come to the Outer Banks for more information. Ronald had come to see me, to show me his findings and to help him confirm his suspicions.

Our station manager forwarded us the video snippet we'd thought might exist. Without an exact time of arrival to the Outer Banks, the manager watched hours of security camera footage before seeing the clip of Ronald's car entering our parking lot. On the video, we saw Ronald pull into a parking space, a tree blocking his face and much of his body. Behind him, a truck pulled up with two men exiting it, the trees keeping their identities hidden like a secret. When Ronald approached, there was a blinding flash, a stun gun used to incapacitate him. The men dragged him into the truck, and Ronald's remains found days later in Buxton Woods.

We also believed Janice Stephen's death came because of her stumbling onto Sully and Gould's practice of drugging young women. She'd told her parents she'd found it in the charts. And she had. What we might never know is if she'd been witness to the pair stealing the newborn babies. The young medical student had worked close enough to have either seen it firsthand or maybe even been approached to join in the criminal activity. We couldn't prove or disprove it. But in either scenario, the outcome was the end of her life.

I took a sip of my coffee, watching the FBI in action. The case of Violet Gould and Benjamin Sully remained unfinished and felt like an open wound like the cuts and bruises that I'd wear for a time. Nichelle wore them too. I thought she needed to take a day, or even a week or more, but she insisted on helping. From over my shoulder, I saw the top of her head. She'd returned to her desk, her kinky hair parted in the middle by a pair of headphones, her monitors painted bright green and black as she scoured through more data.

The coffee was bitter like the feelings I had about the way the night in Buxton Woods had unfolded. To free us, I'd almost killed Nichelle. And while she didn't look at it the same way as me, it had me questioning the dangers of the job. It wasn't long ago when Tracy had become a victim in one of the investigations. And before that, I'd found myself on the wrong side of a brutal serial killer. That one had nearly cost me my life. That same case did cost a life, an unborn child of mine and Jericho's, an unexpected miracle that would never be. Like a distant star its dim light was a reminder of what was. The ache of losing our baby would haunt me a lifetime. Jericho must have seen the look on my face, his joining me outside the conference room, a second cup in his hands.

"Thank you," I said, knowing he'd come to the station to submit his statement in the case of arson being brought against Jerry Stillwell. In the bed of Stillwell's truck, three ten-gallon gasoline jugs were discovered. Forensics would take a sample and use that as comparison to the unburnt gasoline found in the rear of Jericho's house. We all knew forensics would find a match. It was just a matter of finishing the paperwork to close the arson case. With fresh gauzy bandages around my fingers, I sleeved the new cup with the old and drank my coffee black.

There were questions on Jericho's face, his passing a glance at Tracy's cubicle and then to me. When he was close enough to whisper, he asked, "How she doing?"

"Good," I said, nodding encouragingly. "Working through the old archives to try and find links and pictures. Nichelle and the FBI are teaming up on that too."

The archived web pages for the Adopt Me Agency were in pieces, the archaic markup language broken and only providing us with names and the testimonies from adoptive parents. We had no pictures of Tracy or her adopted parents from that time. I was certain her parents' names were going to be found in Sully's ledgers. And when that happened, the name of Tracy's mother would surface. She was another victim, another woman who'd been drugged and then told that her baby had died in her womb. Stillborn.

"I'm sure if Nichelle is on it, they'll find something soon," Jericho commented as we watched Tracy leave her cubicle, a scowl on her face telling me she'd gotten no results in her efforts.

From Nichelle's cubicle, I heard the sounds of typing and mouse clicks. And I think with all that happened, it was the broken links and missing pictures that brought Nichelle to the station today. She needed to help Tracy piece together her past. Uncomfortable with what I knew I had to do, I leaned against Jericho, telling him, "I've made the call and asked Tracy's parents to come down to the station. They'll be the first adoptive parents we'll interview. I hope they didn't know what was going on."

"Daniel's sister and husband?" Jericho asked. He'd been a lifelong friend of Tracy's uncle, Daniel Ashtole, and knew Tracy's parents. "I can't imagine they would have knowingly participated. They're good people."

I brushed his bristled cheek, telling him the raw truth of what could be. "Good people or not, when the pain gets great enough, desperation can make you do just about anything."

"Casey, what about the security video showing Gould with Hannah?" he began to ask, his wondering if my daughter could have been circulated through the Adopt Me Agency. "And now there's Tracy being adopted—"

I was too afraid to consider it and put my fingers to his lips, my eyes closing with the thought. It wasn't just a thought though. The Gould video was proof that she had taken my daughter. Ronald's laptop showed he'd been investigating Hannah's kidnapping. And now we had proof of a baby-selling ring that dated back years. Learning about Tracy and her parents being involved had immediately triggered hundreds of ideas. How often had I noticed Tracy's dimples, or that her hair was like mine? There were Ronald's eyes too, the resemblance to him I'd seen and then shook off as a wishful coincidence. But for so long I've noticed the ghosts of those we love and miss are forever found in the faces of others. Of course we see them. It's because we want to.

Jericho was right to ask though. There was the question of who Tracy's real parents were. But during those years, the Adopt Me Agency had placed hundreds of babies, maybe thousands. What were the odds? Where was the evidence? I couldn't dare wish for it. I wouldn't dare to let myself begin to speculate anything. Not yet.

"I've got to go do this thing," I said to Jericho, nudging my chin toward the investigation rooms with the Stillwells and the district attorney working them back and forth. "Wait around for a few?"

"Sure," he said, leaving his question unanswered. I loved that he knew not to push. Jericho understood what came with patience, what came with waiting for the answers rather than forcing them. "I'll be here when you need me."

THIRTY-ONE

By the noon hour, Nichelle was working with the FBI while I continued working with the district attorney. I'd removed the murders of Violet Gould and Benjamin Sully from the case, clearing the path for the district attorney to develop the charges for the other crimes. If I was wrong, and our continued investigation showed it was Jerry Stillwell, then we'd cross that bridge then.

When I stopped back in to see Jerry Stillwell, we made him aware that in North Carolina with the district attorney's recommendation, the final ruling of a penalty would be death by execution. There was terror on his face. His color was pale, his face damp with sweat. The ramification of what remained of his life was settling into the crevices of his mind and ripping into his soul. The look of him was everything I wanted to see, everything I wanted to instill. It was a shattering fear.

The district attorney prepared a plea deal, an offer to remove the death penalty in exchange for life in prison without any possibility for parole. *A caged animal*, he'd said, and that's what he was facing. Life behind bars was an option on the table, and Jerry Stillwell was willing to sign anything if it meant it would save his life. If only he'd given his victims such an option.

We'd moved him to an interview room so we could use the desk, an officer guarding the door while I stood outside. His mother was less than twenty feet away, a muffled cry coming from behind the closed door. I could only imagine what the FBI was talking to her about. Jerry was working a second cherry cola, the heel of his shoe clapping the floor as his knee bounced. There was one aspect of the murders we had to finish discussing, and it was the highlight of the plea deal.

"Jerry," the DA said, sounding personal, her slim figure perched over the table as she shoved a yellow legal pad across it. She wore an easy smile, gentle and inviting as she spoke softly and encouraged him to write. "If you want this plea deal, we need it signed. We need you to write in your own words what it was you did to Janice Stephen and Ronald Haskin."

His gaze wandered to me for a moment. Regardless of what he'd said earlier, Jerry Stillwell knew who I was. "Don't miss any of the details."

"Agreed," the district attorney said without looking away from him. "That includes what your mother's orders were behind the murders."

He wiped his mouth and picked up the pen, clicking the top of it rapidly while he stared at the blank paper. "I did those things in the woods. But like I said about the doc and the older nurse?" he began, glancing up at us. "That wasn't me. I would have done them different. Done them right."

The district attorney side-eyed me, seeing if I agreed. I gave a brief nod. "Your confession doesn't include them," she said, continuing to nod until he understood. "It doesn't include Violet Gould or Benjamin Sully."

He rocked his head. "That wasn't me," he muttered, repeating himself as he wrote his name across the top, the nerves I'd seen earlier easing.

"You'll need to add the specifics of what your mother told you to do," the DA said.

"She will face prison," I said, making sure he was aware of it.

"Prison? You mean one of them country club federal prisons?" he asked.

Without conferring, I told him, "As part of your plea deal, your testimony helps prove that she ordered the murders. She'll see prison. And it won't be a federal prison."

"That means you'd need to take the stand if we bring her case to trial," the DA said.

The door opened, an agent with the FBI rapping his knuckles gently. He looked at me, asking, "Ma'am?" He wore slacks and a dress shirt, a dark hat embroidered with the FBI logo in bright yellow-gold letters. A younger man, only a few years out of college, I recognized that he was one of the forensic accountants.

In the FBI agent's hands, he carried one of Dr. Sully's ledgers. "What is it?" I asked, palms up as I stood to receive the ledger. Jerry Stillwell sat up, craning his neck to see what it was. The agent motioned to the hallway outside the room, gesturing for us to leave, "Might be best."

"Emanuel?" I asked, his entering to take over.

He waved me on, answering, "I got this."

I closed the door behind me, the accountant pointing to a line in the ledger. He said, "Ma'am, I was told to show you this."

Nichelle was waiting with her laptop, and added, "Casey, I thought you should see this."

"Let's see what you two have found," I said, looking at the top of the ledger and a date from fifteen years earlier. I followed the accountant's finger until I saw the name, Daniel Ashtole, and the entry listing multiple payments. Each was made to cover the expenses and fees involving the adoption of a girl, birthdate unknown, and approximately three years of age. I sucked in a breath. "Wait. Fifteen years ago. And a three-year—"

I covered my mouth, the image of Gould carrying away my daughter flashing in my mind. Jericho entered the hallway, still with the fire chief, the smell of cigarettes arriving with them. He saw my reaction and clutched my arm gently. "What is it?"

My heart was beating fast and hard with the will of a wish I'd tucked away deep inside me. I let the air out of my lungs, my chest drumming painfully like it had the day I'd lost Hannah. I told the accountant, "Thank you." When he tried to take the ledger, I gripped it hard like it was a lifeline. And in some ways, it was. It had only been a minute since leaving the interview room, and suddenly I felt like I was facing a life-changing moment. "If it is okay, I'd like to hold on to this."

"Does it mean what I think it means?" Nichelle asked, eyes glassy even in the dim light of the hallway. "I mean, we know the baby adoptions were fake. That the paperwork was falsified and made to look legitimate. There's the donations to the agency too." She pegged her finger against the ledger entry. "It says a three-year-old!"

"Do you remember anything about this?" I asked Jericho, trying to feel doubtful. He took my arm in his hand and led me to a chair. His relationship with Daniel Ashtole went back decades, their having grown up together in the Outer Banks. "It says here that he paid twenty thousand to the agency for adoption services and listed his sister and her husband as the adopting parents."

"I remember the adoption," he answered, but shook his head. "I remember they needed money to help with all the legal fees."

"Do you remember the girl?" I asked him and bit my lip when hearing the emotion in my voice. This confirmed Tracy was adopted through the Adopt Me Agency when she was three. "And you've seen pictures of Hannah…"

Jericho smiled with disbelief. "Casey, it was fifteen years ago. I don't remember, but the evidence—"

"He doesn't have to remember!" Nichelle blurted, her face buried in her laptop screen.

"What do you mean?" I asked, my voice and hands shaking.

Nichelle knelt next to me, speaking softly, "Casey, those are the names from the agency's web archive." She held her laptop, adding, "That testimonial Tracy found? The one with the broken web links and images?"

"You found one of the pictures?" I nearly yelled, suddenly

terrified to see it. Terrified that the deepest notion of hope would be another unforgivable disappointment. My heart fluttered wildly with huge anticipation. But I wanted to guard against having them dashed again. I'd barely survived when the DNA results proved a girl I thought to be Hannah was somebody else's daughter.

"Just the one," Nichelle answered, her eyes strangely bright as Jericho gently braced my shoulders. She flipped her laptop around, the screen showing the same web gibberish, but with one of the images appearing in the testimonial. "Is this Hannah? Is this your daughter?"

I looked at Daniel Ashtole's sister first, seeing the resemblance to him. My mouth fell open then when I saw their adopted daughter. She was smiling, her dimples showing, and her baby-blue eyes sparkling. My insides crumbled and the walls of the hallway tumbled until they were gone. "Oh, Jericho!"

"That's his sister and brother-in-law," Jericho said, confirming the web archive. "Casey, is that Hannah?"

"That's my daughter," I answered, barely able to speak. It was the first new picture of my daughter I'd ever seen since seeing the grainy hospital video. "That's my Hannah." I grabbed my phone, the background on it unchanged in years. The faces of Jericho and Nichelle blurred as I waved it in front of them to show the last picture of Hannah I'd ever taken.

"I knew it," I heard Nichelle say, her voice distant like a choir rejoicing in song.

As though I were a mile away, I heard Jericho next, "Casey, I'm so happy—"

"Is this really possible?" I asked, my head throbbing, emotions rising. Since discovering the Adopt Me Agency, I'd fancied this like a daydream, even made a wish. But the wish was just like the thousands of wishes that had come before it, so many I'd spoken in a whisper, only to lose them as my search for Hannah continued.

Jericho took the ledger before it fell from my lap. "Casey, the picture Nichelle found is real." He gave my arm a squeeze, a gentle pinch as though assuring me I wasn't lost in a daydream. "Casey, this *is* real."

My heart was racing fast enough to threaten a blackout. I began to speak, "But I—"

"Did you guys get a confession?" I heard Tracy ask. Nichelle moved aside. At the end of the hallway I saw Tracy in silhouette. She held her fingers, pulling on them the way she does when nervous in meetings. "I was passing by and saw you guys huddling."

My legs were like rubber as I tried to stand. Suddenly, it wasn't Tracy I was seeing. It was Hannah. It was my baby girl standing on the lawn of our home in Philadelphia. She was barefoot in the tall blades of grass, a dandelion ball floating errantly around her head. Jericho held my arm as the strength returned and I straightened. "Tracy, there's something I need to talk to you about."

A look of fright, of disappointment showed in an instant as she pitched her toe and tugged on her fingers, a knuckle popping. "That's one of the ledgers! Did you find my mom... I mean my real mom?"

"It is," I answered, touching the ledger. "Maybe we can go—"

"Uh-uh. Here is fine. I wanna know." Her eyes came alive with questions. "Was she like a druggy or something?"

"No, your mom wasn't a druggy. Your *parents* were quite normal," I answered her. My lips trembling, I said nothing else while I moved to stand with Tracy, to smell her, to breathe her in like a flower and take her hands in mine. It took every ounce of me to not wrap my arms around her in an embrace that I'd waited for the last fifteen years.

"Parents?" she asked, glancing at Nichelle and then at me. "Not just my mother?"

"Let's start with your father," I said, the station disappearing around us, my baby's eyes fixed with mine. "Your father was a kind and gentle man who loved you with all of his heart."

She cocked her head, regarding my choice of words. "You said *was?*" Tracy asked, her look souring. "What do you mean? What happened to him?"

Fighting the tears, I told her, "I'm sorry, but he was killed recently." The uncontrollable bouncing in my chest was with such force that I thought I would fall over. "Tracy, your father was murdered."

Her head dipped, but it wasn't out of sadness or surprise. She was thinking through the events of our case. I could see her mind working. She looked up, her eyes searching Jericho and Nichelle and then my face. "You're talking about Ronald Haskin?" she asked, figuring out what it was I was trying to tell her. "Aren't you?"

"Yes. I believe that Ronald was your father," I answered, bracing with uncertainty, feeling blind, unable to read her. "He came to the Outer Banks looking for you."

Her hands jumped out of mine with shock. She asked, "Are you saying that my name... my *real* name is Hannah?"

Weakness raged over me, Jericho supporting me as I answered, "Your name is Hannah White." She shook her head, confused. I tried not to feel hurt by her reaction. After all, until a day ago she'd only known of her perfect life growing up in the Outer Banks. "Tracy, I am saying... you are my daughter."

Tracy took a step away, Nichelle going to her, the look on my daughter's face shedding any hope I had of her remembering who I was. She looked to leave, saying, "I can't... this is all too much."

"Wait!" I pleaded. Tracy stopped her retreat, Nichelle holding her. From my bag, I fished out the one thing I'd kept from the day my daughter was kidnapped. Originally, I'd thought it to have been lost, but it was discovered when I first moved to the Outer Banks and worked a case which led us to finding Hannah's kidnappers. "I don't know if it will help, but this was yours. You were wearing it the day you were taken from us."

My arm outstretched, daring to close the distance between us, I extended my fingers, a plastic charm bracelet dangling. Tracy hesitated as she stared at the colorful shapes of moons and stars. She'd been three the last time she wore it, her kidnappers keeping it and then later giving it to another child they'd abducted. But I got it back, and now I was returning it to Hannah.

"I know this," she said, her face hard with concentration as she took the bracelet and pinched a broken charm. There was a perplexed look that came with a question. "But those were only dreams, weren't they?"

"You used to wear it all the time," I said, a warm calm in my voice. "Even at bath time. You never took it off."

Her harsh look softened then, easing the pain that came with the rejection. She held the bracelet up so the plastic charms caught the sunlight cast through a station window. "I do remember this."

"You do?" I asked as I dried my face. Jericho's hand stayed on the small of my back, assuring me he was there. While it was only a charm bracelet, there was a look in Tracy's eyes that gave me hope of something more. I wanted to offer her my hand but offered a smile instead. To my surprise, she returned it with her dimples showing like the charms I remembered them being. My long search for my daughter was over. I gushed a cry that I couldn't hold back and told Hannah, "It's a start."

THIRTY-TWO

It was Friday afternoon, a few days since the long search for my daughter ended. I couldn't quite explain the feeling, but there was a solace, a kind of peace, a massive relief that I hadn't thought was possible. It wasn't just a mental thing either. There was a physical change in me too. I could breathe easier. I could relax. I felt fifteen years of stresses and the weight of mounting fright drain out of my fingers and toes.

If I had to put a finger on what it was exactly, I think it was finally knowing that my daughter was alive. More than that, it was also knowing that she was well and happy. After all, isn't that what every parent hopes for their children? I'd forever regret not having been a part of her growing up, having missed so many years of her life. But I'd come to know and love Tracy, and I knew her adopted parents did an amazing job bringing my daughter into this world.

With the breaking headlines, Maureen Henson, the woman we'd interviewed outside the candle-making craft store, reached out to me and asked about her baby. I assured her it was only a matter of time before the FBI was in touch. I heard the joy in her voice, and felt it in my heart, knowing what the reunion would be like for her. As a thank you to us, Maureen Henson had a candle-making class and asked to have the team come in as a grateful gesture. While I didn't know a candle wick from wax or how a candle was even made, I floated the idea across the team. I needed to pay them back for working the previous weekend and offered an early dinner and drinks afterward to celebrate. It would be a restaurant of their choosing with Jericho offering to chaperone the team. I knew what that meant, and couldn't wait to spend the evening with them.

We drove north on Route 12, traveling into Duck and returning to the popular Outer Banks town. Once parked, we found the popular boardwalk with its waterfront stores and amazing view of the sun sinking in the west. When we passed the alcove bench where we'd interviewed Maureen, we found her waiting outside her Wicks and Stix candle-making store.

"You made it!" she said, gently clapping her hands as each of us entered, a wrist wrap on her right hand. "I've set aside seating just for you guys. The front row. There should be plenty of room."

"Thank you," I said, Jericho's hand on my back as we made our way to the seats. I looked at the tight bandaging around her hand, guessing it to be a sprain, and asked, "From the dangers of candle-making?"

She eyed her thumb, the tip of it protruding enough to see the bruising. "Yeah, something like that."

"Wow that's strong," Emanuel commented, the aromatic smell wafting through the door.

We passed shelves of oils and candles and diffusers, with names like Lime Basil and English Pear, the scents overwhelming. "Smells wonderful."

"Uh-huh," Jericho replied, crinkling his nose and batting his eyelids.

Emanuel did the same, his mouth drawn down as he tried to breathe through the change in the air. "Why's it so strong?"

"Oh stop," I told them. "Admit it, it smells nice."

"I think it smells wonderful," Tracy said, walking arm in arm with Nichelle.

Nichelle picked up a mint green candle, bringing it to her nose and asked, "For the apartment?"

"I like that one," Tracy agreed.

"To be honest, I'd rather smell the ocean," Jericho said, pulling a chair out for me to sit in. "But I guess this is nice too."

When we were all seated, Nichelle laughed and held up a ball of candle wick, saying, "I have no idea what you'd do with this."

Tracy sat next to her, answering, "You do know that's the part you burn."

"Funny!" Nichelle chided as Maureen took to a short wood platform, and arranged her workbench. For the class, she had a camera on the table which magnified the work area and displayed it on a large monitor. "I love the setup she has."

"Kinda something, isn't it?" I said, Maureen overhearing us.

"I record every class and make them available online," she said. Maureen turned her attention to the room, chair legs scraping as people sat. "Class, today we're making decorative candle jars." She held up a completed jar, the inside colorfully pink and blue like an Outer Banks sunset.

"Awesome," Tracy commented. She jumped ahead and unrolled the wick to lay one end in the bottom of an empty jar. "I wonder how we get it to stick? Like, make it stay center while we pour the hot wax."

"That's an excellent question," Maureen said, continuing to listen to us, the front row having its advantages. "That's a good segue to discuss the hazards we want to avoid."

"Hazards to avoid," Tracy whispered fake-seriously to Nichelle, bumping her shoulder and making a face.

"Don't make me separate you two," I joked.

"A wick that isn't centered properly can burn the jar, even scorch the glass and cause it to crack and break."

"That's a fire hazard," Jericho said, sensitive to the topic, the irony of being in a candle-making class lost on me until now.

"Sorry. I didn't think this through," I told him. But he shook it off, shrugging as though it didn't bother him.

"There are a number of techniques for centering your wick," Maureen continued, the girls sharing another laugh between them. "Glue is one option, but I prefer to use a piece of thin metal or even a small stick and knotting the end of the wick as such."

My focus locked on the monitor's close-up of Maureen's fingers. She worked the wick around a tiny stick, looping the end of it to tie a basic overhand knot. I whispered past Jericho to Emanuel sitting next to him. "Emanuel?"

"I see it," he answered.

"Is it the same?" I noticed Nichelle's smile disappear, her staring at the knot on the monitor. Tracy was looking at it too, the four of us becoming perfectly astute students.

With Violet Gould and Benjamin Sully, I'd considered the motive of jealousy. Focused on it even. What if the motive was revenge?

Tracy tapped the worktable to get my attention and nudged her chin toward the far corner where rows of candles were draped from a rope. They were drying, or it might have been called curing, the part after the wick is dipped, creating two candle sticks. What was of interest was the rope they hung from. It was a clothesline, the kind seen on Violet Gould. "Casey?" Tracy asked.

"I know," I told her as Maureen continued to make a second overhand knot. The two knots were in a row and were identical to the knots we'd discovered on Violet Gould's ropes.

"What's going on?" Jericho asked, dropping a wick into his jar.

I leaned over to whisper in his ear, not wanting to risk anything. "There's rope over there we recognize. There's also the knots—two overhand knots, back-to-back, like the ones we found on Violet Gould."

"That's common though. Lots of people who don't know knots pair up the one they do know," he said, scratching at the bandages on his face.

"Yeah, that's true," I said, turning back to watch Maureen repeat the procedure for the class. Maureen Henson must have seen the news report about Ronald's murder and how he was tied up. I leaned back toward Jericho, adding, "But only one person I know had a protective order to stay away from Violet Gould."

The sun sat on the ledge of Currituck Sound, turning the water into a splash of fire. It warmed our faces as we stood outside of Maureen Henson's candle shop. We sat through the class, saying nothing more about the knots, not wanting to let Maureen know our suspicions yet.

Violet Gould's murder had stood out differently from the others. The ropes were used in similar manner to Janice Stephen and Ronald. Only, the likeness didn't go beyond what was reported in the newspapers. It didn't have any of the particulars that we'd seen with Jerry Stillwell's—the arbor knots used alone and without overhand knots. The look on the team's faces shared the same gut-wrenching sentiment I'd carried since seeing the candles curing. A part of me wished that I had never accepted Maureen's invitation. None of us wanted what we were thinking to be true.

Nichelle was first to say something. "It's got to be a coincidence."

"I know, right!" Tracy added. "She's what? A week maybe less from being reunited with her child."

Tracy's mention of a reunion tugged at my heart, the thought of it ripping through me like a winter wind. "Nobody wants this," I began as Emanuel and Jericho shared a look, their having an uncanny manner of looking only at the evidence. I knew, because I did the same. That's what being a detective is about. But this felt different. "It isn't just about the knots."

"Her wrist?" Jericho asked.

"That's what I can't shake," I said, the bandaging on Maureen's wrist telling me she'd suffered a stress fracture or a sprain.

"She jammed a joint?" Nichelle asked. "So what?"

"The gun found at the Sully residence was a snub-nosed .38 revolver with .357 caliber bullets," I said, explaining Maureen

Henson's wrist injury. "It's a big piece of hardware with a powerful kick for anyone."

Jericho held his hand and closed his fingers to shape them like a gun. "For the untrained, the recoil is tremendous."

"Also, there was evidence the killer was untrained with a handgun," I went on to explain, covering Jericho's makeshift gun when catching a passing couple staring wide-eyed. "An initial shot was through the window, missing Dr. Sully."

I began to see the change in their faces. They were accepting guilt as a possibility. "Two powerful shots and an untrained shooter. The injury to Maureen's hand, the timing of it, and the protective order from the court for Violet Gould," I said in a single breath. "Guys, we have to bring her in for questioning."

As I finished, Maureen Henson appeared, face turning ashen, her lips stretched thin. She looked toward the end of the boardwalk as if to run, but then crinkled her brow. I was certain she'd heard the discussion and was looking to escape. There was no place to go from here though. She held her injured hand and looked me squarely in the eyes, lips trembling as she spoke to us, "I heard my baby crying. I knew it then and she knew it too."

"She?" I asked, but I knew she was referring to Gould. "Could we have a discussion at the station and ask you some additional questions?"

With the sunlight on her face, skin shiny like wax, her expression twisted and she raised her voice. "He knew it too. They did it! They deserved—"

"Maureen, for your own sake, I suggest we go to the station—" I explained, wanting to get her to the station and in front of the district attorney. I'd seen this before, the burden of guilt becoming too much. She was going to pop. She shook her head hard, cheeks wet with her focus jumping randomly. I stepped toward her, telling her, "Maureen! Look at me."

She did as I told her, a calm settling, her eyelids fluttering before her gaze was on me. The tears came then as she asked, "Do you think they'll let me see my baby?"

There were times when I hated my job. This was one of them. "We can discuss it with the district attorney. Do you want to go with us to the station?"

Maureen Henson didn't mince words. She gave the end of the boardwalk one last look. She stood in front of her candle-making store, the setting sunlight beaming from her glassy eyes as she answered, "I think I need a lawyer."

"We can do that," I told her, a mix of emotions rolling through me. I was relieved to be able to close the case of Violet Gould's and Dr. Sully's murders, but was sickened by the bittersweet outcome. Maureen Henson wasn't the type of murderer to hide in her lies. The guilt was going to get to her eventually. For her crimes, Maureen would face prison time. She'd spend her life behind bars. And she'd spend it away from the child she'd fought so hard for.

THIRTY-THREE

We'd gone to say goodbye. It was a blustery summer day, large leaves spitting from Philadelphia's tallest and oldest sycamore trees that lined the street of the funeral home where Ronald was being viewed. His family, some distant and who I hadn't seen in almost twenty years, spoke to me as though we'd only just talked the day before. Ronald was like that too, able to pick up a conversation with someone at any point in time. I think that was one of the first things I loved about him. And I suspect I'd seen the same in our daughter, in the way she handled homicide cases and crime-scene investigations. Like Janice Stephen and the memory bones search Dr. Swales helped me perform, the DNA test results for me and Ronald confirmed that Tracy was our daughter. I think I could always see me and see Ronald in her. And it gave me a comfort knowing Ronald would live on through his daughter.

Tracy joined me for the trip back to Philadelphia, her identity remaining known only to those directly involved with the baby-selling case. We knew we were on borrowed time though, Hannah's kidnapping case flirting with national attention more than a few times over the years. Reunions were always a great story, and selfishly, I wanted to tell mine. I deserved to tell it. Looking across the funeral parlor, I stole a glimpse of my daughter, a deep sense of gratitude reminding me how lucky I was. A thought came to me. I'd told my story already. Maybe the ending wasn't mine to tell. While I'd waited long enough to find my daughter, this was Hannah's story too.

Ronald's casket was open for the viewing, his head and face and neck looking eerily normal, but his color flat like the empty faces on a mannequin. Considering what he'd looked like when we'd found him, I was impressed with the transformation. I braced the wood and metal that were a part of his final resting, the cool touch of it in contrast to the satin lining inside. Uncomfortable with saying goodbye, I reached inside until the tips of my fingers touched his suit jacket. It was a gray tweed, the kind I knew he liked, his sister Patti picking it out from the suits found in his apartment closet.

"You are my enlightened eagle," I mumbled, wishing that Jericho could have joined us. With Nichelle's access to Ronald's laptop, his online persona as Ahren was revealed to me. I scoured the online sleuthing forum, but from Ronald's perspective, discovering that he'd been helping me all this time. Deep in my heart, I wished he'd reached out to me as the man I knew and had married. I feared it was my anger during our last conversation that kept him away, gave him a reason for wanting to stay hidden behind the veil of an online account. I'd never know why that was and it saddened me.

Tracy must have seen me struggling and came to stand next to me. Her only childhood memories remained those she'd made with her adopted parents. But there was the charm bracelet. She'd remembered it, and that might mean another memory would return some day. Tracy took my hand, placing hers with her father's, my heart swelling with our precious, but bittersweet reunion. "Thank you for finding her. Goodbye, Ahren."

A week had passed since we put Ronald in the ground. And during that time the charges against Laura Stillwell were formalized and released, her arrest and arraignment processed. She and her lawyers decided to go forward to trial, which I had expected to see happen. She would face a judge and jury for the murders she ordered her son to execute, the charges carried being murder in the first degree. There was a basket of other charges, which would come from the FBI, and require a separate trial. For now, we had her, and the district attorney was certain we would win.

What helped with the case was having Laura's son. He faced the rest of his life in prison in exchange for taking the stand and testifying against his mother. From Jerry Stillwell, we also learned whose handprint it was we'd discovered on Ronald's arms, the blood thinners he was taking giving us the unexpected clues. We'd known the first handprint was his, and I'd thought with certainty that we would match the second to Jimmy Rush. But the security guard's hands were more than twice the size of the second handprint. It was Dr. Sully's hand that matched the bruises on Ronald's arm. In Jerry Stillwell's confession, he'd named Dr. Sully as aiding in the abduction and murder of Janice Stephen and Ronald Haskin. Jimmy Rush had only participated in mine and Nichelle's kidnapping, his taste for the crimes unfitting, which had led to his murder.

As news of the baby-selling racket spread, so too did the reunions, the FBI and my team reuniting those separated by Violet Gould and Dr. Sully. The press fed on it like sharks, particularly Maureen Henson and her upcoming trial. We'd enter the late summer months with a new reunion story nearly every day, sometimes two and three in a day. The FBI took on the role of reunion maker to track down the women who'd lost a baby to the scandal, pairing them with their children. Nichelle took on the role of liaison, managing the data collected. They began with one of the first women who'd lost her baby over eighteen years earlier when Gould, Sully and Stillwell first incorporated their businesses. Her name was Alison Parker, a mother of two and resident of Manteo.

Alison Parker's reunion with the child she thought was still-born was the first and one of the sweetest of many we'd see. It was also the saddest for me and the team. On that day, I stood in the station next to Nichelle's empty cubicle, a stack of boxes containing her belongings, her computer gear, and an empty cat mug sitting on her desk with dust collecting around it. I was joined by Alice and Emanuel and Tracy, our heads turned up to face the station monitors. On the screen we saw Nichelle wearing a shirt with a yellow-gold FBI logo as she joined the agency, her role expanding as she read from a sheet of paper to tell the reporters Alison Parker's story.

When Nichelle stepped back from the podium, a young man of eighteen entered the camera's view, a sad smile on his face as his gaze darted around the press conference. He wiped his cheeks and shielded his eyes from the flash photography. Alison Parker appeared on the other side, approaching cautiously, weepy and hair carried in a breeze. Camera flashes filled the screen with bright lights as she held out her hands to greet the man at center stage, the reporters' questions going unanswered as mother and son were reunited. When the camera zoomed in on them, I saw Alison Parker's lips moving. I saw her tell her son something, but couldn't make the read. In my mind, I thought of Maureen Henson and imagined her telling her child: *I knew you were alive. I always knew.*

As expected, the press ate every minute of the baby-selling story. It was the reunions that became the national headlines, with evening shows with tearful mother and child embraces. There were so many babies stolen over the years, the FBI had to put a dedicated team on the case, the public dubbing the massive case as the *Rourke Children*. What the reporters didn't show, not at first anyway, was what happened to the parents who had been duped, who had paid an exorbitant amount of money for adoption processing fees and then had their children lost in the scandal. Co-parenting became a thing, the mothers and fathers sharing custody. But some of the cases turned ugly, each side mounting a team of lawyers and filing civil lawsuits with judges facing custody hearings. What we'd discovered and revealed with the help of Dr. Sully's ledgers might take years to work through.

Emanuel was next to leave the station. He'd gotten the promotion I put in for him and he was on his way to take on a bigger stake in battling crime and bringing justice. There was a station on the mainland in need of a lead detective. With my help and recommendation, he landed the position. Our goodbye was only temporary though, the friendship with him and his wife lifelong, particularly on Saturday afternoons when me and Jericho met with them for an afternoon of bowling or to chase a ball around the golf course. I'll never get why we play that game, but I can't stop once I start.

As for Tracy, she remained Tracy Fields. She'd asked her adopted parents to say nothing, to discuss nothing, to ignore any requests from reporters. And as much as it pained me, Tracy had asked the same from me as well. We could keep it quiet, too. Sully's ledger remained in joint custody between the FBI and the district attorney and might never be released to the public. The angst, the nervousness and the fears that had weighed mercilessly on me during my years of searching for my daughter were finally gone too. I found comfort, a new sense of serenity that I hadn't had in what felt like a thousand years. I was complete. I was whole.

It was a meal. Just a simple one. But if there were nerves to be had, it was found with me in the kitchen and cursing a Crockpot that felt too hot for the low setting I'd selected to use. We had guests coming. I wasn't much of a cook, but I could follow the basics of a recipe, or at least I'd thought so. And follow the recipe I did. I'd gone to the market, bought the meat and vegetables and even sliced and diced while watching a video online where Gordon Ramsay had offered tips on how to keep your tips—fingertips that is.

"That smells amazing," Jericho said, entering the apartment kitchen, stepping over a box and making room on the crowded counter. I checked him on his compliment, giving him a hard look to see if he was just being polite. "No, really, I mean it. I can't wait to try it. What did you call it?"

"It's called a Mississippi pot roast," I said as I smashed a lump out of the potatoes, steam rising into my face. "Pass the butter."

As he navigated to the refrigerator, the apartment stuffed with house-fire donations, the doorbell rang. Jericho handed me the butter as I moved around the counter. "I'll let you," he said, picking up where I'd left off. I cleaned my hands and wiped the front of my apron, nerves rising and making me feel jittery. Jericho stopped me before I went to the door and planted a soft kiss. He'd shaved for the dinner, his skin smooth against mine. He took my hand, telling me, "Casey, it's dinner. They'll love it."

"It's not the meal I want her to love," I said, feeling selfish. "But thank you."

He put on a smile, encouraging me to do the same. "She will."

My hands clammy, I wiped them again as I blew the air from my lungs and opened the door. "Hi guys," I said to Nichelle and Tracy, the two dressed for an evening out, the sun setting behind them.

"Wow! That really smells good," Nichelle said, kissing me on the cheek as she handed me a bottle of wine.

"Well thank you," I said, freezing a moment to look at the wine. I stammered and waved a hand, saying, "Please, please, come in, come in. Food will be ready soon."

Jericho joined us, greeting Nichelle with a hug, "Congrats on the big move to the FBI!" he said, taking to shake her hand.

Tracy entered my apartment, her hands together. I could tell she was feeling nervous too as I leaned toward her and kissed her like I had Nichelle. She returned the gesture, stopping to look at me. For a frightening moment, I thought I had mashed potatoes in my hair. And then it happened. Tracy put her arms around me and pulled me close to her. She squeezed me tight as though our hearts could touch. The apprehensions and the nervousness drained from my body. I shut my eyelids and held on to her as long as she let me. I ran my hand across her back and felt her hair run through my fingers. There was only the two of us there. She whispered something then, her breath warm on my ear. "Thank you for never giving up."

"I love you, Hannah," I said, my words heavy with bated breath.

"I love you too," Tracy said, wiping the tear from my face.

We might never be the mother and daughter I'd hoped for, but time does have a way of changing things. It heals and fades our scars. It turns our memories old when new memories surface. We had a future and we had time. What new memories would I have with my daughter? Whatever they were, I imagined they'd be wonderful.

A LETTER FROM B.R. SPANGLER

Dear reader,

I want to say a huge thank you for choosing to read *The Memory Bones*. If you did enjoy it, and want to keep up to date with all my latest releases, just sign up at the following link. Your email address will never be shared and you can unsubscribe at any time.

www.bookouture.com/br-spangler

I am fresh from a few days stay in the Outer Banks where I got to work on book five in the Casey White series. Afterward, back at my desk, I could still feel the warm sand on my feet and smell the ocean while editing. There was the beauty of Currituck Sound too, the massive basin of brackish water was alive with windsurfers, paddleboarders and birds fishing. The images remain as fresh as being there.

As with the previous Casey White books, I also loved revisiting Casey and Jericho's story, along with the rest of the characters. What do you think is going to happen next? With Corolla North Carolina on my mind, I have new chapters written for Casey White Book 6. Sign up with the link provided above to find out.

Want to help with the Casey White series and *The Memory Bones*, I would be very grateful if you could write a review. I'd also love to hear what you think, and it makes such a difference helping new readers to discover one of my books for the first time.

I love hearing from my readers too. You can get in touch with me on my Facebook page, through Twitter or my website. I've added the links below.

Thanks,

B.R. Spangler

brspangler.com

 facebook.com/authorbrianspangler
twitter.com/BR_Spangler

ACKNOWLEDGEMENTS

There are a few people who I would like to thank for their continued help and support with all the Detective Casey White books. They let me talk through new ideas and they read early drafts and they tell me what works and what doesn't work. Thank you to Ann Spangler, Chris Cornely Razzi and Monica Spangler.

From the team at Bookouture, thank you to the extremely talented Ellen Gleeson for her skillful editing, and for being able to see a story's strengths and weaknesses so I can work them in every draft.

Also, my immense appreciation and gratitude to all who work so hard at Bookouture to make every book a success.

Printed in Great Britain
by Amazon